A KILLING MOON
WINGED GUARDIANS

Hope you enjoy!

A Killing Moon:

Winged Guardians

Alexis D. Craig

Book Cover Design by Rebecca Poole of Dreams2Media
Edited by Elizabeth Anne Lance

First Edition
First Edition: November 2019
ASIN: B07YBG9M9W
ISBN: 978-1-7339018-2-6

Published by
Three Fortnights Press
P. O. Box 168401
Irving, TX 75016
Submissions.34Press@gmail.com

TABLE OF CONTENTS

Before You Begin Reading...

A Killing Moon - The Playlist: these songs were ones I used to fuel my inspiration while writing this book. I hope you enjoy them as much as I did as you listen to them while reading.

https://open.spotify.com/playlist/2NFga4avqELlQhwWeyOsW2

Happy Reading,

Lexie

PROLOGUE

CORA

I know better, I do. There are so many good, valid reasons not to be here I've lost count. And yet, as I lean over my half-assed game of pool watching the door, I wait.

Here is the Calumny, a dingy little out-of-the-way bar in a suburb of Boston, catering to a certain clientele. It made its name as a speakeasy back in the day, a place to come and let it all hang out, as it were, and true to its rusted, beer-stained roots, it's still very much that kind of scene, only not in the way the owners intended. Surely as I breathe, that is a fact.

A long bar with mismatched stools, nicked with knife wounds and scarred by cigarette burns, the bartender behind the counter pretends to keep it clean. I appreciate the ruse, even though when I'm here, I drink from the bottle, just in case. The honest-to-Goddess jukebox in the corner has been stuck on Stevie Ray Vaughan's greatest hits for the last hour, and I'm grateful because in a place like this, the musical selections could be a helluva lot worse.

This isn't my normal haunt or neighborhood local. Hell, this isn't even the town I live in, but the assignment I was given puts my target here, so here I am, and here I'll stay until he arrives.

It's mostly empty tonight, a small blessing, but it's the far edge of winter, and there are a good many things to do on a Thursday night in February that don't involve liquor and a pool table with warped cues, worn felt, and a mildly tilted slate. Then the door opens to the night outside, he comes in, and it is absolutely game on.

I don't need to look up to know it's him. The icy winter chill, so foreign in this place, carries his scent—warm woods, leather, and spice—like a winged messenger, full of potent promise. My eyes close for a moment, and I wish my body didn't immediately wash in heat every time I'm in a damn five-mile radius of him, but there it is, and here I am, making sure my grip on my beer bottle doesn't shatter the glass and make a mess.

From the corner of my eye, I watch him, keeping most of my back to him to maintain my anonymity until absolutely necessary. Goddess, he is beautiful. Short, dark hair that looks like he keeps it styled with his fingers, a closely trimmed beard, shoulders that could double as a mountain range in a close-fitting navy sweater that brings out his come-fuck-me blue eyes. His jeans cup his ass just so, and his boots are nice but scuffed enough to look like they might be for actual work as well. Finnegan O'Casey is sexual fucking perfection on a stick and absolutely everything I should not want.

He is gorgeous, he is fun, he is *third in line to the damn throne*, and not in the market for any kind of dalliance except with someone of his status and, um... pack. There is that. He's a member of House Lupine, in line to one day lead Therantia, the unified shifter kingdom—because his sketchy-ass brother would likely abdicate, or at least everyone hopes so—and there's an unspoken rule with Lupines, especially royals, stick with other Lupines. Mostly.

There are rumors—whispers, of course—of Lupines who wandered far afield to join up with Vulpines or Ursines, but those are only fairy stories, or in the case of Ursines, cautionary tales of breathtaking violence. At no point in time was there any kind of legend of a Lupine and a Corvid becoming anything at all other than a ruler and their most trusted advisor. That isn't the job I want.

I could have gotten close to him the conventional way, joined my father at court as an adjunct advisor to King Niall. I have the schooling, the necessary training and skills. But the intrigues, gossip, and politics never really interested me, so I left the family to find my own way. Hell, we knew each other as kids, a cub and a fledgling who didn't have anything in common other than our parents' association, and he was smart and brave... kind. At least, I remember him to be kind. The rumors now suggest some of that kindness may have been bled away from him but preparing to rule a nation can do that to a person.

As for me, kindness is a goal, but it can be a business liability. I do all right as a—ahem—legal advisor to some of the major shifter businesses in the area, the one to call when things have gone to hell and they need a demon hunter. Work doesn't define me, though. At least, I try for it not to, with more or less success. Today, though, and for the foreseeable future, I'm on a mission of a different kind. Certainly nobler than being the local corporate fixer can be.

My sensitive ears pick up his order, scotch and soda, one ice cube, and it's pretty clear I'm going to need another beer before I have enough courage to do what I need to do. Any other person, any other shifter, and I would have been in there, running my game like I own the joint. This one, though.... Gods and Goddesses, this one makes my palms sweat and my panties scorched. Not a position of strength.

The last couple swallows of beer are cool on my parched throat, but they don't quite get the job done, and I catch the bartender's eye with a raised bottle and a finger. He smiles nervously, like he knows who I am or who Finn is and senses trouble, but he nods once and reaches into the cooler under the counter.

I watch him grab a seat at the corner of the bar, pretending to take in the game on the flat screen overhead while watching the door like I am, cautious. I think both of us have enough enemies that even our downtime merits a certain amount of circumspection. The fact he's in here alone says a great deal, but I'm not foolish enough to think he's unguarded or unprotected.

In another life, I would have gone up to him and bought him a drink and charmed my way into his company, but he gets that all the time, at least if the gossip rags are to be believed. They have kernels of truth if you know where to look, so that's not the play here.

No, better I bring him to me. Men in general respond better if they think it's their idea, and he probably would be no different. So, I throw in another row of quarters, rack the balls, and chalk my cue. Deep breath now, moving around to the head of the table, I lean over, line up my shot, and smash my break.

FINN

I saw her when I came in, bent over the pool table in a pair of jeans that were just short of criminally tight. The knee-high boots made her look incredibly tall, but now that I'm a bit closer, I can see that for the optical illusion it is. I didn't come here for that kind of entertainment, but tonight, she's making me reconsider.

The shotgun snap of pool balls being abused by someone with great strength draws my eyes, and I see she's over there by herself and sank three on the opening break. *Damn.* Her face is beautiful and oddly familiar. Her expression as she takes in the billiards landscape is serious, giving her eyes a golden cast, and the way she worries her full bottom lip with her teeth is distracting as hell. She's in a cozy-looking burgundy sweater with a low-cut vee which draws my eyes... well, let's just say the view is spectacular and leave it at that. She's as smoking from the front as she is from the back.

And that is exactly the distraction I don't need right now. My father's dying, and my brother is, for lack of a better word, dissolute. Wouldn't be a problem, really, if not for my father's devotion to the line of succession and the letter—as opposed to the spirit—of the law. *Sigh.* I could formally challenge Brendan for the throne, but that was the aggressive act of a desperate man, and I'm not there. Yet. I'm still trying to find a better solution, but so far none has presented itself, and I'm running low on options.

She comes around the table and lines up a shot, giving me a breathtaking view of her perfect peach of an ass, and I'm reconsidering every decision I've ever made. Damn, but she is absolutely, unreasonably fine. Long black curls brushing the table, dark skin that looks so touchably soft under the fluorescent light over the pool table. I can actually feel my resolve buckling the longer I look at her.

When the bartender comes around the counter and heads her way, I stop him. The bottle in his hand is intended for her, and gods above and below, the Universe has provided the opening I need. He puts it on my tab as he retreats to the other end of the bar, away from her and me.

This intriguing woman doesn't smell like a Lupine, but it's a scent that's, again, achingly familiar. Just out of reach in my mind, an itch I can't scratch. No idea why that would be, really, as we haven't met before, I don't think, but damn if she doesn't exude a sense of peace and *déjà vu*. She is some kind of shifter, though, because Calumny is not the kind of place non-shifters frequent, and with good reason. No one wants to run into a drunk werewolf, not even other werewolves. Or worse, a werebear. I shudder at the thought before squaring up to cross the room.

I move behind her and off to the side, shamelessly enjoying the way her ass looks in those jeans and the long line of her back as she leans over the table. Once she takes her shot, I'm there at her elbow, drink in hand.

She presses a fiver into my hand, murmuring her thanks before doing a complete double take. Her eyes are the most interesting color I've ever seen, a mix of well-aged scotch and gold, and wide as they look me over. I'm happy for the perusal, honestly. The niggling sense of knowing is back, but face to face with her beauty, my mind can't come up with a single idea as to how or when we would have met.

"You're not Mickey," she whispers tentatively, taking a half-step back before straightening her spine. Her sip comes with a raised chin and a challenging expression in her eyes, and while I may be a prince, she looks imperious as all hell, in command, and my original assessment of unreasonable sexiness is all but confirmed.

"I'm not," I admit, crowding into her space a little more. She smells sweetly spicy, like orange and jasmine tea and something else I can't identify, and my curiosity is full-blown. This close, her intriguing facial expressions, sexy mouth, and golden eyes are too much to enjoy from afar. "Anyone got next?"

She shakes her head, her mass of black curls bouncing around her shoulders and wisping around her face. "No one playing me now." Her gaze travels around the room as a reminder we're all but alone. "I'm always up for a game, though."

The seductive drop in her voice is like a lick of fire across my skin, hot enough to burn and definitely leaving an impression. If she's in the mood to play, I'm certainly in the mood to indulge.

CORA

He takes a cue from the beat-up rack on the wall, more sketchily bent tree limb than pool stick, and snags the blue chalk from the scuffed lip of the table.

"Finn." He offers me his hand as he approaches my location at the table.

No last names, but then, this isn't that kind of party or that kind of place. "Cora." His hand is warm in mine, big, confident. Up close, he smells like heaven, some expensive cologne with a hint of the earthy undertone which marks a Lupine. He didn't go to any trouble to mask his scent. No need to with a face as recognizable as his. "Stripes."

"All right." He shrugs with a half-smile as he sets his drink on the edge of the table and lines up a shot. He sinks one ball and leaves himself a very convenient next shot as well. "What brings you to Boston? Business or pleasure?"

He makes the shot and ties up our ball count. I do like a challenge.

"Remains to be seen, no?"

I move around to lean against the table next to him as I tip back my beer. A slight shimmy is all it takes to draw his attention away from the game and cause him to scratch.

"That was dirty."

The way he growls makes me want to do it again just to tease him. Damn but he makes it hard to remember my mission. All my hormones are stuck on fuck-him-now-please, and I'm tempted to let them loose. The way he sniffs as he moves past me tells me he's noticing them, too.

"You don't know the half of it." Dammit, my traitor tongue. More often than not, it does exactly what it wants, and I am left to deal with the aftermath. Still, it wasn't a lie, so I'm going to let it ride and see where it goes.

The way he licks his lips in response to that, looking me up and down like I'm an all-day sucker and he's got nothing but time, only twists the tension in my stomach even more. I'd wear him out like a fresh set of batteries if he'd let me, and I assume that is exactly why I was chosen for this assignment. I'm so his type, and damn if I don't want to take him for a test drive.

"So, really, what brings you here? And to Calumny of all places." As if to make his point, his blue eyes sharpen, and for a moment I'm pretty sure I see teeth, but then he's fine again, so maybe not. He sips his drink, all casual-like, but the way his eyes track me is anything but.

This is the tricky part. If I show myself to him, this gets bad, quickly, in front of witnesses. I know I need to contain the reaction but doing so is... complicated. Then it comes to me, the literal go-for-broke plan that will yield either success or failure, and absolutely no middle ground.

Taking his scotch from his hands, I turn the glass and press my lips to the spot he'd just been drinking from, throwing the contents back in one sustained swallow. Yes, it burns all the way down and tastes like horribly fermented tree bark, but I have shit to do and don't have time to muck about with tentative dancing. "You wanna get out of here?"

Finn's blue eyes are flame-bright, incendiary as he watches me suck on the ice cube from his now-empty tumbler. He rubs the pool cue between his hands as he thinks, looking between me and the table before deciding. Muttering something under his breath that sounds distinctly like "Fuck it," he takes the eight ball in hand and slams it into the side pocket with a decisive thunk. "Where to?"

I don't know why I thought he'd let me drive, but it doesn't matter. I'm riding in this sexy-ass red Maserati, all flash and sass, and his hand is on my thigh, so I think this might actually work out. I'm not here for this, but it's very much a bonus I'm willing to use to my advantage.

We pull up to my three-story brownstone in the older part of town where gentrification is still a few years off, but the tendrils are starting to show. There are purple pansies in my window boxes on the front of my house and rosebushes with the sharpest thorns imaginable outside the ground floor windows. It's very cute and homey, exactly why we came here. Nothing about this screams 'safe house' or 'heavily armed fortress,' which is how I like it. The fact it's both those things, negligible.

He parks in front, and instead of letting me out, he comes around and opens the door, immediately taking my hand to draw me up and into his arms. He crowds me against the car, all strong arms and muscles and heat, and I just want to know how soft his beard is. Goddamn, his lips are soft, and insistent but not demanding. The gentle brush of his lips over mine as he cradles me close has my body in a riot. I don't know if I'll be able to hold back my shift if he keeps this up, and I want nothing else in this world. His tongue delicately swipes across my bottom lip, and my brain shorts out for a second, caught in a feedback loop of sensation. The kiss is anything but aggressive, regardless of how we got here, and I hear a whimpering noise come from one of us as we pull back. The smirk on his lips tells me it came from me. *Hell.*

"Just making sure we're on the same page." His voice, all soft and rough and affected, makes my knees watery for a second, and I'm glad I have an arm around his shoulders and my fingers in his hair. If we weren't on the same page, a kiss like that could write a whole damn novel.

I tangle my fingers in his as I step away, Finn falling in behind me as I fish out my keys from my pocket. He's a silent sentry on my doorstep, close enough for me to feel his heat, and it's all I can do not to reach back and touch him. That kiss told me a lot, like how hard his body is underneath those fine threads, all beautifully defined muscle and strength, and if I play my cards right... At this point, I'm dealing from the bottom of the deck with no damn shame at all.

The house is quiet. A single side-table lamp on in the living room at the back of the house is the only thing visible from the front door and down the hallway. There are pictures on the upper half of the walls and shoes lined up against the bright white wainscoting, but I'm not here to give him a tour of anything but my panties, at least for now.

Once I lead him to the living room, he slips an arm around my waist and pulls me tightly to him next to my couch. This kiss dispenses with the niceties of the first, open-mouthed and wet from the very beginning. My hands on his shoulders are like gripping granite, they're so solid. He lifts me into him again, like I weigh next to nothing, and Goddess, if that's not the hottest thing ever. I'm not short or particularly small, but I'm deceptively light—hollow bones, dontcha know—even if most people don't treat me like it.

His hum of pleasure as I wrap my legs around his hips has me grinding against him, the hardness I feel against my pussy through my jeans not something I'm willing to ignore. All at once, the world spins, and I feel like I'm falling, only for us to come to rest in the enveloping comfy corner of my black leather couch. I'm straddling his lap, and if we didn't have clothes on, this would be one good deep breath away from serious fucking.

"You're trying to kill me?" He huffs a laugh as he rests his head on my shoulder. His hands are blistering through the denim where they rest on my hips, and I'm tempted to wiggle just to see how he reacts to the added stimulation. The hitch in his breath and the way his eyes lose focus for a second make it more than worth it to me.

His question, though.... No, now's not the time. I'm not giving this up solely because of the mission. I've earned this, dammit. "Seems counterproductive, no?" I tug at the hem of his sweater with a smirk to make my point, and his answering grin has my thighs clenching in sheer want.

"Ladies first." That's all the warning I get before my own sweater's gone and—sweet mother of mercy—his hands are on my tits, and it's the best thing ever. His hands are so big, covering them completely in calloused warmth, each slight twitch or breath making me squirm in his lap, even through my bra. "Fuck, yes."

There's a fabric-tearing sound, and my open bra is hanging from my shoulders in tatters, and I don't give a damn because Finn's lips. Damn, his lips, wrapped around my nipple and doing things to me that have me pulling his hair and ripping words out of me, begging as I grind up and down against the hard ridge behind his zipper. The soft shift of his beard against my sensitive skin is making me completely nuts.

"Finn... please..." I don't even know what I'm asking for, but I'm damn close to shredding his sweater and sending him home shirtless with cashmere under my talons. He seems to sense this, though, and pulls back long enough to draw off the offending garment and throw it in the direction mine sailed.

Finn clothed is a special treat. Finn shirtless is a naughty fantasy you indulge in late at night after everyone's gone to bed. So good and such a terrible idea, but not so bad you want to stop. I can't stop touching his skin, so warm and soft, a light sprinkling of freckles across his incredibly strong shoulders, his perfectly sculpted pecs and abs for frickin' days. If I'm asleep, leave me to it. I got things to do.

Unable to help myself, I lean into him and press my lips to his neck, just below his ear. My teeth scraping against the skin make him arch up into me with a curse, and suddenly we're skin to skin, and this is the best day of my life.

He's warm, so damn warm and soft and smells so good. Holy hell. I lick my way down his neck, pausing to bite here and there.

So many places I want my mouth and tongue, my nails digging into his tautly muscled pecs and running down his sides, and then I'm suddenly on my back on the couch cushions with my wrists pinned in one of his hands over my head.

"You, Cora," his breath is heaving as he tries to talk to me, "are a damn menace." His crooked smile as he looks over my half-naked and exposed form tells me that's not an insult. Of course, the heavy feel of his hard cock against my hip also underscores the point. With light fingertips, he draws his hand down my arm, starting at my wrist and trailing up to my armpit, where the ticklishly light touches set me wiggling. "Stop?"

His tone is teasing, even if his eyes aren't. There's no threat here; he's not so far gone he'd overlook my feelings in this. That, and seeing his swollen, shiny, red lips poised over my puckered nipple has me shaking my head.

"Use your words, sweetheart." He nuzzles my breast, his eyes on my face as he waits, his free hand tracing a curlicue pattern on my stomach just above the waistband of my jeans.

I struggle against his hand on my wrists before looking him in the eyes. The only word my brain can manage to force past my lips is, "Please."

His smile is feral, predatory, every bit the wolf he is as he flicks open my jeans and slips them down my hips a bit. My legs are trapped, both by where they're tangled with his and now the jeans, but his fingertips on the tiny scrap of silver silk between my legs is unmistakable.

"So pretty," he breathes against my stomach, the brush of his beard making me arch and groan.

He presses his nose to my skin above the elastic, taking in my unadulterated scent for the first time. There's no masking who I am now, and part of me is nervous to be so vulnerable to a Lupine—an exposed belly can be a killer in the wrong hands—and part of me just *does not care* in this moment because he's dragging down my panties and jeans to my ankles, and the moment one foot is free, he shifts it to the back of the couch as he moves in between my splayed legs.

There's no mistaking the intent here. His hand on my wrists is just as strong as it ever was, but as he looks me over, I start to feel like a four-course meal in front of a starving man.

"Leave them here." He presses on my bound hands for a moment before the pressure lightens considerably. I nod, and he raises an eyebrow. "What do you say?"

Part of me wants to balk, but damn if this isn't the hottest thing I've ever done, so I respond, "Yes."

His now free hands move to massage my inner thighs, not moving up, fingertips rubbing circles into my flesh and so good. "Yes, what?" he prompts.

"Yes. Sir."

A slow grin unfurls across his lips as his eyes glitter in the shadows of the room. "Good girl."

FINN

Seeing this woman spread out before me is transformative. I'm not normally this... aggressive on a first time, but something about her brings out all my inner dominance, and fuck yes please. Indulging a bit, I lean in to mouth the point of her hip bone, maybe with a little teeth, but every time I brush my teeth or beard against her, she makes this noise that leaves my dick throbbing in my jeans, and damn. So much perfect brown skin, and she's all mine for the night.

"Now," I'm rubbing circles on her inner thighs again, fingers up minutely higher, "where was I?" The closer I get to her heat, the more she squirms, but to her credit, her hands stay exactly where I put them.

My favorite thing in bed, if anyone were to ask me, is eating a woman out. Her taste, the feel of her tender flesh against my tongue and lips and face, goddamn, the *sounds* she makes as I drive her insane. I live for that, and I know beyond anything else, any woman who spent time horizontal with me is guaranteed at least that much pleasure, though I've always been an overachiever.

When my nose brushes her damp curls and she trembles beneath my hands, I can feel I'm in for a wild ride. Licking her taste from my lips, I make sure she's watching as I nuzzle in closer. Her moan is nothing short of pornographic, and it makes me smile. Then I spread her lips and take my time learning her folds and doing everything I can to make her insane, following each and every gasp and moan and plea for more. Every brush of her clit by my lips and tongue is greeted with a helpless wail as her hips rise to my mouth. She's close, and gods, I want it.

"Such a sweet pussy." I make a point of humming the compliment against her clit, and the keening whine that accompanies it has me grinding against the couch for just a little more friction. She's going to make me come in my pants if I'm not careful. The way she twists her hips and moans when I tease her clit with my lips and beard are so perfect. She's close, and I want to blow her mind.

I slip two fingers deep into her, curving them to rub the swollen spot inside her tight channel, and suddenly she's falling apart all over my face and hands. So slippery and responsive, I can't get enough of the way she groans and grinds against every gentle abrasion of my mustache and beard against her tender flesh.

Her second release hits immediately on the heels of her first, heralded by her strong thighs wrapping around my head to hold me in place as she rides it out. I may suffocate, but damn, what a way to go. And, yeah, it's hard to be humble when I sit up and she's lying there, mouth open, breath sawing in and out of her lungs, face flushed, and hands exactly where I left them.

"Good girl." I chuckle as she half-opens one eye at my comment, and I make sure to give her a show of running a hand down my face and licking her juices from my palm. "Delicious."

CORA

If that was not the hottest thing I've ever seen, I'll eat my phone. I groan and stretch, still breathless and feeling tiny aftershocks from a pair of truly spectacular orgasms. That normally only happens when I'm alone with my battery-operated friends, so Finn's skill is definitely commendable.

"May I?" I wiggle my fingers, but don't move my hands, and he drops his head, snickering. Normally, submission isn't something I'm into, but in the moment, he'd been quite persuasive.

Finn nods, streaks of color across his cheekbones as he gives me a hand up, pulling me until I've straddled his lap again, arms wreathing his neck. There's just something hot about being naked and he's still half-clothed.

"That mouth could be a weapon of mass seduction," I purr against his neck as I nibble at his earlobe.

His fingers contract on my waist as he throws his head back in laughter. "You're terrible." Even as he scolds me for my questionable—awesome—pun, he can't seem to stop the sigh my attentions generate.

I grind my hips against his in a tight figure-eight and he thrusts up against me, biting my neck and collarbone as he breathes my name, a soft, needy sound followed by a very filthy curse. I do it again, because holy crap is that hot, and bite his neck at the same time along the muscle right where it meets his shoulder, and he thrashes underneath me, damn near hard enough to unseat me.

"I think," I whisper after I take my time tracing the shell of his ear with my tongue, "turnabout is fair play. No?" His groan as I slide down his chest to my knees in front of him is the kind of thing I'll be hearing in my dreams from now on. My nipples rubbing over his skin makes it hard to remember my destination.

He watches me through hooded eyes as I take advantage of my position to explore his fantasy-fulfilling abs, one lick at a time. I'm shameless and do not care even a little bit. Feeling the muscle jump under the pressure of my lips is such a damn heady power trip, every hiss of pleasure and whispered plea only riling me up further.

Opening his jeans, the first shock is he's gone commando. It's damn cold outside, and he's in his altogether. "Laundry day?" I smirk and press kisses and nibbles to his recently revealed v-line, tearing a groan from him that makes my thighs clench. I'm not worried about the answer as I get shock number two.

Whoever got the intel on Finn's—ahem—assets hadn't lied. Impressive size, proportional to his overall frame, and holy gods thick, I might as well have received a winning lottery ticket. "Jackpot," I mutter to myself as I start to stroke him. He's been hard for a bit, sticky precum flowing down the sides of his cock, and I make sure to maintain eye contact as I stroke him and then lick my palm to sample the main course's salty, musky flavor.

Rather than sprint to the main event, I take my time, learning the terrain, swiping my tongue against the shaft in spots, licking and finally taking his balls in my mouth for a thorough tongue-lashing. He whimpers as he drops his head against the back of the couch, his hands fisted in his lap.

The amount of trust he shows in me is amazing, and I'm not going to wait anymore. Content I've teased him enough, I settle in for the floor show. I flick my tongue around the head of his cock, finding the essence from the source even better than my secondhand taste.

"Look at me." I wait until it's all eyes on me to take him in my mouth, moaning at the heavy feel of his flesh on my tongue, inching my way down with one hand holding his hips in place while the other massages his balls. *This?* I love this, I live for this, and pride myself on giving a phenomenal blowjob, or at least the one by which all others will be judged.

"Oh, fuck, Cora," he grinds out as I slip my mouth further down the shaft, taking him in and out in an easy rhythm that lets me take more of him in a little at a time, until my lips are finally flush against the base. If I stick out my tongue, I could lick his balls. I do that once or twice, just to hear his needy whines and because deepthroating is an art, not simply a skill. Once I'm comfortable, I pick up the pace, sliding all the way up and down, milking him with my tongue as I go, listening for the telltale signs he's close, and easing back just enough to keep him right on the edge. It's cruel, but when I do finally let him, he'll thank me. Right after he regains consciousness.

His hips are trembling under my hands. I look up to see his chest heaving and the cords of his neck standing out as he strains to keep still, then finally, finally, I slide all the way down, swallowing his cock with my tongue massaging the underside of the whole length as I take him down to the base and hold it, my throat working him, pulling him over the edge with a shout that makes me glad my neighbors are on vacation.

When I finally let him slip out of my mouth, clean as a whistle, he's growling and wheezing broken, shuddering breaths with his arm thrown over his eyes and his head too heavy for his neck to lift from the back of the couch.

I may be a terrible human being, but I give great head.

FINN

The icy cold wetness of a bottle of water pressed into my hand brings me back to this plane of reality. When I open an eye, which takes a surprising amount of effort, I see Cora situating herself at the other end of the couch, still naked—bless her—cracking the seal on her own bottle. Like she didn't just leave me completely wrecked and spent in her living room.

"I… that was… thank you?" I chuckle because clearly the ability to string words together coherently is still a way off for me. After tucking myself back in my jeans, I kill half the water bottle and try again. "*That* was impressive."

Her grin is all teeth and dimples and adorable as she holds up her bottle in toast. "You, too. Certainly hadn't been what I was looking for, but I'm glad I found it. Damn."

While we both ponder our next move, I finally look around the room. Spacious, with both east and west walls nothing but built-in mahogany bookcases stuffed to bursting, and the wall in front of us is dominated by two sets of French doors separated by a mint green wall with a rolltop desk and a TV mounted above it. It feels very lived in, authentic.

"So, what's a Corvid doing slumming it in Calumny?" The bar's a dangerous place on a good day, known for fights and a lot worse. The idea of a refined woman like her making time in a place like that doesn't really sit well with me, but I also don't want to overstep. It's a conundrum.

She drops her head with a rueful grin. "Honestly?"

I gesture for her to continue because I'm legit curious.

"I was in a mood." She rolls her eyes, likely at herself as much as the situation. "Shifter bars are hard to come by outside of major cities, and I didn't feel like driving all the way into the city or catching the Red Line."

I can appreciate her point, so I nod. "All the same, maybe not that one, okay? I'd worry." Thing is, I really would. Corvids are known to be intellectual, delicate, smart as hell but physically on the fragile side. That's not a good fit for that place at all. "I'm not in there all the time, and I'm definitely not their normal customer. I just..." Feeling like an overprotective asshole, I figure I should go for broke, and she'll either go with it or she won't. "It's a rough place, and I'd feel bad if you got hurt."

Her lips twitch as her smile evolves into pure mischief. "Perish the thought." She sets her empty bottle of water down by her foot.

"Thank you." She doesn't shut me down completely, so I feel a little better, at least until I see my watch. "Damn."

"Something wrong?"

I'm expected back at the palace at some point tonight, and there's nothing like an APB to put a damper on an otherwise stellar date. "So, I hope you don't think this is terrible," her raised eyebrow is expressive as hell, speaking volumes with just a tiny quirk as she rearranges herself on the couch with her knees pulled up and her arms wrapped around them, "but I have to head out. Not that this wasn't incredible."

Her dark eyes sparkle in the faint light. "Ah. Okay. No worries. I enjoyed myself as well. Excuse me for a moment?"

"Of course." She is a living, breathing, work of art as she glides in front of me on the other side of her coffee table, naked as you please. It's enough I'm rethinking my whole exit strategy and considering postponing until the morning, damn the consequences. An ass that fine deserves to be worshipped. Early. Often. *Thoroughly.*

Cora leaves down the hallway and up some stairs I hadn't noticed on my way in, only to reappear a moment later wrapped in a little gray bathrobe that is really only sexy wrapping paper the way it falls to her mid-thigh, revving the engine on my imagination. Again. "I'll walk you out."

She's completely unselfconscious as she waits for me to put my sweater back on, offering me a bottle of water for the road. Honestly? I kind of feel like slipping her my number for a do-over if she's available.

"So... what happens if I want to see you again?" We're at her front door, and cowards die a thousand deaths and all that.

Her shrug is nonchalant, noncommittal, but her eyes are sharp, warily intrigued. "I don't think that'll be a problem."

"You don't?" Maybe I misread...

"I mean, Lupines and Corvids run in the same circles. We're bound to know some of the same people, so yeah. Seeing each other again is definitely a possibility."

Her straight face has me wishing the floor would swallow me whole, right here, on the spot, so her evil grin a moment later is a bit of surprise.

"I'm sorry. I'm an asshole. I couldn't help it. You're being so prim, I just..." She giggles, clearly tickled with her little joke, even though my self-esteem is still staggering from the hit. "Lemme see your phone."

She holds out her hand expectantly, and now that I'm paying attention, I can see how delicate her hands are, how delicate she is all over. She texts herself and gives it back with her hand on the doorknob. "It was interesting to meet you, Finn."

The way she gives me another thorough onceover makes it hard to remember I have to leave. Especially when she says my name like that, all low and soft and sexy. "Likewise, Cora."

I crowd in close as she throws back the locks, plural, as in more than two, which is concerning but not terrible for a woman living alone. Before she opens the door, she hooks a finger in my collar and yanks my mouth down to hers one last time. A hand over her head braced against the wall, I can't help but run my free hand over those luscious curves hidden in that too-damn-soft, thin bathrobe. So good.

I love the way her breath catches when I touch her baby-soft skin, just above her knee and sweeping up under the robe, because it's not like I have anywhere to be or anything, and damn, but she's fine. The way her body rises into mine, arching like a wave to press against me with a moan as I nibble her jawline is what brings me to my senses. I hate having to do the responsible thing, but in a house where that type of action is somewhat limited, I have to do what I can.

"I'm sorry," I whisper against her lips. They are so perfect and soft and suckable, and why can't I just be a normal guy for another hour or so?

She hums, and I can still feel the heat of her hand on my neck as she leans against the wall away from me. "Me too." We stare each other down a little longer before she smirks. "You should probably go because I don't have the restraint to stop again."

Her candor startles a laugh out of me, but hell yeah, I love a woman who knows what she wants. "Fair enough. 'Night, Cora."

"'Night, Finn."

CORA

The moment I open the door to the quiet night, I know something's off. The kind of not-quite-right that has the adrenaline goosebumps spreading over my skin and my toes curling. I don't know if the air smells wrong or sounds wrong or what, but when the random car engine starts down the block, I'm suddenly in motion.

I grab Finn's arm, and when he would have yelled, I shove him inside and down to the floor, immediately putting myself and the ballistically reinforced door between him and the hail of bullets incoming. I hear the glass in my guest room and kitchen windows exploding, and I know my flowers are going to be in a shambles, but we're safe for the moment so long as they don't try to breach the house. This isn't something I signed up for, but regicide in my ground floor hallway is frowned upon in this establishment, and I won't allow it.

The moment the firing stops, I shove my hand in the umbrella stand and come up with my weapon, a compact 1911 .45 caliber kept for just such occasions.

"Stay down, Highness," is all I tell him as I throw open the door long enough to slip outside. There's a dark colored pickup truck parked next to Finn's now bullet-riddled car, and it guns the engine the moment I make an appearance and starts to peel out.

I don't even have to think about it and open fire, walking and firing as I make my way out to the street. I know from the way the glass explodes I scored at least a couple hits, but I don't know much beyond that. As it is, I need to go make a phone call. And have a conversation I'd have just as soon gone without.

Finn's not on the floor when I get back inside, causing another spike of adrenaline as I make my way further into the house, gun in hand. I'm out of ammo, but I can make it work if I need to.

"All clear out front. You okay?" I call out because if that was a distraction, I will kick my own ass.

"Who *are* you?" His slightly tremulous voice is coming from the floor in front of my rolltop desk where I find him holding one of my sturdy, wrought iron bookends. His blue eyes are wide with fear, and he's folded his tall frame into a tight ball with his arms around his knees and his head back against the desk.

My skin feels hot as the shift begins to come over me, my fingers becoming claws and the feathers I keep hidden from view making a brief appearance, as his eyes widen. It's gone before it really kicks in, thankfully, due to rigorous training, but I kept the talons just in case I have to fight hand to hand. One thing Corvids are known for, besides a clear lack of fucks, is our ability to defend our territory. Whoever's out there picked the wrong one today.

Blowing out a deep breath, I look down at myself, naked under my damn bathrobe, with an empty magazine weighing down my thin pocket, the hottest bachelor in the kingdom on my floor and under my protection for the moment. I'd be amused if this weren't such a messed-up situation. Going over to the couch, I lift one of the cushions and pull out two fully-loaded magazines for my pistol and slap one in, chambering a round before putting the other in my pocket. "Funny story, Your Highness. My name is Coretta Westgate, and those men were here to kill you on behalf of your brother."

BRENDAN

"It's done?" The silence that met him on the other end of the phone line had him pulling the slim pre-paid phone away from his face to check the connection.

"There were... complications." In the background was some sort of melee. Screams of pain, numerous voices shouting, car doors slamming. It was impossible to discern the circumstances, but complications were not what he paid for.

"I see." Taking a deep breath, he pinched his nose and looked out the window as several figures in gray suits poured out of the guard house into a line of idling Range Rovers. "Your contract is terminated. I'll be in touch to settle up the balance owed to you."

He closed the phone, hanging up before the other man had a chance to respond. If he crushed the phone and left tiny bits of electronic detritus in his trash, that was no one's business. Just as well, considering the wrath flowing through him had the air tasting like copper pennies and smelling like ozone as he fought his body's desire to shift. There would be time for that soon enough.

"I have to go out," he informed his aunt as she relaxed in front of the fireplace with her late night book and cup of tea. "I won't be long."

"Be safe, my dear." She didn't even look up from her reading.

Into the darkness he wandered, unnoticed, unhindered, naked as his black fur melted into the night. He had some things to attend to before the guards returned, and it was just as well they were otherwise occupied.

In his head, he could hear her say, "That's what you get for sending a jackal to do a wolf's job." A mistake that would be corrected directly.

CHAPTER ONE

FINN

"*Funny story, Your Highness. My name is Coretta Westgate, and those men were here to kill you on behalf of your brother.*"

Those were certainly words, but damn, if he could figure out what they meant. She may as well have been speaking Greek. "Are you saying my brother—?" He had to stand, and when he did, his knees immediately betrayed him by going all squishy and that was not okay.

"It's alright. I gotcha." Cora's right there, though, this woman, this goddess, this super spy? She held him up with an arm around his waist like it's whatever, like she's not mostly naked in her living room and he'd recently gone down on her. "...your retinue?"

Words started making sense again all at once, but not in time to catch her whole question. "I'm sorry, what?"

"Your people, your personal guards, where are they? We need them here. Now." Suddenly she's handing out orders like a seasoned field commander. "Are they close?"

As much as he didn't want to, he admitted to the truth right away. "I... kinda left without them." He just wanted one night, was that so wrong?

Her dark eyes shimmered with gold for a moment as she squinted up at him, disbelief writ clear across her features, right down to a fairly twitchy left eye. "Okay," she breathed out deeply, rubbing her fingers against the bridge of her nose. "Here's what we're gonna do. I gotta make some calls, so I need you..." She pushed him onto the couch and shoved her half-empty bottle of water into his hands. "Right here. Drink."

He wasn't proud of how his hands shook opening the bottle but apparently, she liked what she saw because she turned away to open up the desk and scribbled something on a piece of paper.

"You're going to call your retinue. Get them here, *now*, and tell them there was an attempt on your life at your girlfriend's house but leave off the part about the who." She pressed the paper into his hands before stalking over to a table in the entry foyer and pulling open a drawer. Cell phone in hand, she turned to head upstairs. "I'll be right back. Don't answer the door for anyone."

Girlfriend? What? Hearing the sureness of her voice, as well as the confidence of her movements, even in as few clothes was jarring. And this was a lot to take in, like *a lot,* a lot. "Wait—what? Where are you going?"

If she noticed how hyped up he was, she didn't mention it as she paused on the stairs. "This situation is going to get weirder before it gets better, and that's gonna require actual clothes. I'll be right back." And so maybe he took one last long look at her beautiful, mostly naked form as he dug in his pocket for his phone, it's between him and the gods, and they were not speaking at the moment.

And so there he sat, alone in her living room that still smelled like sex and gunfire and holy fuckshit. Her words played over and over in his head like some kind of weird, warped loop. Why would Brendan want to kill him? How does she know all this? What's the play here?

She was upstairs for a moment, and he could hear her talking to someone, maybe yelling, so he sent a text to the Commander of his personal guard, the man who would flay him alive for this little stunt as soon as he got home. Needless to say, texting Vasily Brețcu was probably not the highest on the list of bad things so far this evening, but likely a strong contender for the top three.

"...you know what? Do better, or the next time I get shot at *because of you*, you *will* be dead because of me. Your anonymity is luxury I allow. Don't test me." The way Cora pounded down the stairs only underscored how pissed off she was at whomever she's talking to. He might feel bad, except that he was the whole reason she got shot at. Apparently.

Goddamn, but she was glorious. Gone was the sexy, soft bathrobe and sweet face, and in their place, a very proper sleeveless gray dress that buttoned down the front and clung in all the right places, *holy gods.* It stopped at the knees, showing off her gorgeous legs and delicate-looking heels. She was a vision in prim and proper and damn if he didn't want to mess all that up right now. He knew it wasn't the time, dammit, but he still wanted to.

Stalking over to the TV cabinet, she reached behind it and pulled out *another* pistol and chambered a round before rucking up the skirt of her dress to secure it to a holster on her thigh. When she smoothed the skirt down again with no discernable bulge, he had the most inappropriate erection since that time in eighth grade with Meghan Karwoski in math class.

"'What am *I* gonna do?'" she asked as she wedged the phone against her jaw and tied up her hair in a very proper bun that showed off her beautiful neck. "I'm gonna unfuck this, because that's what you pay me for, and when this is over you and I are going to have a conversation. Face to face." Snarl on her lips, she turned to him and her face... softened, for lack of a better word. She went from razor sharp ice queen to Cora, the girl he met over a game of pool at Calumny. "We'll speak soon."

The so-very-proper way she perched on the couch next to him made him smile, despite the situation. "You good?"

"Yeah." His phone lit up for the eleventh time in three minutes, with Vasi becoming increasingly irate as the messages went on. Yeah, he's his best friend, but damn, this was excessive. "My Watch Commander's en route and is likely laying waste to every single traffic law between Westie and here."

The shifter palace was on an acreage not far from West Roxbury that had been in the family since before the US was a country. Hell, they predated the colonies.

"As he should." She nodded, not looking at him while she put on a shade of lipstick that had clearly been made from the blood of her enemies. "Not that I minded spending time," she grinned when she said it, "but all things considered, this was dangerous as hell."

As much as he knew he didn't have to justify himself to her, he thought she'd get it. "I just needed... I needed to get away. Get some room to breathe, ya know? Life at the palace, it's pretty intense most of the time and even though I'm not next in line to the throne, I still have a lot of expectations of me."

The wail of police sirens cut through the background noise of the night and grew louder as they approached.

"Sometimes it's hard to be the responsible one." Her gentle smile was surprisingly comforting. Cora rose to her feet and brushed an imaginary wrinkle out of her skirt the moment car doors start to slam outside. "Girlfriend, right?"

"Yeah." The fact she seemed to know what she was doing was the only reason he hadn't pushed back yet. He still had a *lot* of questions, but he wasn't dumb enough to think now's the time.

"Alright then." The pops in her neck were audible across the room as she tilted her head then rolled her shoulders, waiting for the knocks that came a moment later. "It's showtime."

CHAPTER TWO

CORA

In the decades since the shifters revealed themselves to the human populations, numerous treaties had been negotiated between the kingdom and the world outside the protection of the palace. Most shifters opted to live among them, but that made for some interesting legal difficulties.

One of which that was absolutely inviolable, though, was all incidents concerning matters of the crown were the purview of the Royal Guards. No half measures, absolutely no exceptions.

Dealing with the human cops had been a breeze compared to dealing with Commander Vasily Brețcu, head of the Night Watch for the royal house of Lupine. The moment the Strigine rolled up on the scene with his crew of tastefully dressed minions, the cops ceded jurisdiction almost instantly. Their fearful expressions were politely ignored but noted. Vasi, as Finn called him, had a rightfully earned reputation as a dangerous, scary dude. 'Eyes in the back of his head' wasn't a metaphor when you're an owl.

Head and shoulders taller than her, he would look right at home on one of those firefighter calendars she pretended not to buy. With his silver-streaked dark hair in a bun at the base of his skull and in his flawless black on black suit draped expertly over the body of a minor deity, he looked like he'd just as soon bite everyone in the room as look at them. The ability to engender that level of wordless terror was the mark of someone damn good at their job.

The intel that came with the job indicated he may be a good ally eventually, but the client was still vetting him. Son of Romanian immigrants, he had been Force Recon with the Marine Corps before coming to work at the palace. He was fastidious, smart, and going to be a damn nuisance to keep ahead of if she planned to remain hidden in plain sight. Fortunately, this was something she'd trained for as well.

With a flick of his wrist to dispatch his cadre of agents throughout my safe house-disguised-as-a-townhouse, he glided right up to Finn, giving me a passing glance that would strip bark from a tree. "Highness, a word."

That Finn moved to place himself between the two of them spoke well of him, though it was unnecessary. The day she couldn't take an owl was the day she turned in her wings. Eh, okay, maybe not take *him*, but she'd certainly take great pleasure in fucking up his pretty face if it came down to it.

When Finn pulled her to his side with his arm around her waist, it was all she could do to suppress the shiver down her spine. *It's not fair how attractive he is, and I still have a job to do.* "Go," she whispered as she turned her face to his chest. Playing the coquette was the easiest course of action right now. Vacuous party-girls got little in the way of second glances. "Talk to him, I'm not going anywhere."

She could feel the brush of his lips against her head and a quick squeeze before he stepped away to talk with his personal Guard by the French doors to the backyard, and she busied herself tending to her lipstick and makeup while watching his crew root through her abode. She was pretty confident that anything truly incriminating was either out of the house or well-hidden. It wasn't like they'd brought in ground-penetrating radar to look through the walls. Then maybe she'd start to sweat, but for the moment, she was cool.

A pale-skinned, scarecrow of a man in a dark suit similar to Vasily's wandered over with a notebook in his hand a look of carefully banked trepidation in his dark eyes. Approaching her was clearly not high on his list of life's desires, but a necessity of the case.

"Yes?" She kept her tone clipped, playing the wary girlfriend part to the hilt.

"Ma'am," his cheek ticked as he smiled shyly at her, "I'm Lieutenant Commander Osian Driscoll and I have some questions for you."

From her preliminary notes, she knew the young Cathartine was relatively new to the squad, Brețcu's second in command, newly promoted with an above average record. The dossier had been shorter on some of the more personal details but for right now, she had what she needed to handle this kid easily. "Call me Cora," she offered with a tremulous grin and her arms wrapped protectively around her middle.

His questions were pretty standard, and she kept her answers to mostly truthful. They met in person tonight—and for the last few weeks, so far as anyone was aware—and went back to her place. She found out he was the prince later. She didn't really pay attention to politics. Worrying caused premature wrinkles, after all.

For all the sharpness of his features and attire, his temperament was actually kind of sweet. He reminded her of a cuddly puppy, eager to do the right thing. His methods of interrogating were very casual, non-threatening which was impressive given his size. He loomed as a matter of fact, but he went out of his way not to be intimidating to her and she appreciated that.

His questions were brief overall, and she didn't have a lot in the way of information she could share, so she played up her overall delicacy and daintiness. He seemed to take her exactly as she presented. All the better for her.

It's hard when the cover you had to work with was yourself, or at least most of her. It was her burn identity, a last name of little renown locally, a socialite from out of town. It was all accurate, more or less, and held up to the deepest scrutiny because of its veracity. She even looked like herself, more or less. Opting to use a witch's glamour as insurance because as much as she wanted to be herself as possible with Finn, this was still a treacherous assignment. She didn't bear a lot of resemblance to her childhood self, but with the glamour, this was her, in as authentic a form as she could manage. He'd deserved that.

The only potential downfall would be her. Letting too much slip through would out her to the king and court in no time, and that's the last thing *anyone* wanted. Still, this was as much of herself as she could give right now, so hopefully it would be enough.

"Finnegan. What the actual fuck, man?" Vasi's supremely pissed-off growl reached her ears, bouncing off the glass nicely. "I can't even tell you how many ways this whole thing is completely fucked but it's an impressive number. I'd expect this from Brendan, honestly, but you?"

The deep sigh that followed made her toes curl. It was probably wrong that she could recognize his voice from a mere exhalation, but it wasn't like she had a shortage of secrets she could take to the grave. "None of this was supposed to happen. I just came to see her and..." he trailed off on a heavy sigh and she watched him card his fingers through his hair in frustration.

"And that's another thing!" The sharp tone in the Commander's voice made her glance at the two men just in time to catch him snarling directly at her until her unrelenting gaze forced his silver eyes to the ground in front of her. Wuss. "Who is she?" he hissed with his face just inches from Finn's. "What do you know about her? I have nothing on her in my files."

"We were keeping it off the radar. She doesn't want to be a public spectacle and frankly, neither do I. This was just something for the two of us."

Damn if he didn't sound sincere, he was surprisingly good at this. Cora exhaled so deeply she shrank two whole inches, not counting the heels. She'd been holding her breath waiting to see how that conversation would go, and he held up beautifully.

"Uh huh." Not that she expected Vasi to buy into it, but it was enough to back him up a bit. "I'll still need to check her out, of course."

"Oh, of course."

That was a cue if she ever heard one. "Sweetheart," she purred as she slinked up to Finn, slipping a proprietary arm around his waist as she nestled into his side, "should I be worried they're going to make off with my lingerie? You know I bought that little lacy pink thing for your eyes only..." And the way he slipped an arm around her and blushed at just the right moment felt like victory.

"Are you sure you don't want me to get rid of this Corvid *muistă*?" Vasi asked the prince with a viperish grin.

"How's about you *mânca-mi-ai pizdă*?" At his slack-jawed stare, Cora made a point to blink at him innocently with her head snuggled against Finn's chest and kept her lips in a flirty pout, even if her words were filthy as hell. Under other circumstances, she'd snatch out his tongue, but that was not her role tonight. "I mean, since you know all about Corvids, I'm sure you're aware of our facility with languages, no?" The wink wasn't necessary, but the mortified red in Vasi's cheeks and Finn's subtle snort of laughter was worth it.

One of the flying monkeys from Vasily's forensic team approached them with several small plastic bags in his hands containing bullet fragments and gods knew what else, followed closely by Driscoll. "Miss Westgate, I'm sorry, but it appears we're gonna be here all night. Do you have a place to stay?"

Cora opened her mouth to reply, but it was Finn's voice that responded, "With me."

Vasi was suddenly struck with a fit of coughing, but the prince was unfazed as he turned to his friend. "She saved my life tonight, Vasily, and she didn't have to. Having her as my guest at the palace is the least I can do."

If he was going to challenge it, the Commander of the Night Watch clearly thought better of it. "Of course, Highness," he clicked his heels with a deferential head tip. "As you wish."

CHAPTER THREE

VASILY

Vasily was fit to be fucking tied. Of course, he could not show that, watching over her shoulder as Finn's *curvă* packed a bag for the night. It was difficult to pin down what bothered him about all this, but it was more than simply a matter of not knowing what was going on in the life of his best friend. It was something Cora Westgate-specific.

She spoke Romanian like a Slav. Like she learned it from a Slav. There was an accent there, something just to the left of center that set off more flags than a July 4th barbecue and it had his feathers ruffled and his talons dying to come out. He'd have to keep that to himself, though, because Corvids, though much smaller in size, were incredibly smart on the whole and vicious if provoked, not to mention the ability to rally more to her cause in an instant. It was one of their gifts. She wasn't scared of an owl, and he'd bet money there wasn't much that scared her at all.

A drive-by shooting, aside from how incredibly old school the method was, usually was cause for quite a bit of alarm, and yet, she'd been as cool as the other side of a pillow. Unbothered, unruffled to the point where he actually wondered if she'd taken fire before. She was too calm, and even as she played at being a flouncy little vapid side piece, her eyes, the way they slide from almost black to gold and back, told a different story, with longer words and a great deal more swearing. She knew something about this, a lot of something, and getting her to come up off that information was not going to come cheaply.

Watching her pretend to doze with her head on Finn's shoulder, with her long legs thrown over his lap and his hand protectively on her thigh, it would have made for a cute picture if it wasn't abundantly clear that something truly hinky was going on, and somehow, some way, this Corvid was smack in the center of it.

FINN

Pulling into the gates of the compound always felt a bit like a prison sentence, all guarded gates and intractable rules. It was a heavy mantle that settled over his shoulders the instant he set foot on the grounds. Yet, as he rode in the back of the Bentley with Cora snuggled up in his lap, he felt surprisingly peaceful.

It wasn't appropriate, especially now since apparently someone wanted him dead, but the warm weight of her soft body curled up against his shoulder, her strong thigh under his hand just below the hem of her skirt, they imparted a kind of peace on him that burrowed deep under his skin. This woman was dangerous in a lot of ways, but it was the potential damage to his heart that concerned him the most.

From the front seat, Finn heard Vasi murmuring to someone on his phone before he turned around with a somewhat bemused expression. "We have a welcoming party."

"Do we, now."

Given the late hour, the only ones who should have been up were the royal guards, so a welcoming party was neither warranted nor normal. He must have stiffened at his friend's inference, since Cora stirred in his lap, whimpering softly as she turned her face into his neck. He shushed her with a kiss to her forehead as held her closer. It was hard to believe the warm woman in his arms, so soft and snuggly was the same one who'd shielded him bodily from gunfire and shot at his assailants.

"Tell me no one woke up my father."

The King was terminally ill, a fact that hung over each and every moment in Finn's life like a pall, and there was no need to get him out of bed for something as mundane as him being out without a minder. Especially since he was physically fine and none the worse for wear for the assassination attempt. His father's fragile health was his motivation to seek the throne instead of his brother. To carry on his legacy in good faith as opposed to... well, otherwise.

Vasi shook his head as they rounded the final curve that led through the massive stone interior gate to the house. "Even weirder."

Leaning against the doorframe with his arms crossed was the lithe frame of his dear older brother. Long black hair burnished with gold highlights from the streaky light overhead, he waited in a white undershirt and dark flannel pants over bare feet, looking more 'average' than he ever managed in daylight.

Brendan O'Casey was the face of House Lupine, the green-eyed cover model and the sexy heir to the throne. He got all their mother's looks and enough of her charm to be dangerous. Born to the spotlight, he was effortless in his manipulations of both the media and everyone around him. He reveled in his status as a 'man of mystery', banking on the royal mystique to smooth over any rough edges that occurred in his wake.

He guarded his true self like a cranky dragon, and honestly, it had been so long since Finn had seen it, he likely wouldn't recognize it if it were in front of him. They hadn't been what he would consider 'brothers' in a very long time. But this? Now? Brendan hadn't really cared about him since BSB was around. The first time. It was one more shouting voice in a headful of them, not the least of which was Cora's confident assertion at essentially gunpoint that the man in front of him, the man whom he loved as his family, wanted him dead. It was a lot to take in.

He fell on them the moment Vasi opened his door. "Thank goodness you're home."

Ignoring his overbearing presence, Finn unfolded from the back of the SUV and then turned to hand Cora out of the car, holding her possessively to his side. "Is something wrong with Father?"

Brows drawn in confusion, Brendan shook his head. "Not at all, but I heard about tonight and I was very worried. Do you know anything about who might have done this?"

Almost out of reflex, his eyes cut to Vasi, who shook his head almost imperceptibly. Now was not the time. "Not yet."

"Well I know the Guards will look into this and keep us safe." He smiled warmly at the waiting retinue before locking his emerald gaze on his brother. "I'm glad you're okay, Finn."

This. This was the brother he remembered. Before their father fell ill, before everything went to hell between them. The level of affection he still held for this man was almost painful to acknowledge. "Thank you."

"Of course, Brother." Focusing his attention on the silent but watchful woman at his side. "Who is your friend?"

"Highness," she murmured with her face downcast in an exhausted approximation of a bow.

Unsure if he should let her continue to speak or not, Finn tightened his hold on her to convey his intent as he replied, "I was with her when all this happened. She saved my life."

Brendan's expression never wavered. If anything, his smile broadened as he took her in. "Well, then I owe her a debt of gratitude." He dipped his chin to her deferentially, a move his older brother rarely practiced. Turning back to Finn, he held a hand out toward the door. "Tonight was such an ordeal. Why don't you head upstairs to bed and truly, I'm glad you're alright."

Away from the strange interaction with his brother, Finn didn't know what to think. The silence that followed them through the muffled halls to his chambers was offensive. This place was his home, had been his home his entire life, and this woman, who moved mutely beside him like a wraith, had, in the course of an evening, blown his whole life to hell. And he wanted answers.

As soon as Vasi drew the doors to his antechamber, he turned on Cora. "I need to know everything you do. Tell me who you're working for."

CORA

Returning to the palace had been hard on her, feeling like the air was slowly being pressed out of her the moment their car turned on the property, one painstakingly manicured tree at a time. She, too, had been raised here in this imposing stone compound, in the diplomatic wing, and the scent of her father was in every breath she took.

Her family and the O'Caseys went back to the beginning of time, practically, at least to the time of King Arthur. Their families had occupied Castle Bisclavret since its construction sometime in the 1100s. Initially built in Brittany, France outside the town of Carnoët, it had been moved to the New World a brick at a time to avoid the house of Valois's penchant for hunting shifters. With all the history behind it, it was as much a prison to her as it was never a home.

Keeping silent and playing sleepy with the crown prince and then on the quick walk through the ground floor of the royal wing had been both her best plays and the easiest, lest she be recognized, and her cover summarily blown in spectacular fashion. This was now an infinitely more dangerous game, and any time her family was involved, intrigue and treachery were the default settings.

And all of that was before the masterclass in duplicity as performed by Brendan O'Casey. Prince Brendan, scion to a lineage of wolves that dated back to Sir Marrok in the court of King Arthur and the Faoladh in Ossory before that. Beautiful, beguiling, and as dangerous as any viper. Oh he'd poured on the charm when they'd arrived, all sleep-warmed and welcoming to hide the oily sheen of his rage. She'd seen his face when he laid eyes on Finn, lips pulled taut to bare the teeth, the vein between his perfectly manicured brows throbbing, and then it was gone, the expression ethereal like a mist. It was easy to see how he was able to fool people, but that didn't make listening to him simper about his 'concern' for his brother any easier.

The room beyond the dark wood cloister of the antechamber was immense. Paneled walls lined with intricately patterned lead glass windows, the space was dominated by a recessed sitting area furnished in burgundy velvet mausoleum chic and a glistening black grand piano in the corner. She didn't even know he played, at least it wasn't a ready memory for her.

Wandering through the room, checking lines of sight from the windows and potential escape routes, she moved by rote, allowing her mind to wander. There was a lot they didn't know about each other as adults, though that was by design, at least on her part. She'd studied him, as much as one could through media files and a prepared dossier from her crew of two skilled analysts and a few operatives, preferring as recent information as possible, to blot out the sweet, fragrant nostalgia of their childhood together here. It was all she could do to keep everything straight, and the consequences could not have been more dire.

This was just supposed to be a job, and now she was leading a drunk and clumsy wolf through a minefield that could easily obliterate them both. Still she supposed answering his question as best she could was only fair, given that their lives were so intimately intertwined.

"You suddenly hard of hearing?" He grabbed her arm, abruptly pulling her out of her musing. The steel in his voice was new, as was the cold look in his eyes, but given their location, she knew he wouldn't hurt her. "I asked you a question."

Cora held up a finger as she shook off his grip, unflinching at the arctic chill in his blue eyes. Opening her valise on the bed, she immediately removed all the clothes before feeling around for a moment. Seconds later, she emerged with a small electronic device pulled from what appeared to be the false bottom of the suitcase.

Ignoring his unabashedly curious gaze, she toed off her shoes next to the bed and made a nearly silent circuit of the room with the device in her hand flashing with red and green lights. It was difficult to plant listening devices with Lupines, what with their advanced hearing, but it wasn't impossible. Satisfied when the little black box remained silent, she crooked her finger at him to follow her.

"I was hired," she acknowledged softly as she strode deliberately over to the sitting area and poured herself a tumbler of whiskey from the crystal decanter disguised as a globe side table, "to keep you alive."

To his credit, he was right on her heels. "Hired by whom, and why?"

Perching delicately on the edge of a couch cushion, she sipped her drink. "Don't know and given how we both ended up in your quarters tonight, I would think the second question would be obvious." The whiskey burned on her tongue as she tracked him through the room with her eyes.

The wolf in him was restless, pacing, occasional huffed growls of annoyance and irritation as he stripped out of his sweater and returned from his wardrobe in white tank top undershirt over his jeans. It was wrong that the image made him even hotter. "Before that, though. You were hired before that. What was the threat to me? You said my brother...." It was clear from the tight set of his mouth that he couldn't even bring himself to voice the accusation. "He couldn't do this! You've met him! You've seen him!"

She'd seen him pull wings off butterflies when they were kids too, but she didn't want to go there just yet, because the confidence in his voice chilled her to her core. "I've seen what he wants us to see. What is most beneficial to him that we see. Nothing about your brother is what it seems."

"What is it you think I should be seeing?" he sneered.

"Brendan is the crown prince of Therantia, and there are many people who fancy being in his good graces. For every misstep, mistake, and transgression, there's a favor given, a sin overlooked, an absolution unearned but granted anyway. He's in deep to too many people. Too many people whose agendas run contrary to the well-being of the kingdom. It's too dangerous for him to become the king."

The longer she spoke, the golder his gaze, the firmer his jaw set, until his cheek ticked, and his every breath was just south of a growl. "And me? Where does killing me fit into all this?"

Cora met his steady gaze with one of her own. His understanding here was absolutely essential to making this job work. "Your death is a safety net. A stopgap against his own assassination or deposition. You are, in short, a threat to his potential reign. Especially since you lack all the baggage that is part and parcel to your brother's being. You're the better choice, honestly, and he wants to eliminate you before someone who can do something about it acknowledges it. I'm here to make sure that doesn't happen."

"You still haven't shown me proof," he demanded as he folded his long limbs to sit across from her on the couch.

"And here, I would have thought the drive-by shooting would have made that self-evident," she noted dryly, pouring some whiskey in a chunky crystal tumbler and handing it to him.

Finn took the glass from her with a sniff and watched her over the lip carefully as he sipped. "It's hard to take the word of someone who slept with me for a paycheck. Who's to say you aren't paid to lie to me as well?"

Cora stiffened at the insinuation, using all her inner poise to refrain from answering his little dig with a gouge of her own. She'd taken a risk by giving in to her attraction to him, and this was the price she would pay. Throwing the rest of her drink back and slamming the glass down on the table, she rose to her feet and looked him in the eye. "I'm not a whore, and you will not call me one again."

Grabbing her belongings, she stomped into the bathroom and quickly donned her nightclothes. She didn't normally wear them, but since she was on the job, she figured black leggings and an oversized Eagles jersey were preferable to naked. Not to mention easier to hide armaments on her. Leaving in the middle of a dispute with a client wasn't exactly the most professional of moves, but she figured she could be forgiven considering the completely messed up start to her night that didn't seem to be getting any better. By the time she returned, he'd refilled her glass and left it sitting on a coaster in front of where she'd been seated.

"So you slept with me because you wanted to."

"Still on that, huh?" She couldn't help the bored tone in her voice as she twisted her hair up for the night. This was a fight they would be having for a long time and if he didn't believe her now, nothing she said was going to change it in this moment.

His bright blue eyes narrowed as he crossed his arms, showing off muscles that were absolutely cruel in their perfection. So rude. "Considering no one was shooting at me until after we slept together, maybe they weren't gunning for me. You have any angry exes or anything like that?"

As 'gotcha' moments went, this was a bit lifeless, but it was late, and she clearly wasn't successful in challenging his overall state of denial tonight. Folding her leg under her, she curled up in the corner of the couch with her drink. "Not any that know about that particular safe house, no."

Finn's unfairly perfect lips frowned as he stroked his beard. "We fucked around in your safe house?"

Seeing no point in lying, she hitched up her shirt where it sagged over her shoulder and nodded. "Not quite, but that's the gist. Yes."

"For your job," he clarified after another sip.

Rolling her eyes, she sighed. "The job is separate."

Nodding, eyes focused on the middle distance between them, he worried his upper lip with his teeth. "Would you have slept with me otherwise? Approached me? Anything?"

Cora glared at her charge. What the hell kind of question is that? She'd *wanted to* approach him since she was old enough to know what that was, but as far as seeking him out for that purpose? "No." Their lives were at the same time too disparate and yet too intermingled to allow for the luxury of romantic discovery. Honestly, she'd taken the opportunity tonight because of an impulse, a desire that stretched back years, and one she was surely regretting as the night progressed.

Ticking them off on his fingers, he enumerated her transgressions. "So you manipulated me, ruthlessly slept with me, on the orders of someone but you don't know who. Why the hell should I believe what you're saying about my brother?"

Growling in frustration, she held up a finger. "It was a blowjob. And I *didn't* sleep with you because of the job I was hired to do." Why she needed him to understand that in that moment was a mystery, but she did not plan to relinquish her certitude any time soon.

"So then why did you?"

"I've been asking myself that all fucking night." Yes, it was mean, yes, it was petty, but damn if the look of affronted shock on his face wasn't a little bit worth it. "Look, it's late. We've both had a very traumatic day and could probably do with some sleep."

He looked like he might protest but then his whole body was overtaken by a massive yawn that rolled through him starting at his toes and ending with his arms stretched over his head. "Sounds good. I'll take the couch and you can have my bed."

Cora shook her head as she stood up from the couch and stretched. "No dice. I'm on the couch as a first line of defense. You sleep in your bed, and in the morning, I'll call my handler and get someone else assigned to you." She had no idea if such a thing were even possible but made the offer as a kind of olive branch between them.

His lips curled into a sad, sleepy smile as he headed into the bathroom. "Whatever floats your boat."

It was as she collected a pillow and blanket from his bed that a terrible thought occurred to her. "You don't have..." she frowned as she searched for the word. "A valet, right? Someone who comes in the morning to pick out your clothes?"

"This isn't a Disney movie," Finn called from the bathroom, sounding like he was talking around his toothbrush before he swore over some running water. He emerged a moment later in a pair of comfortably loose blue plaid pants and nothing else, flawlessly beautiful chest on display all the way down to his v-line. "I don't have anyone who dresses me. The only person I see in the morning is the member of the kitchen staff who drops off my breakfast."

"And is me bunking on the couch the kind of thing they'd notice? Maybe talk about later?"

Finn's eyes narrowed as she spoke. "You angling to share my bed?"

"Don't get your panties in a bunch. I'm asking questions because I'm concerned about your safety. Besides, even if I did sleep in your bed, it would take me and a search party three days to make it over to your side. I promise I won't sully your virtue further."

His lips twitched as he blinked slowly at her, climbing into the bed on the far side. "Whatever, asshole."

"Fuck you, too, then." This was not how she intended to go to bed with Finn, back to back with miles of mattress and unreasonably soft sheets between them, but he was safe, so she'd done her job for the moment and everything else could wait until the morning.

CHAPTER FOUR

FINN

He'd been sleeping by himself since childhood, and as much as he'd made a point of sticking to one side of the bed for Cora's sake, somehow his sleeping-self missed the memo. Starfished across the center of the bed, he woke to an unfamiliar weight on his shoulder and a strange warmth against his side. It took a second to orient himself to the situation, Cora's head cushioned on the junction of his shoulder and bicep, though in fairness he did steal her pillow at some point, and the way she was curled against him kept her facing the door, a physical barrier between him and anyone who meant him harm. His hand spread out on her stomach was just a happy accident.

It was a lot to take in, her accusations against his brother, but it was hard to argue against a drive-by shooting. He was surprised Vasi hadn't spent the night in the room with them, but in the years he'd known the man, he was many things but not a cockblock if he could help it. Not that there was any danger of that happening.

Fuck, the night had gone to pieces in front of him. It had been going so well, from his sneaking out and meeting a beautiful woman, to getting hot and heavy in her living room. Well, the living room of her safe house. Holy fuck how had this situation gone so far off the rails?

He'd been taken in by her wicked smile, lethally dangerous curves, and the air of mischief and fun that floated around her like her cock-stiffening perfume. She was a succubus, he mused with a soft grin dancing at the corners of his lips, in the form of a Corvid who could beguile a saint. And, as he drew the back of a finger slowly down her silken cheek, he knew he was not a saint. She was just so damn tempting, in a way that the usual socialites and dignitaries his family lined up for him just... weren't. In a word, she was unexpected.

Much like Cora going from a dead sleep to sitting straight up with a gun in her hand trained on the door and her other hand plastered to his chest holding him down flat in the bed behind her was unexpected. He had a second to process the slow motion train wreck of the soft knock, followed by the click of his bedroom door and the bleating scream of the kitchen steward rolling breakfast into the room who definitely hadn't signed up for a Glock to the face before everything snapped into fast forward.

"Christ, Cora!"

Finn was up and between the two of them immediately, arms out like he could truly prevent a catastrophe naked but for his boxer briefs because apparently, he'd kicked off his pajamas sometime overnight. On the one hand was a gentle young Hircine kid named Francis who was working to pay for school who looked like he was a good deep breath away from passing out with his hands to Jesus and doing his best to cower behind the food cart and silver domed trays of food.

For her part, Cora had her implacable golden eyes trained on the young man in the white coat and her aim didn't waver except to adjust for Finn's sudden insertion into the scene. There was no doubt in his mind that she could shoot the poor kid without even ruffling his hair. The way she cocked her head to the side, never blinking, was spooky as hell and in as much as he appreciated her devotion to the cause, bumping off the kitchen staff was going a bit far.

"Francis," he called, his eyes never leaving his bedmate.

"Highness?" The high-pitched, reedy voice was surprisingly steady considering the stench of sheer terror overtaking the room.

"Back out of the room, go down to the kitchen, take a break, then resume your duties. We'll speak later." He was answered by the door opening and closing, and only then did he look back at the door. Bringing the cart into the room and parking it next to the bed, he wilted as he sat beside her. "You can put the gun down, we're all alone."

Her response was a hum of disinterest as she lifted the tablecloth to examine the rest of the cart before slipping her weapon back in its holster behind the headboard. How she'd even managed to plant it there was a question he was pretty sure he didn't want an answer to, but it was marginally comforting to know that she was prepared to fight for his well-being if it came down to it.

Watching her closely as she gracefully rose from the bed and threw open one of the windows, Finn removed the domes from the plates of bacon and eggs, sliced fruits, and cottage cheese, and began organizing their meal for her return. She looked so temptingly *soft* in the morning, in her leggings and jersey that gapped to reveal the sharp edge of her shoulder blade, and the way she moved... it was delicate, deliberate, it reminded him of one of his mother's porcelain ballerinas.

"So... that's a thing that happened." Finn's tone was remarkably light considering.

Cora's gaze, now returned to their normally dark state, slipped over him on him like a shroud as she sat next to him and poured some coffee.

Sipping primly from a delicate bone china coffee cup, pinky out unobtrusively, she wouldn't meet his eyes. "I don't wake up well."

Hot coffee threatened to lurch into his sinuses as he snorted. "Couldn't tell."

Buttering a triangle of toast, she was the picture of understated elegance in the early morning light. The barest hints of sunlight caressed her cocoa skin, giving it the appearance of fine velvet, and damn if he didn't want to touch.

"I might still be a little jumpy after last night."

"You're lucky he's not a fainting goat."

"I'm not sorry." The twitch of her lips may have been a smile, but she covered it by biting a piece of apple.

Finn hummed in chagrined humor and scratched the back of his neck. "I wouldn't expect you to be." The eggs were perfect as always, over medium with yolks just runny enough to merit dipping toasts in them. He poked the golden dome and watched its contents bleed onto the plate before picking up his toast triangle. "Vasily's gonna have a fit. He takes traumatizing the staff very seriously."

Cora's annoyed grunt came with a darkly self-satisfied smirk. "He's the one that didn't search me before leaving me in your room."

"You'd have taken his hand off if he tried." Pride and amusement warred in his voice, even if he did his best for his face to show disapproval. "So what are you gonna do about Brendan?"

"I have my people running down every lead we can. Known associates, financials, some kind of leverage to convince him to leave on his own. If that doesn't work, then we'll go public and let the chips fall where they may, legally. Maybe with a little help, but still."

"And me? Where do I fit into all this?"

"My job is to keep you alive and safe while we do all that." She took a drink of her coffee and dropped in another sugar cube. "Normally I'm all about staying in the background and running this kind of thing from behind the scenes. This time, it just so happens I have to be a little more hands on."

"'A little'?" he scoffed, shaking his head. "So much for staying low key so the servants don't talk."

The way her shoulders bunched up as she cringed made him chuckle. "Yeah... pretty sure that ship has sailed." She pulled herself back to her full height, and sniffed daintily, then drained her coffee cup and poured some more immediately. "The striped boxers were a nice touch."

Finn barely got the napkin to his mouth before spitting out his food with snickers. "Yeah, you didn't leave me a whole lot of options."

"Should I be pissed? I mean, I seem to recall you going to bed with pants on."

Rolling his eyes, he sprinkled pepper on his bowl of cottage cheese. "And you were unarmed, so let's call it even, shall we?" When he went to spoon some into his mouth, Cora's hand shot out and seized his wrist. "What the hell?"

"Don't eat that." The humor was gone from her expression, her eyes now vibrantly gold and fingers shifted completely into talons.

"Coretta, what's wrong?" he asked cautiously, lowering the spoon back into the bowl and never taking his eyes from her. She cocked her head, looking from him to his plate. "Did you want some?"

"No, don't eat that," she repeated, her voice now gruff as her hold on her shift slipped. "It's poisoned."

Finn pushed the cart away immediately, now completely focused on her. "What? Why? How? How can you tell?"

After releasing his hand, she shivered, her shift immediately receding back into her as she took the bone white saucer from her coffee cup and dumped some pepper into it, bringing it to eye level. "Looks wrong."

He unclenched immediately then, rolling his eyes at her theatrics. Nothing about this breakfast smelled like anything other than eggs and toast. He was a Lupine, dammit, and he's pretty sure he would have noticed anything amiss. "Really? Looks fine to me."

"You don't wanna eat this." A hand up as if to stop him from talking, she went to her luggage and began to root around again, eventually coming up with a magnifying glass. After spreading the pepper out on the plate with a fingernail, she examined the flakes until she thrust the plate and magnifying glass into his hands. "Look."

Not sure what she was on about, he humored her and gazed at the tiny flakes of cracked black pepper. He was pretty sure there weren't supposed to be shiny bits in there. Lots of unusually shiny bits. "How did you even see that?"

Cora blinked at him slowly. "I'm a Corvid. Built-in 'shiny shit' detector."

Finn coughed to cover the chuff of laughter at her statement. "I guess." Even looking murderously serious, she could joke. It was an interesting juxtaposition. "So what the fuck am I looking at, exactly?"

She shook her head, taking the plate from him and covering their breakfast with the domes. "No idea. I need to make a phone call."

Cora was all business again, a snarlingly terse conversation with the phone wedged between her shoulder and jaw as she gathered her things and went into the bathroom to dress. When she emerged, she was no longer the sexy, sleepy nymph with questionable taste in football teams, but the well-dressed and pressed socialite with her blood-red turtleneck, houndstooth skirt, oxblood boots and matching lipstick. She looked alluring and dangerous and the urges to whimper and submit were difficult to ignore.

She was just hanging up from whomever she was speaking to when she joined him sitting on the side of the bed. Digging through her makeup bag, she came up with a small silk pouch of jewelry. "Okay, we have a plan now."

"Do we?" It was hard to think around how suddenly exhausted he was. There was so damn much to consider now. The shiny shit in the pepper was definitely there, and not something to ignore. Someone clearly wanted him dead, even if it wasn't his brother, and was brazen enough to make an attempt in the palace. His fucking home. Vasi was gonna have a stroke, kittens, and possibly a nuclear meltdown when Finn informed him of this. Provided he could be trusted. At this rate, he couldn't even trust his best friend, and honestly that hurt more than someone trying to end his life.

"Well, first, they're sending someone to come collect the food and test it. If it's poisoned, it's slow acting or we both would have noticed by now." She blinked at him meaningfully as she fastened a silver hoop to her earlobe. The fact they weren't dead was a good sign, apparently. "Whatever it is, we need to figure that out, and the sooner the better."

"Agreed."

"Next, you're gonna get your shit together and dress, we're going to go on about your regular day." She spritzed an intoxicating scent on her wrists before fastening on her watch and a bracelet.

There was literally nothing regular about this day. "My... normal day? Are you serious?"

She nodded as she deftly replaced all her belongings. "The cover is you're showing me around your work."

The mundanity of it, the audacity of it. Finn was on his feet driving his fingers through his hair as he paced just trying to release some of the anxious tension that was twisting up inside him. "And then what? Your people, whoever they are, send me a new minder at the end of business today? Is that how this works?"

Cora shook her head, shifting around on the bed until she faced him. "Look, I'm the best trained, best armed, and I'm the closest to you we can get right now. There is no one else to send. I asked, and I'm sorry."

The worst part about that was she seemed to be telling the truth, at least from what he could tell, considering how fluid veracity was where she was concerned. "So... what then? You're stuck with me?"

The corner of her sexy mouth lifted into a crooked grin, surprisingly affectionate and not at all unkind. "I got the impression you were stuck with me." Taking his hand in both of hers as he passed by her, she enfolded it in their soft warmth. "I promise I will keep you safe until this is over. You have my word."

Looking down into her face, she was beautiful, guileless, and his heart truly wanted to believe her, regardless of their past interactions. "No more lies?"

Her flinch at his question was miniscule and fleeting before she nodded. "No more lies."

Out of options, and all but bruised by the truth pressing in around him, he had no choice but to accept her offer of protection. "I believe you."

CHAPTER FIVE

CORA

For all that Crown Prince Brendan was known widely for his ceaseless carousing and philandering, and less widely for his gambling and other assorted vices, Finn was the exact opposite. His inherent kindness and goodness were practically his brand, on the boards of hospitals, museums, and other shifter charities. His fundraising efforts were legendary and the tour he took her on of his not-for-profit charity, the Society of Angels, in honor of his beloved mother, the late Queen Angelica, showed the breadth of his desire to make the world better for all shifters.

Goddess, the shifter kingdom had wept at her death. An icy road on a dark night, it had been an accident that had devastated a family and the entirety of Therantia. The whole world mourned the loss of a queen, one devoted to her not-yet-teenaged sons and to children everywhere. Her good works lived on through Finn, and yet the memory Cora most associated with her was lemon-lavender tea and shortbread cookies on a Sunday afternoon after Midsummer. Something about teddy bears and fancy dresses with gloves before her feet could touch the floor in the dining room chair. It was hazy and faded with the mists of the intervening decades, but it was warm and the affection it engendered was as fresh as it ever was.

Finn, with his little grins and openly caring nature, had a lot of her in him. He was... soft, but in the best possible way. Gentle, from the way he hugged a child who'd run up to them outside of his headquarters, to the way he squired her about with an arm around her waist and his hands perfectly respectful in their placement at all times.

She, however, was so very not soft. As his sweet nature made itself more evident, it inspired in her a protective instinct that was razor sharp and possibly rigged to blow. She would lay on the wire for this man, not just as a future king, but because of *him*. He was way more than just a pretty face. The more she got to know him, the more keen the desire to keep him safe had become for her. Maybe that was why she'd been chosen for this assignment, but whatever it was, she would be with him, keep him safe and cared for, until The Morrigan came to take her home.

Not that looking at his pretty face was any kind of hardship for her. With his stupidly broad shoulders, nipped in waist and museum-quality ass, he had a body made for suits, and no matter how many times she saw him, he was always breathtakingly beautiful to look at. Impeccable slate gray worsted weight three piece cut to absolute mathematical perfection, with a white shirt and an amusingly aggressive fuchsia tie, on anyone else it would have been comical, playacting at being an adult, on him, it just worked. He wore a waistcoat as a matter of course, dammit, and it made her knees weak.

"I'm terrible at my job," she muttered to herself as she watched another dignitary walk away whose name she'd dutifully recorded for later research by her team. For the umpteenth time, she reminded herself that she had no business noticing how sexy his beard was or how unreasonably distracting his luscious mouth was.

"I truly hope not," he murmured out of the side of his mouth behind a fake grin as he greeted someone else.

Lunch was a prestigious restaurant within walking distance— under guard—of his office, a white tablecloths and taper candles type of affair with a private dining room, and best of all, no cameras allowed.

Cora draped her linen napkin across her lap as the server poured coffee for them. The moment they stepped away, she licked her lips and pronounced, "You do a good job of carrying on your mother's good works." The pink flush on his cheeks above his beard was endearing as hell as he pointedly studied the menu, only glancing up at her through his lashes, the action igniting in her a desire to cuddle him close.

Rubbing his beard absently, his lips curled into a small, but genuine grin. "I'm glad you think so. If I can bring half as much light to the world as her, I'll be happy," he replied softly.

The urge to reach out and take his hand burned on her fingertips as she curled them into her palms. Just like the memories of her time spent with his mother and her own remained locked behind her lips, forbidden to be shared. She was here for protection, not comfort, and that she had to keep reminding herself was burdensome. "I think you could do that from the throne."

Eyebrows almost to his hairline, Finn dropped sugar cubes into his cup of coffee, making a point of not looking directly at her. "You're suggesting treason," he murmured softly, even though they were alone in the room.

Sitting up straight, she crossed her legs and assumed her most confident pose as she drew her finger around the rim of her coffee cup. He may play the innocent, but he was not a stupid man. Not to mention that her employer had all but explicitly stated the intent was to install him on the throne by any means necessary. She wasn't here for a coup, but the good of the kingdom was at stake. "I'm not suggesting anything. I'm sure you know keeping you safe from him has but one conclusion. We're not in a Dumas novel."

Any commentary he may have had was silenced the moment the doors to the dining room opened, revealing a terribly flustered server, plus two more of the staff, as well as Finn's two personal

Guards from the Day Watch, Xander and Devon.

"Is there a problem?" he asked, sitting perfectly still as the table in front of them was straightened, another place setting lain down, but no chair.

Xander was the taller of the two guards, willowy thin with wild blond hair styled into unruly spikes over what she assumed to be the standard working uniform of the Royal Guard: gray suit, black shirt and tie, brown shoulder holster and one on the hip for show. Smelled like family, an Avian cousin of some sort. Definitely a Bird of Prey, if his sharp features and unsettlingly piercing gaze were anything to go by. He dipped his head briefly before addressing them. "No, Highness. Your father—"

"Is he alright?" Finn cut him off, blue eyes wide and immediately a bit feral.

Devon, Xander's partner, put up both hands and stepped back from the rare display of Lupine aggression. He was dark-skinned, Finn's height so over six feet, and built kind of like Vasily with the wide shoulders and thickly muscled thighs, only with an infinitely more pleasant personality. His easy smile and dark eyes gave him an approachability that Vasi and even Xander lacked. He smelled like family, too, strangely enough, though closer to Xander than her in relation. "Yes, the king is fine. In fact, he's here."

"He's what?" Napkin tossed on the table, Finn was on his feet and buttoning his suit jacket on autopilot she could tell as he approached his Guards. "How— He— How—?"

Cora rolled her shoulders to shake off the rising tide of agitation she felt flowing off him in waves, going to his side and slipping her hand in his. It wasn't normal protocol, but she felt like he could use the assistance, the desire to comfort clearly winning the day. He immediately laced his fingers with hers without speaking.

Xander's sharp eyes caught the motion, but here merely looked her over and said nothing else about it. "His Majesty desired an outing, and his nurse agreed. He'd asked after you, and we told him you were here. He took the liberty of ordering for all three of you."

On cue, more waitstaff appeared with serving carts and domed dishes. Apparently, this was now her new normal. As the table was set, an escalating sense of urgency moved though Finn, translated through his stiffer posture, tighter set to his jaw, damn near crushing grip on her hand. This wasn't fear, it was nerves.

"Have you never introduced anyone to your father before?" she murmured, doing her best to be out of earshot of his guards as she aired out the conclusion she'd arrived at in her mind as a question.

"Not in this context, no," he bit out, barely turning his head in her direction.

"I see," she exhaled. Knowing this next interaction would likely make or break this case, Cora took matters into her own hands. Literally.

Reaching up, she cupped his chin as she shifted in front of him, drawing his anxious blue gaze to hers as she brushed a thumb over his cheekbone. "Cora..."

Ignoring the warning tone, she slowly lifted onto her tiptoes and drew his lips to hers, his hands falling immediately to her waist and sweeping her closer.

Her other hand braced on his shoulder, her eyes fell shut as she brushed her lips back and forth lightly across his. His warm breath on her face made her toes curl and she couldn't resist the temptation presented by his sexy bottom lip, pulling it between her teeth and tugging gently. His whimper when she did was like a molten fluid, rushing over her, bathing her in slippery liquid heat as she sealed her mouth against his.

He tasted of coffee, warm and sweet, the flavor made her want to melt into his strong arms. It was hard, so fucking hard, not to sink all the way into the kiss, to let her tongue twine with his as she breathed in his quiet groans and sighs, but somehow, she maintained. It wasn't quite chaste, but delicate, open-mouthed kisses and the occasional nip of his bottom lip were enough to calm him right down. Or at least alter his focus enough to ease his anxiety a bit.

"Goddammit, Cora," he breathed against her lips, his forehead resting against hers. His voice was soft, blissfully winded as he ran a hand up and down her back. He pressed a kiss to the corner of her mouth, and it was all she could do not to go up in flames around him. His was not the only one whose focus was divided.

Xander clearing his throat theatrically was the next sound she heard, and right before she stepped away from Finn, she met his stormy blue gaze with her own heated gold and smoothed a hand over his lapel. "You'll be fine."

She only hoped she could say the same. Theoretically, she should be fine, the glamour strong and intact, with no issues. The problem came in the proximity. Effecting a glamour around family was always a tricky business, requiring both skill and finesse on the part of the witch and the user. All it took was one familiar turn of phrase or mannerism for the whole charade to crumble to dust.

Her father was the king's chief advisor and closest friend. The king had held her as a baby, hugged her as a child and treated her as family. At least for as long as her own family did. *Before...* The idea that she'd left of her own accord was a polite fiction that neatly encompassed a terribly complicated situation. It was easier to say she left than to talk about being cast out. Let's just say Corvids in general have a long memory and excel at holding a grudge. Like as both a faith and a profession. Shaking off the dark thoughts, she figured it was too late to turn back.

That Finn and Brendan didn't recognize her was not a surprise. She looked nothing like her childhood pictures, with her teeth and broken nose corrected, enough so she could probably disavow them if she wanted. The additional cushion of the witch's glamour was only to hedge her bets, though only with Brendan, because of her current closeness to Finn. Either way, she was granted the anonymity of a life without a past.

The monarch, though, she could not afford for him to see her true self, because the moment her father became involved, everything about this situation would fall directly to shit. Game face on, she watched as the Guards snapped to attention as the leader of the shifter kingdom His Royal Highness, King Niall, of House Lupine, wheeled into the room accompanied by his nurse, a squat woman in an austere navy blue suit with a face like the business end of a mechanical pencil.

The last time Cora had seen the king in person, he was smiling, hair barely tinting silver at his temples, summer weight suit, still on his feet, at her high school graduation party. A private family affair, more adults than children, it was a way for her father to show her off, his last child out of the house and successfully into an Ivy League school, on an equestrian scholarship to Cornell. She was the picture perfect daughter of a diplomat, effortlessly straddling the human and shifter worlds and showing her family in the best possible light.

What she remembered most from the day, however, was that King Niall hugged her. Touching royalty was forbidden, generally speaking, especially the King and Queen. The queen hadn't been as strict about it, because Cora and her siblings had been children, but the king? Outside of the general understanding of childhood exuberance, no. His affection that day traveled with her through the years.

The intervening years had not been kind to him and seeing him in the chair with a cashmere blanket, hunched over with papery yellowish skin and mostly translucent gray hair was quite the shock. She dropped into a deep curtsey to cover her shocked and somewhat alarmed reaction to him when he was wheeled to a stop in front of her.

"Finnegan." His father smiled at him weakly, reaching a shaky hand out to his son. "I hope I'm not interrupting your day too badly."

"Of course not, Da. Never." Finn's smile was unlike any that she'd seen so far, such an expression of love and joy from just a turn of his lips. He leaned down and hugged the man as best he could in the awkward position before stepping back to her side and wrapping his arm around her waist. "May I present, Coretta Westgate."

Mouth dry, she relied on all her training and manners to origami fold her features into a smile that could pass for genuine as she gazed down to this shadow of the man she knew. "Majesty, it is lovely to make your acquaintance."

There was a heart-stopping moment as he cocked his head and met her eyes, the blue in his sun-faded to pale gray, as he reached for her hand. With a sidelong glance at Finn, she clasped his fingers lightly with her own, disconcerted by their softness and delicacy.

"You look familiar, Miss. Have we met?"

Feeling the additional weight of Finn's curiosity, her smile warmed as she folded his frail hand between both of hers. "I imagine I would not have forgotten meeting such a handsome man as yourself."

The man in the chair beamed, nose wrinkled and dimples on full display. "Aren't you a charmer," he giggled, looking approvingly over her shoulder to his son. "Shall we eat?"

Lunch was a multi-course affair, with every single gripe and growl she'd ever made as a teen taking etiquette lessons echoing in the back of her mind as she deftly chose each correct utensil and glass. Small talk wove its way around and through each dish and expertly paired glass of wine.

"Your brother informed me that you had quite the evening last night. You know that once Brendan is installed on the throne, your nightly, ahem, adventures, will be nonexistent. At least those without a security detail. You will be next in line for the throne, and your actions should reflect that."

Bright blue eyes snapped to hers over the floral centerpiece. The offhand way he said it and the expectant look on the king's face were out of line with a question about the drive-by. Blinking at Finn in the Morse code equivalent of 'bitch, be cool,' Cora picked at her dwindling side dishes before spearing a bite of grilled asparagus, sipping her wine to keep her mouth occupied.

"I'm sorry, Father." Finn spoke the words into his plate, shoulders rounded in the posture of a chastened little boy. "I wasn't thinking. I just—"

"Of course you weren't," the old man chuckled, winking at her, "you had much more important, and beautiful I might add, things on your mind in that moment."

Cora felt her cheeks flame even if it couldn't be seen and was gratified to see the flush in Finn's cheeks as well.

"So, will we be seeing more of you, my dear?"

Blinking at the sudden shift in spotlight, she smiled bashfully, relief coursing through her when he didn't mention the previous night's gunplay. "I suppose that would be up to Finn, Your Majesty."

Licking her lips, she set aside her fork and the waitstaff stationed around the room appeared at her side in an instant to remove the plate and flatware. It was easy to forget they were there, paid as they were to fade into the background, and yet it was a bit unnerving to be in a situation where her every need was anticipated and met without request or question.

"Well, in the event that he does, I'd love a chance to get to know you better." The old man's nose wrinkled as he grinned, and he patted her hand in a distinctly uncharacteristic show of affection. "If that would be alright with you, of course."

Nodding before she'd even thought it through, Cora beamed. "Of course, Majesty. I would like that very much."

"Excellent." The moment he set his fork down, all of the dishes on the table magically evaporated with the help of the waiters standing by. Immediately small plates filled with interestingly layered pastries and new silverware were placed on the table. "I hope you don't mind, my sweet tooth goes unindulged most of the time and well? Sometimes, it's good to be the king." His wicked little grin made her want to hug him.

"More coffee, Miss?"

"Yes, thank you." Cora smiled up at the young girl with a nod. Another place setting was laid out, the cozy lunch for two now becoming a foursome apparently. "Are you expecting a guest?"

Waving away his own coffee refill, the king took up his fork. "Marius LeStrange, my Chief Advisor, wanted to speak to Finn, and since we were here, having lunch, I invited him along. I hope you don't mind."

"Of course—oh *hell*!" All the klaxons in her brain sounded off at once when she heard the name 'Marius LeStrange', or as she knew him *'Dad'*, and the start made her flail and now there was blistering hot coffee all over her. Scalding liquid quickly soaked through the arm of her sweater and skirt, sluicing down her leg to collect in her boot as she shoved herself back from the table.

"I'm so sorry!" the server squeaked, gray fur and whiskers creeping out in her twitchy cheeks.

Finn was by her side in an instant with a napkin blotting the rapidly spreading stain on her skirt. "Are you alright?"

"I'm good. It's fine." Two hands up, she deflected his attentions and the well-meaning deluge of staff. "Is there a bathroom?"

"Of course, Miss," the server who doused her held out an arm to lead her to the room, her delicate pink tail swishing behind her in agitation was hard to miss but nothing Cora could do anything about in the moment. "This way, please."

"One second." Moving to Finn's side, she whispered, "Talk to your father, spend time with him. You both need that. I'm going back to the castle to change clothes, or at least, get these washed, okay? The guards are here, and you should be fine. Watch the condiments."

She'd never get used to that slow blink, crooked grin thing he did when he was really happy, like even smiling was part of the enjoyment. Something about the expression hit her in an unprotected soft spot in her heart and made her chest ache a little in the best possible way. "Understood. I got this part." An arm around her waist, he hugged her close to him and tipped her chin up with a knuckle, his bottom lip caught between his teeth as his face filled with apprehension. "I know we haven't really discussed this, but I'd really like for you to stay. If that's alright with you."

Licking her lips, she nodded slowly, hearing both the spoken and unspoken statements in that question. "For as long as you need me." Part of this whole interaction may have been for show for the staff, but the warmth in his bright sapphire eyes told another story entirely, at least some of the more intriguing parts.

Finn brushed her nose with his on a happy sigh. "Then I'll send Vasily back to your place to get you some more clothes."

Dipping her head in a playful show of deference, Cora winked. "As you wish, Highness."

CHAPTER SIX

VASILY

"**I** haven't even been awake for an hour," he growled out loud to no one as he cut through the crime scene tape to enter Cora's townhouse. Finn had asked him as a friend to retrieve her belongings because she would be staying in the royal guest quarters at the palace, saying that he'd like very much to keep her unmentionables unmentionable for his Guards. Nothing travels faster than cop gossip.

That was the sole reason he was looking through her painfully organized closets for a suitcase to toss her shit in. He did not want to be in that house any longer than he had to. Being in her space just felt wrong, or maybe it was just the space itself he didn't like, but either way, the moment he found a bag, it was open on the bed and he was grabbing her stuff.

Designer dresses from the closet, a couple pairs of shoes,

and— "Who in the hell has this many pairs of panties and bras?" he wondered out loud, his outrage spiking the longer he had to touch her silky bits. They were small scraps of fabric that he tossed by the handful into the duffel bag, clearing out the drawer, or so he thought. One last check revealed a hot-rod red pair, and holy hell there was an image he'd just as soon not have of his friend's lover, stuck in the corner of the drawer. When it didn't come with a perfunctory tug, he was just about going to leave it when he heard a shift in the drawer.

Another tug of the elastic and the bottom of the drawer pulled up at the corner, not revealing her bra drawer underneath, but a passport, no, make that three passports. US, Dominican, and French passports, all with her picture, with names like Liza Gibbons, Isabella Ortiz y Velsaco, and Elsa St Denis, two bundles of several thousand Euro and a couple of at least five grand in US dollars. Oh, and a small black velvet bag stuffed with diamonds, because why not? Driver's licenses, birth certificates, the works. This was a stash spot and not just for an errant bag of weed. There was a void where a pistol should have been, and he made a note to frisk her when he saw her next.

Finishing his first objective, he zipped up her duffel bag and loaded it onto his shoulder along with her garment bag. In the kitchen he grabbed a large reusable grocery sack and loaded all of her 'other' belongings. She would answer for this. He had no idea who or what she was, but today was her last day anywhere near his best friend and his family. His instincts had borne out and he'd been right to be wary of the Corvid *traseistă*. He only hoped his best friend wouldn't pay the price.

Dialing the phone the moment he turned on the Jaguar engine, he flexed his fingers on the wheel and organized his thoughts. There was no work without a plan and without a plan, nothing ever worked.

"Daywatch Comm," came the computer-generated voice over the speakers as he pulled down her street, eyes open for paths of egress for the would-be assassins as well as potential tails.

"This is Commander Brețcu, access code Echo-Lima-Bravo-Three-Two-Charlie."

A different voice picked up a moment later, this one clearly human... ish. "Commander, a little early for your shift, no?"

"Mos, my man. I have some weirdness going on that I need you to look into ASAP." While not a Royal Guard, Nicodimos, with his diplomatic and intelligence community liaison skills, was the man Vasi trusted when he needed the whole, unvarnished story. Not a bird of prey, but you'd never know it with hunting skills like his. Smart, fast, focused. He was known for finding ghosts in secluded closets and that was exactly what Vasily needed now.

"Are you alright? How can I be of assistance?"

CHAPTER SEVEN

FINN

Lunch with his father and Marius stretched on for another couple hours, but Finn didn't mind. It moved quickly from policy issues to stories of the fabled old days and the shared recollections of two men who'd spent a lifetime in each other's company as friends, comrades in arms, and family in every way but blood. He could learn as much from their conversations as he could sitting in lectures and seminars, easily.

Still, Finn found his thoughts straying to Cora. With her letter-perfect manners and comportment, she went from an intimate lunch for two to an audience with the king without even batting an eye. He knew she wasn't there to really be his girlfriend, but the next one he had, that was definitely the quality he'd look for. She was categorically unflappable, and that level of calmness was pretty damn sexy.

Though he did his best to hide it, sometimes the anxiety of his situation got to him. He wasn't prepared to lose another parent, in all honesty. The fact that they'd had a couple years to watch him waste away hadn't really taken the edge off the finality of the situation and knowing that everything he was doing was in preparation for that? It could be incredibly heavy on his heart and mind.

Which was why Cora's effortless transition from 'guard' to 'girlfriend' in front of Xander and Devon had been so damn welcome. Her brand of distraction was... well, he wanted to feel bad about indulging in her offered kisses, but that'd be a damn lie. He knew the power of those full, sexy lips and wasn't about to turn down the opportunity to sample them again. He just wasn't that strong.

She was a mercenary, protecting him for money or country or whatever, but a part of him still really liked her. She was easy to talk to, understanding, smart, and so damn sexy his body practically vibrated with sheer want at least once an hour, more if he was directly in her company. It was unseemly and unlike anything he'd ever experienced before. Maybe it was her toughness, or sharp edges and remarkable unavailability, but he wanted her badly and denying himself was becoming more and more of a fulltime job.

And then he had to go and ask her to stay. It was both a kindness and the most exquisite form of torture he could imagine. Her house *was* shot up, and as his pretend-girlfriend, she would be spending a great deal of time in the palace anyway, so it stood to reason having her stay in an adjoining suite to his was the easiest and most sensible solution. Even if he worried that 'morning' wood was quickly becoming an all-day affair the more time he spent with her.

Her smile when he'd asked, the way her dark eyes widened in pleasure before she smiled at him kept playing over and over in his mind on a loop. He was pretty far gone already and while he had every reason to run in the other direction, he couldn't seem to manage even a step that way.

Opening the interior door to his suite, he found Cora pacing back and forth in the recessed sitting area with her phone pressed to her ear. Curls twisted into a bun on top of her head, she was positively swimming in a fluffy white bathrobe that hung almost to her ankles, with the sleeves rolled up several times, but still came down to her hands. Even without the contrasting color belt that matched the monogram on the chest, he knew it was his, and honestly, seeing her in his clothes, or lack thereof, hit him like an etch-a-sketch, shaking all other thoughts out of his head but her.

Her and her bare feet on the Persian rug, the way she bit at her thumb's cuticle as she talked, the tiny wrinkle between her eyebrows that showed her annoyance. She smelled like sunflowers and amber, warm and gentle like a summer afternoon. It was a study in fascination, and he was there for it.

"You're sure, right? I don't have to tell you exactly how bad this is gonna go if you're wrong, right?" Her all-business voice was so damn sexy to him, so in control, in command. Finn had no problem imagining her commanding legions to do her bidding. He sure as hell would. "Yeah, I need the paper on that. Email it and I'll get it printed out. Thanks for expediting that."

Finn felt the moment her dark eyes catch on his form, the way her whole body seemed to relax and a smile that just seemed to blossom across her face. "One minute," she mouthed to him, holding up a finger.

Nodding in acknowledgement, he dipped into the closet to hang up his jacket and dispose of his tie, waistcoat, and shoes. He was done being 'on' for a bit and just wanted to kick back for a minute of peace. Listening to her murmurs, he came out just as she slipped her cell phone into the pocket of the robe. "You doing okay?"

"I'm good. I'll tell you about it in a minute." She sighed as she collapsed onto the couch in a swirl of French terrycloth. "How was your meeting?" When she reached for her tumbler on the coffee table, he saw that she'd made one for him as well.

Setting his cufflinks on the table, he rolled up the sleeves on his dress shirt before starting on the buttons. "Eh, it got better once I got them talking about the good old days. Marius has the best stories."

"Yeah, that sounds like him," she grumbled quietly into her cup before throwing back the remainder of her drink in one long swallow.

He paused reaching for his drink, watching her assessingly. "You know Marius?"

Shaking her head with a sad smile she focused at her lap, she replied, "No, but old timers are good for a tall tale or two."

Finn waited for her to continue, then refilled her cup with a couple fingers of whiskey when she kept her silence. The air about her was still, darker than he normally saw from her and it concerned him. "Father had nothing but compliments for you, by the way," he offered as a change of both subject and tone. He held his tumbler up as a toast before sipping the rich amber liquid. "If this were real, I'm reasonably certain he'd be seeking to marry me off. He still might."

She snorted into her drink and flashed him a smile that seemed grateful for the conversational detour. "He was very sweet. I enjoyed our lunch very much." The way her eyes sparkled when she spoke of his father ignited a warmth in his chest that felt almost like a hug. "And no offense to you, but I hope not to be here that long."

Her lips smiled but it was hard for him to take joy in the sentiment. "None taken. Any movement on that front?"

Stretching out to cross her feet on the table, Cora cradled her drink on her stomach. "I'm waiting on an email now. Nothing moves as fast as I'd like."

If Finn were a better man, he'd ignore the way her robe gapped open high on her thigh, revealing miles and miles of perfect, soft, sexy legs. He'd ignore the way her toenails were incongruously hot pink and glittery, a flouncy touch he would not have associated with her overall cool and measured demeanor.

Setting his drink on the table, he slid across the couch to the spot right next to her. "Are you really alright?" Finn let his hand rest on her bare knee, the warmth of her skin too potent a draw to let pass.

"As well as I'm gonna be I suppose." Her dark eyes narrowed as she sipped her scotch, brushing her lips with her thumb afterwards. "Why?"

Following the line of the robe, he trailed his fingers up the top of her thigh, exposing more and more skin incrementally. "I wanted to make sure you weren't burnt by the hot coffee."

"Oh, I see." Her eyes widened as she grinned knowingly. "Worried about my well-being, are you?"

Finn reared back with a hand over his heart, the picture of affront. "But of course." His pose dissolved into a dark chuckle as he crowded up against her, destination clear as his hand resumed its position high on her exposed thigh. "I wouldn't want anything to happen to this beautiful," he brushed his lips over her forehead and tugged at the robe's sash, "soft," his tongue teased her bottom lip as he gently peeled back the lapels the white terrycloth to reveal body to him, naked but for a tiny pair of black mesh panties, "un-fucking-believably sexy body."

His wolf growled in pleasure at the sight of her, all that beautiful, touchable brown skin displayed against the stark white robe, all full breasts and long legs and goddamn. Biting his lip, he trailed his fingers down from her collarbone down between her breasts. "Fuck," he breathed, the need for air suddenly paramount as he felt more than a little lightheaded, "I know I shouldn't..."

"And I know I should stop you. And yet..." Watching him through half-closed golden eyes, Cora's face relaxed into a wicked grin as she dragged his hand to her mouth and wrapped her lips and tongue around his finger.

The softness of her clever tongue broke him, leaving him hot, wanton, breathless as he surged over her, her face in his hands as his mouth claimed hers. He swallowed her moan as she dug her fingers into his waist and bicep, just sharp enough for him to wonder about her talons. She arched underneath him, her breasts pressed flat against the wall of muscle of his chest separated only barely by his cotton undershirt, his fingers plucking at the tiny satin bow of her underwear at her hip, a request, an invitation.

Her lips on his cheek, her teeth tugging at his earlobe, her tongue tracing the pulse on his neck, everything about her made him crazy. This was a terrible idea, but he needed it like he needed oxygen. Wrapping his arms around her body, he fell back onto the couch, leaving her naked and sprawled on top of him with squeals of laughter.

The bathrobe slipped off her shoulders, collecting at her elbows as she pushed herself upright on his chest her hips settled firmly over the hard ridge of his cock. "Unexpected."

"Necessary," he retorted with his tongue out to tease her. His hands on her hips holding her to him, grinding up against her to underscore his point.

Mouth open to moan or argue he didn't know, she was interrupted by her cell phone ringing in the pocket of his robe. Shoving a hand in her pocket and retrieving her phone, she held up a finger. "To be continued."

Finn chuckled as he rested underneath her as she spoke in hushed tones into her phone, one hand behind his head, the other running up and down her naked thigh under the robe. He could be patient, for a moment.

No sooner had the thought crossed his mind than his own cell phone rang, followed by the bang of the antechamber door slamming open. "The hell—" He hadn't even had a chance to attempt to sit up when Vasily, Xander, and Devon burst through his bedroom door, guns drawn and pointed at them.

"Get off him!" Vasily snarled, eyes bright yellow and exuding all of his threatening predator aura. His gun was trained on Cora and did not waiver at all.

"Oh Jesus!" Eyes averted from the scene, Devon's gun dropped immediately as he cringed. Xander had no such delicacy, smirking and not looking away at all.

"Imma call you back." Smooth as you please, eyes bright gold and dead-looking like they were at breakfast, Cora slipped her phone back into her pocket and hiked the cloth back up onto her shoulders to almost cover her tits without even a hint of self-consciousness.

Finn pushed to lean up on his elbow, hard to do when she refused to yield his lap, eyes on his best friend and personal Guards. "What, and I cannot overstate this, *the fuck* is going on here?"

CORA

In her entire career, she'd had more than a couple severely awkward situations, but none quite this bad. But the look on Vasily's face? Yeah, he wasn't going to get the satisfaction of seeing her upset or cowering.

"Get off of him," he repeated, reaching for her arm.

"I'll clip your goddamn wing, fledgling. Try me." Maybe it was the threat, she made sure to keep her tone soft and conversational, or the shimmer of feathers that danced across her skin, but his hand stopped before it made contact, and he stepped back from her, out of arm's reach. She'd fight, and she'd likely lose, but there would be blood.

"She's not who she seems, Highness," Xander supplied helpfully, gun still out and on her, but without the urgency with which they'd entered. Everyone started talking at once at that point with the words 'whore' and 'liar' making an appearance more than once.

"I know she's not." The warmth of Finn's hand on her thigh never moved even an inch. Maybe she would feel differently about that later, but in this moment, it was kinda nice. Finn's proclamation brought the arguing to a halt and she could see them all mentally working to regroup. "Here's a thought. Why don't you spit out whatever it is you feel you need to and then we'll get back to what we were doing before you all got here, okay?"

"But Finn, you don't even know her real name." Addressing Cora, he pulled her multi-colored collection of passports from his pocket. "Liza Gibbons." He slapped the first one down on the coffee table next to their drink coasters. "Isabella Ortiz y Velsaco." He slapped the next one down.

"*Claro*," she murmured, still bored with his little display. Apparently, she'd managed to go from Skinemax to Showtime at the Apollo without ever leaving her seat. She hadn't expected him to lay siege to her underwear drawer and was minorly impressed with his work even if it was blowing her life apart at the moment.

"And finally, Elsa St Denis. Am I missing anyone?"

Even if he was just asking rhetorically, the slow grin that spread over her lips was more than enough of an answer to visibly raise his blood pressure. He was an easy toy and she was just mad enough to make use of him. A hand squeezing her thigh got her attention, though.

Finn's eyes, normally so blue and warm when he looked at her, were cold, distant and reserved. "You promised no more lies."

Scooting back out of his lap a bit, she shook her head. "'No more lies' is not the same as 'confess everything.'"

With a triumphant swoop of his arm, Vasily held out his hand as if presenting her as a debutante. "Finnegan O'Casey, meet *Commander* Coretta Ashai Westgate, née LeStrange, Royal Guard. On paper, she worked out of Operations and Base Logistics."

"On paper?"

The Strigian nodded smartly. "Yeah, on paper. In reality, the Commander was assigned to the Special Protectorate Division, a specialist in firearms, language acquisition, subterfuge, clandestine operations, and espionage." On an afterthought, he threw out, "Honorably discharged." And then the mood in the room blew the hell up.

"I'm sorry, what?" Finn asked.

"You're a Guard?" Devon exclaimed.

"You're nobility?" Xander questioned.

"*Commander*?" Also Devon said.

"LeStrange? As in *Marius* LeStrange, Chief Advisor to the king?" Xander again.

"And what the hell is Special Protectorate Division?" Finn questioned.

"You're a spy? Are you running an op?" Devon again asked.

Everyone was talking at once again, but at least the guns were all abandoned back in their holsters. Taking advantage of their distraction, she unfolded herself from Finn's person and closed up the bathrobe with a knot in the sash. Snagging the glass with the most whiskey, she threw it back in one sustained swallow until all the voices died out and she was left with four very interested sets of eyeballs on her.

Rubbing a line between her eyebrows, she focused on releasing the tension that was gathering in her shoulders as she leaned against the arm of the couch farthest from Finn. "Yes, I am the daughter of Marius LeStrange, Marquise of Ravenscroft. No, he does not know I'm here, and that's by design. I used to be a spy, now I do some freelance work."

"You're not a raptor." Devon's puzzlement was clear in his narrowed dark eyes and skeptically arched brow, even if his question wasn't. It wasn't strictly required that a Royal Guard be a raptor, merely heavily suggested.

"Nothing gets by you, huh, Chief?" she snapped before closing her eyes and taking a deep breath and held up a hand, physically warding off his retort. "Sorry."

The dimple in his cheek made a quick appearance as the corner of his mouth twitched. "No worries."

As she spoke, Finn pulled in on himself, emotionally and physically, knees to his chest with his arms wrapped around them. She wanted to comfort him, but clearly that ship had both sailed and been set on fire. "I do mostly corporate fixer-type stuff, nothing that would require your attention normally, but then I was hired for a job. This job."

"This job involve fucking my best friend?" Vasi's mouth was clearly still full of acid from the way he spat questions at her.

"That's a longer conversation I don't intend to have with you," she replied with a forced cheerfulness. Her situation with Finn was complicated and the very last thing it needed was more external input.

"Who hired you?" the Strigian demanded.

"I don't know."

"What's the job?" Xander inquired, looking mad enough to strip her feathers, and she was tempted to entertain him, just to have something to hit.

"Get next to him and keep him alive, whatever it takes."

"If the prince is in danger, we need to know." Devon crossed his arms as he took up a position on the arm of the couch beside Finn.

Cora nodded. "I agree. Someone's tried to kill him. At least twice since yesterday."

"*Twice?*" Vasi's owl screeched and everyone in the room flinched. "What the fuck do you mean, 'twice'? I'm still working the shooting." Turning on Xander and Devon, he railed, "Did you have anything?"

Xander's hands came up in the universal symbol for 'not it'. "No! Nothing." Turning to her, he demanded, "Explain yourself."

She sighed and wished, not for the first time, this conversation could wait until she was wearing actual clothes beyond a borrowed bathrobe and panties. "Don't yell at them. They don't know because we didn't report it, because we needed to be sure."

"Sure of what?" The way Vasi's chest was heaving, he looked close to hyperventilating.

"That you weren't part of the problem." To Finn she said, "That's the phone call you walked in on. I wasn't going to bring them in without assurances."

The Night Watch Commander looked clearly mad enough to spit three penny nails. If she'd been any other animal, she would have been terrified. "Who the hell do you know that has the clearance to pull our jackets?"

"Classified," she replied with a smile, clicking her teeth at him like she would with her beak just because she could. "Though I could ask you the same thing, since my actual service record counts as state secrets."

Devon's hands came up in a 'T'. "Hold up, time out, wait. So you're telling me you were hired for a job by an unknown party and told to protect Finn, *our job* by the way, and then had us investigated like *we* were potential assassins?"

That hit all the salient points more or less. "Yeah, that's exactly what happened."

Xander stalked over to her, leaning down to get in her face, his brown and white feathers and beak shimmering just below the surface of his skin. "I have worked with this family, for the *king*, for my *people*, since I was *eighteen* goddamn years old. I cannot fucking believe you would think—"

Cora held up a hand. "Hey, I agree. Your record is exemplary."

Looking over his shoulder at Devon and Vasi, she nodded. "All of yours are. Beyond reproach. But when I was tasked with this, I needed to know I could trust you, and not just because of a work history." She shrugged.

"Says the woman trained to lie for a living." Snarling, Xander stalked over to the writing desk and flounced himself down in the chair.

"Oh fuck off, you'd do the same."

Vasi grunted but didn't reply to that. "So, what? Now you're gonna read us in on your little op?"

"Wait a minute! Wait a goddamn minute!" Finn shot to his feet, stopping with his face mere inches from hers. "Coretta LeStrange, the daughter of the Marquise LeStrange. The man I had lunch with a little over an hour ago?"

"Yes. That's why I facilitated the coffee incident. The whole 'slightly clumsy socialite' cover works when you have enough truth in it." And she learned from the best, considering her mother definitely qualified as a flouncy, foofy, socialite.

"You have two sisters and a brother, and all of you were raised here in the diplomatic wing."

She nodded halfheartedly, not liking the direction this was taking, but helpless to stop it.

"Which one are you?"

Brows down, she was confused. He really didn't know? "What do you mean which one am I?"

"You're not married, right?"

She shook her head again, watching him work it out with a growing pit in her stomach.

As if they didn't know, he informed the guys, "The two oldest sisters are married to varying nobles, your brother is an adjunct adviser to the king, so that leaves the youngest—Holy Fuck!"

Annnnnnd there it is. Her split with her family had not been exactly broadcast news, but it was pretty damn noteworthy. She'd left for college and she and the O'Casey brothers would see each other on breaks but not like it had been when they were young. When she went to law school, she came back with a non-shifter husband and a desire to leave the family business.

Realistically, her family could have absorbed one hit, but a human husband with the potential for halfling children, *and* abandoning a family duty that stretched back centuries? Yeah, far too much to ask, and to say her father never forgave her and likely never would was an understatement. He just happened to take the rest of the family with him when he left, or rather, had her leave.

Of course, her marriage dissolved because of certain fundamental philosophical incompatibilities, so when the Special Protectorate of the Royal Guard recruited her after her law school graduation, she went, with the understanding that she was not required to interact with her family. Easy enough to do with so many undercover and covert missions she'd lost count. Westgate was her married name, and she just never changed it back, finding it to be the perfect cover to keep her family in the dark about her life.

The moral of the story was the damage to her family, her reputation, and her standing among the nobility was irreparably razed. And then she went and slept with the prince. For reasons.

He closed his eyes and sank back down on the sofa, head in his hands as he mulled over this new/not new information. "I've known you my whole life." She couldn't tell from the tone of his voice if it was a good thing or a bad thing, but the vibe she was getting was definitely leaning toward 'bad'.

"More or less. With a few notable exceptions," she confirmed.

Finn pulled a hand down his face, stretching his features, even as he couldn't even look in her direction. "I—I need some time."

"As you wish, Highness. You're coming with us." Vasi was on his feet and reaching for her again with a snotty little smirk on his lips.

Again she ducked his attempt to manhandle her. "I'll hurt your feelings," Cora promised him with a vicious grin as she walked over to stand next to her overnight bag of belongings. "Shall we?"

* * *

VASILY

How someone managed to strut down the hallway barefoot, and in a bathrobe, while under guard, he would never know, but damn if Cora didn't manage. Back straight, chin up, her eyes didn't wander from the front as she marched alongside them.

The suite they'd placed her in was directly next door to Finn's. He unlocked the antechamber and held the door for her as they entered. It was all mahogany coffered walls and ceilings with royal blue brocade furnishings, and as far as guest rooms went, it was almost larger than the whole of his apartment.

"I instructed the staff to put your things away," he opened tentatively as he dropped her bag on the bed. The mood was different now, sharper, without the buffer of Finn between them. There were no doubts in his mind that she would make good on her threats if pushed. His hold on his temper was fragile and as much as he wasn't in the mood to pick a fight, he was not opposed to scrapping if she wanted to.

"Thank you. Does that include the rest of what you pulled out of the drawer with the passports?" Her words were clipped as she turned to face them, hands falling to parade rest likely without her even noticing.

"It does, but I don't think you'll need that here." Hell, between him and the staff, she hadn't even carried her own bags. She didn't need money as a guest of the crown.

"I'm surprised the vulture didn't find it when he was working the crime scene. Is he here?" Smugness dripped from every word.

"He's not on yet, and he's still new. He and I will discuss this later." He did not have to justify himself to her, even as he felt the need to defend the kid from her verbal barbs.

Cora seemed to consider his answer for sniffing like she was no longer interested. "So then am I a prisoner?"

"In these accommodations? You're joking. Though arguments could be made." Part of Vasi wished it was just the two of them, both of equal stature and understanding and they could just hash it out as they needed to. Having Xander and Devon along for the ride complicated things, in addition to providing possible unintended witnesses.

She rolled a shoulder with a secretive little smile, heading over to the sitting area and going straight to the globe which hid the liquor cabinet. "Not my fault you're not as good as you thought you were." After pouring a finger of whiskey into four glasses, she nestled herself into the corner of the couch. "So, did you burn any other aliases I should know about besides those three?"

Vasi froze for a second reaching for his drink as Xander snorted in amusement. He was off duty for another hour yet so he could afford a sip or two. "If it makes you feel any better, SPD called me after I ran the third one."

"I actually don't feel better but at least you didn't get the chance to fuck anything else up."

"Wouldn't have been necessary in the first place if you'd'a come clean right away," he mused as he leaned back to occupy the other end of the couch with a cushion between them that may as well have been a demilitarized zone.

"Oh yeah, because a drive-by shooting scene with forty million people around is exactly the place to say 'hey, nice to meet you. I need to talk to you about attempted regicide.' Just rolls off the tongue." She sniffed and took a mouthful of bitter amber into her. "You find the truck yet?"

Devon shook his head. "Not yet."

"Nothing personal, but I doubt you will. I know I hit at least one of them, if you haven't started checking hospitals yet."

The Day Watch Commander pulled his cell phone from his pocket and fired off a text. "Noted. So you think this was a professional job."

"I know it. I just don't know how deep this goes, so I had to take precautions."

"Our crew is solid. Our investigators do good work. They are not involved in," he gestured around the room, "whatever this is."

"I'm sure you believe that. My reports bear that out so far but they're far from complete."

Vasi slammed his glass on the table, drops of amber liquid sloshing over the side. "You're *auditing my staff?*" The outrage was so swift, he didn't know where to begin to articulate it. "You can't possibly believe that one of us..." he trailed off, too incensed to even finish the sentence.

Sitting up, she turned to face him head on, obviously unafraid of his wrath. "I have reason to suspect the attempts on Finn's life are coming from his brother. You remember him, our crown prince and the current heir to the throne?" Closing her eyes, she made an effort to call back her sarcasm. "I don't know what to believe. And I'm auditing *everyone's* staff. All I know is someone is gunning for Finn and my employer wants me to keep him safe. So that's what I'm gonna do. Whatever it takes." Taking a deep breath, she scooted back on the couch like she was physically disengaging from the conversation. "You don't have to like it; you just have to stay out of my way."

Devon and Xander were watching the conversation like a tennis match, doing their best to stay out of the line of fire. As staring contests went, this one seemed to have a greater potential for bloodshed than most.

"I assume you have proof of you claims."

Nodding solemnly, she reached into the pocket of her robe. If everyone happened to stiffen up until she came up with a cell phone, well, that was just a hazard of the job. "Give me your number."

"Why?"

"So I can send you what I have."

The exchange was made, and his phone began to chirp as she inundated him in reams of research and legwork. He rousted Xander from the desk so he could sit and read over it uninterrupted.

From the corner of his eye, he watched the Cooper's hawk circle the sitting area before taking up a spot on the other end of the couch from Cora. "I have questions," he announced as he folded his long limbs delicately on the leather cushion. Normally he was the one Vasi tapped for complicated interrogations. The tall blond came off as an idiot, a bit of a buffoon to Devon's driven straight man, but his around-the-way style disarmed more suspects than any of them and coaxed more confessions and lead information inadvertently than any threats or hard sell did.

"Knock yourself out," replied, her cajoling, silky tone immediately drawing Vasi's eyes to make sure she wasn't gearing up to rush anyone and stab them in the neck with some sort of previously hidden or improvised device. Satisfied she was lounging with her hands laced across her stomach and feet on the coffee table, he went back to his reading. Xander, more or less, could fend for himself, and Devon was there if he needed backup.

"Why doesn't your family recognize you? They're all over this building."

She cocked her head to the side. "Do you look like you did when you were twenty?"

A slow, amused smirk curled his lips. "More or less."

"Then I count as less, I suppose. Not the first time."

"And Finn? You grew up with him and he didn't know you?"

Her annoyed hum brought Vasi's eye to her but when she didn't do more than shift positions and retie her robe, he let it go. "That one's a little more complicated."

"Explain."

"I look a little different, yes, but in both cases, I've been using a technique..." she hedged, her tone clearly one of calculation and deliberation.

"I'm listening," he coaxed, his tone friendly even if the look in his eyes was nowhere close.

She hissed a breath in, clearly reticent. "There are methods... used by other magical beings, to disguise—"

"A glamour," Vasi cut her off and rolled his eyes. "Just say it's a glamour. You're using a glamour." It wasn't legal, by human or shifter standards, but like any black market item, the emphasis was always on 'market.' And there were so many other problems to address, her using illegal magical implements was not even on the radar.

That tripped Devon's interest immediately. "So then you don't really look like that?"

Cora's lips twitched. "Like what?"

"Like this sexy chocolate smoke-show with legs for days?" That comment brought the room to a screaming standstill as all eyes turned to him. "What? I'm not the only one who was thinking it."

She coughed, choking out her thanks while Xander merely side-eyed his partner. "*Any*way. Have you been lying to the prince this whole time? Does Finn know what you really look like?"

Vasi kept up the computer screen but watched her closely as she answered. "He does." Satisfied with her open body language and immediate answer, he let it go, because while she was a trained liar, she did seem fairly devoted to his best friend.

"How's that work?"

"I really don't look like I did when I was a kid. I went through a very serious Ugly Raven period, like the Ugly Duckling but fewer feathers and much, much angrier." Xander chuckled and waved a hand for her to continue. "The glamour is just in addition to my own physical changes. And it doesn't work on sex partners."

"Interesting." His Day Shift compatriot sat forward and looked like he was going to continue that line of questioning until Vasily cleared his throat loudly. He did *not* need that much information about his best friend's sex life, thank you very much.

The blond man's blue eyes met his and he nodded before turning his attention back to Cora. "Do you know the person who hired you?" The change of topic was jarring, but that info was of great interest to all involved.

"Maybe." Her tone was bored and a quick glance at the couch showed she hadn't moved and Vasi decided to let it ride.

"Maybe you know or maybe you don't wanna say?"

"I haven't met them in person for this job, but that doesn't mean I don't know them. They reached out to me, so clearly I was on their radar at some point."

"And you really believe someone is gunning for the prince?"

"I do."

"And that involves you staying close enough for him to stick his dick into?"

"Xander." Devon's choked warning was swifter than the Night Commander's.

"Keep it civil."

Cora's snort of amusement eased Vasi's mind. "No one bitches at James Bond for banging his marks."

"M does. Question stands."

Vasily closed his eyes and consciously unclenched his jaw. With these two at the helm it was gonna be a long night.

Chapter Eight

FINN

The smears of pink and purple across the sky announcing the impending arrival of the sun were what greeted Finn's exhausted eyes before he went around the room closing each and every opaque curtain before falling back into the disheveled bed. He had no intention of greeting the day, cheerfully or otherwise.

It was hard to imagine that two days ago, he'd had a relatively normal existence. He'd walked into a bar to get a drink and relax and his whole life had been slowly pulling apart ever since.

Meeting Coretta Westgate, LeStrange, whatever the hell her name was, had been simultaneously the best and worst things to happen to him, ever. Because now, in addition to his father dying and his wantonly cruel brother taking the throne soon, he had to deal with someone actively trying to kill him. Admittedly, that could have happened regardless of her being there, but he was still going to blame her. At least a little.

He groaned in annoyance into his pillow as he pulled the blanket over his head. Why did she have to be so fucking amazing? And brave. And smart. And apparently quite cunning. When he thought of her, naked but for her ultra-soft bathrobe holding off the world at gunpoint, she was fire personified. The way she moved left him half-drunk with lust and that was before she ever opened her mouth. She was practically fucking perfect in person. And yet...

On paper, she was an F5 tornado produced by a Category 5 hurricane. Cora was a divorced ex-spy who was prepared to kill his brother on his behalf if it came down to it. Talk about making family reunions awkward as all hell. And that was just *his* family. Her own family had cast her out, for not joining the family business, for marrying a non-shifter, or conversely, she left rather than be tied down to outdated notions of familial obligations. It depended on which side you heard, but oh man, news of that had bathed the palace in Corvid gossip for weeks. She was *'escandala'* personified. It was a wonder she would come back and do anything for his family at all, especially since it put her in such close proximity to her own.

Rolling over with a growl and harrumph, Finn shielded his eyes from the emptiness of the room with his forearm. Strange as it was, a part of him felt bad that he didn't really remember her when they were younger. Her sisters were classical beauties, tall, elegant features, he seemed to remember Brendan seeing one of them for a short while in high school. Something about the coolly sensual beauty of the class valedictorian meeting the royal badboy.

That could have been his story with Cora, if both of them hadn't been so trapped in their own little worlds. Two bookish younger siblings, dedicated, determined. In his mind he associated her with pigtails with weaponized solid plastic ball hair barrettes wearing dark blue plaids, maybe glasses? He hadn't been much better, growing into his current body somewhere around the summer of his junior year. By then the shyness had cemented as a mostly-permanent fixture for him and while he saw and occasionally interacted with her and her family, there was never a hint of... well, anything.

A soft knock at his inner door caught his attention, and the scent of food and livestock that followed the door opening moved his feet to the floor.

"Don't shoot! It's just breakfast!" Francis called softly into the room before rolling the cart in. Poor kid looked like he hadn't blinked since the previous day and like he couldn't get out of there fast enough.

"No worries, kid. She's not here."

"Ohthankthegods." The young Hircine man about melted into a puddle just outside of the sitting area. A few deep breaths were all it took for him to collect himself to roll the cart to the bedside. "If you don't mind me saying so, Highness, your girlfriend is a bit... scary."

It was telling to Finn that his first impulse was to refute that she was his girlfriend rather than her being scary. His inclination to truthfulness was going to get him caught up if he wasn't more diligent. "Certainly before coffee she is," he agreed as the young man poured. "She was very sorry about upsetting you yesterday, she was just..." it took him a moment to settle on a word, "startled. It wasn't your fault."

Francis shrugged and gave Finn an easy grin. "No worries, Highness. Once my asthma calmed down, I was fine." He turned to leave and made it about three steps before he turned around with a remarkably serious expression. "I'm glad actually."

"Oh yeah?"

With his head cocked to the side he looked like the world's most earnest golden retriever. "Yeah. Everyone needs someone in their life to look after them, back them unconditionally. You have that in her. It's a good thing."

That his mind filled in 'for a price' made his chest hurt but he nodded his understanding. "Thank you, Francis." It would do no good to point out the crushing naivete there, a naivete he himself was guilty of, but he did appreciate the sentiment. Pushing away the salt and pepper shakers to keep from using them by accident he shook out his napkin. "Good day."

"Good day, Highness."

CORA

She slept like hell, but that wasn't exactly unexpected. Alone in a strange place, not exactly under guard, but definitely not free, family lurking in every shadow and around every corner, it was enough to tune up her aura, so it looked like one of those plasma orb lamps she loved as a kid. A sound caught her attention, a knock at the inner door of the antechamber that had her laying her hand on her gun in the bathrobe. She wouldn't pull this time unless she had to, but she was wary when the breakfast cart was wheeled in, not by the young goat to whom she owed an apology, but a whole different animal. A longhaired black wolf, to be exact, doing his best to pretend he wore sheep's clothing.

"Good morning, Miss Westgate."

Brendan was all smiles, slicked back hair and muscular forearms visible below his sleeves as he wheeled the cart into the room next to her bedside. He was dressed in a royal blue button-down shirt that emphasized his eyes with the sleeves rolled up and gray trousers with razor-sharp creases, giving him the air of artfully messy, dressy approachability. "Did you sleep well?"

"Morning, your Highness. I slept fine, thank you. To what do I owe the pleasure?" Cora found him deceptively pretty, his beautiful face a beacon to bring you closer for much darker ends. Him being in the same room with her made her uneasy, but being alone with him? Yeah, that made her wish she had a sharp-edged weapon. The comforting weight of the pistol in her pocket did nothing to dispel her disquietude where he was concerned.

"Well, a little birdy told me you could use some company this morning, so I thought we could spend some time getting to know each other." Pausing in the middle of the room, he looked from the sitting area to the bed, a slow and decidedly lecherous grin slithering over his lips. "Would you like this in the sitting area or in bed?" His voice made his preference quite clear.

Clutching the robe around herself like armor as she made her way to the sofa, she gestured toward the table. "This is perfect, Highness. Thank you for your kindness."

"Of course, my dear." His smile seemed genuine as he unveiled the steak and eggs and fruit with a flourish, but she still kept an eye on his hands. If he truly was homicidal, she didn't want to get taken out by something he slipped in her food.

Cora felt a little better about her situation, since the place setting he put out in front of her came with a steak knife. She waited until he was seated and tucking into his breakfast to pick at the pile of berries and fruit on her plate. "So what would you like to know, Highness?"

"You simply must call me Brendan," he instructed as he held up a carafe of coffee for her.

She nodded and he poured. "Then you must call me Cora."

The corner of his lips twitched but he didn't look up from his plate. "Thank you, Cora." Her name was a purr on his lips that sent a chill straight up her spine. "Are you enjoying your stay?"

"Yes, thank you. Your brother was kind enough to offer after the previous night's drama." She played the simpering socialite enough, every breathy whimper and shaky bite of fruit was second nature to her. Playing games with apex predators had a high price if you lost.

"Of course he did. He said you saved his life." He laid his hand over hers with a look of earnest gratitude and a gentle squeeze. "You'd think he'd be more grateful."

She glanced longingly at the bacon and just couldn't trust what was on her plate where he was concerned. "What do you mean?"

"One would think he'd be more intimate with the girlfriend who saved his life. So tell me, what did my dear brother do?"

"Do?"

"Well," he gestured with a bite of steak on his fork, "considering the prince's girlfriend is no longer staying in his suite, what would you think?"

"I'd think that it wasn't my business to pry." She grabbed a strawberry and popped it her mouth, careful to watch the food he chose versus that he eschewed. It was not at all beyond the pale to think he'd poison her if he had the opportunity.

His soft chuckle made her tighten her hands on her cutlery. "Fair enough."

"So then I'm curious as to what your thoughts are." Fighting her shift became more of an active job as her apprehension rose. As it was, her eyes were gold and there was no reversing that for the moment. Damn if she didn't wish for more clothes, though.

His nose twitched as he sipped his coffee, regarding her over the rim with a smarmy kind of sneer. "Knowing my brother as I do, I knew there'd be trouble in paradise, but it takes a special kind of idiot to screw up this soon."

The bluntness of his statement startled a bark of laughter out of her. "I..." she giggled in spite of herself, he'd caught her so off guard. "What makes you think he's the problem?"

"Honestly?" She raised her mug in a gesture for him to continue. "Experience. He's *terrible* with women." Leaning back with his cup of coffee, he sighed dramatically. "Oh, his face and his brawn get him far, but when it comes to closing the deal, well..." Brendan shrugged as if he were truly sorry about this state of affairs. "My understanding is their time with him is less than satisfying. Frankly, a woman who saved his life should be lavished in every way possible, not left to fend for herself in a strange place. I'm sure there's many a man in this wing of the palace who would be more than happy to take care of any wishes, wants, or desires you may have, my dear, if you but say the word."

It was hard to squelch the shock that flooded her senses at his shamelessness. Even if she wasn't his brother's girlfriend he was so far out of line, he was two or three coloring books over. "And I suppose you're such a man?"

His golden-eyed slow blink was a mirror image of Finn's, the first time she'd really seen a similarity between them, and it spooked the hell out of her. "Perhaps. I just believe that a breathtakingly beautiful and refined woman such as yourself deserves to have a man who appreciates and can meet," his voice dropped to a rumbling growl, "all your needs."

"I..." Cora licked her lips and reached for more coffee in an effort to avoid meeting his gaze. Fortunately the deep brown of her skin allowed her to hide the flush that came from his blatant flirting. This was certainly a strange start to the day. "At the moment Finn and I are quite happy, even if we have had a difference of opinion on a few things. I do, however, appreciate your concern, Brendan."

"Of course, my dear." He swept to his feet then, all grace and swirl like smoke as he moved to brush a quick kiss across her cheek and ghost his fingertips down her neck to her collarbone. "But do keep me in mind in the event your circumstance should... change."

Brendan was fast, too fast for her to casually break his fingers for touching her and she hated that she had to let him get away with that one. He left with a wink and it was another five minutes of silence before she felt comfortable enough to relax into the couch cushions. Goddess, this job was going to kill her, or she was going to end up in jail, one or the other.

FINN

He had just grabbed his wallet and keys to leave when Cora came stomping through the door. Well, as much as one could stomp in her sky high black heels with the red soles that went with her gray dress that appeared to be part silk toga, part cling film, all unreasonably distracting. She was on the phone, and the look on her face could have quailed generals, and when he opened his mouth to ask, he was met with the single finger of direction. That direction being, "I'll deal with you in a moment." Not exactly how he anticipated their reconciliation starting.

"Yeah, we're on our way there now. I'll advise." Snapping her phone into her clutch that matched her shoes, she fixed him with the yellow-eyed glare he'd come to view with concern.

"Where are we going?" He slipped his keys in his pocket as subtly as he could manage and hoped she didn't notice.

"You need a doctor; we have to go." The low pitch of her voice telegraphed the seriousness of the situation to him as it showed how fragile her grip on her shift truly was.

Hoping to alleviate some of her stress, he folded her hand in both of his. "We don't have to go anywhere. I have a doctor. I can just summon them here."

"No, you can't. I'll explain along the way." Lacing her fingers through his, she led him from the room and down the hall away from the front of the palace to the library. "We need to ditch your minders."

"What? Why?"

Ducking inside, Cora went straight to work, down the bookcase to the far interior wall third shelf down from the top, Chronicles of Narnia. "Hopefully this still works," she muttered, pulling on the book like she was going to remove it from the shelf.

Finn blinked as the shelf receded into the wall and slid to the side to reveal a blackened hallway. "Holy shit! I don't know if I'm more surprised that this is still here or impressed that you remember it."

"You never forget your first secret passageway." She winked over her shoulder at him as she grabbed his wrist and dragged him inside, ensuring the door sealed behind them.

He hadn't thought about this place in years, and he *lived* in the palace. "Won't they come looking for me?"

She shook her head as she turned on her cell phone's flashlight. "Nah, I called you in sick already and hung a 'Do Not Disturb' sign on your door when I walked in the room. That should buy us a few hours."

The sheer scope and scale of her efficiency was frightening to behold.

It was a winding walk through the narrow hallway as she led them farther and farther from the relative safety of his rooms. He wanted to know what was wrong, demand answers from her, but something told him this was neither the time nor place. Just when his frustration reached its peak, they came to a barred steel door that opened to reveal a metal culvert tunnel with a disc of bright sunlight at the end.

They emerged in a copse of trees with a lot of groundcover, and about thirty feet away in a pile of leafy branches made to look like especially dense underbrush was a covered graphite-colored Infiniti Q60 coupe. Blackened windows, matte accents, it was the vehicular equivalent of a shadow, quick and transient, a mirage out of the corner of your eye that vanished before you really saw it.

The radio came on the moment she turned over the engine, a 90s alternative station playing Stone Temple Pilots loud and proud. "Shit! Sorry," she cringed as she leapt to bring the music down to something a bit less brain-rattling.

"No worries." Rubbing a hand over the interior and the dashboard, he took in the height of luxury of this ride. With all the bells and whistles, plus some he was pretty sure he wouldn't know to want, it was nicer than his own personal vehicle. "Is this your car?" At this point he knew that just because she had the keys and the radio was on a good station did not make this her personal ride. "It's comfortable."

"Yeah, it's my personal. I would have had them drop off something work-related, but we needed something inconspicuous that I could fit your tall ass into comfortably." He caught her sly sidelong glance even as she flexed her fingers on the steering wheel.

"I appreciate you thinking of me," he said as he nestled back into the unfathomably comfortable passenger seat. "Your people just left it for you?"

She nodded. "Yeah, I told Mookie where to leave it and he did. He's good like that and he knows what's at stake."

Finn laughed. "What the hell kinda name is Mookie?"

Her chuckle was soft and knowing. "Mookie and Samson are a Felid/Canid pair who were referred to me because they had nowhere else to go. They do work for me off the books and I keep them housed and fed. It's a good arrangement."

"A Felid and a Canid pair..." he enunciated the words to make sure he wasn't getting them wrong. It wasn't exactly abnormal for those two animals to be together but it sure was rare. "And those are their given names?"

She shrugged. "I would assume so. It's not like I gotta issue 'em a W2."

"Touché." The casual way she talked about her unorthodox hiring practices and associates made him want to ask so many more questions, but he had other, more pressing things on his mind. "So, where're we headed?"

Looking in the mirror, then over her shoulder, she hit the turn signal and switched lanes. "Witch Mecca."

He snorted at her description and did the math, about an hour from their current location. "What's up in Salem? This doctor you want me to see. What's that about, anyway?"

Cora tapped a button on the steering wheel and then turned slightly in the seat to face him. "Dr. Bauer is an associate of mine whose primary currency is discretion, followed closely by cash."

"Well, that wasn't an ominous description at all." He didn't realize he'd spoken out loud until he heard her snort of amusement. "Is this some kind of weird underworld doctor? Am I gonna lose a kidney over this?"

She waved off his concern with a flick of the wrist and a quick smirk. "Nah we just needed a place to go for you get some tests. Any time you so much as sneeze, it makes the news. We can't afford that right now."

Sounded reasonable enough. "What kind of tests?"

The casual nature of her shrug seemed disingenuous as she reached over to adjust the AC. "Blood, and whatever else is needed."

Finn's anxiety spiked right then and there as he gripped her wrist tightly. "Alright, I've indulged you long enough on this, but let me be clear: you are not getting a drop of blood out of me until you tell me what the hell is going on."

Cora's blinking silence was the only answer until he released her wrist. "Copper and glass."

"Stained glass windows?" It was literally the only thing he could think of with that combination of things off the top of his head, and that answer was straight out of left field.

"The food tests from the other day. The shiny shit on you breakfast. They found ground glass in your saltshaker and copper dust in your pepper. Now, either one of those things would not be a big deal for a shifter immune system or metabolism, but together? The glass makes it so the copper can penetrate deeper into your system and build toxicity. I need to know your level of exposure and you need to know if you're dying any faster than you were when you woke up this morning."

It was like all the air had been pressed out of his lungs, underscored by the sensation of choking on his tongue. He didn't even notice he was gasping for breath until he felt her long fingers on his wrist, petting and soothing as best she could while driving. Concentrating on the soft susurrations of her voice, he began to breathe deliberately, doing his best to calm his racing heart and pull himself back from anxiety's cliffs.

Finally feeling less like a heart attack was imminent, he remarked wryly, "You are just a tiny pearl of joy, you know that?"

Cora winked as she flashed him a cocky grin. "I'm paid to keep you alive, not blow sunshine up your ass. That's an extra fee my client refused to sign off on."

"Lucky me."

The rest of the drive through the Massachusetts countryside was peaceful and unremarkable on a day that had taken on a shadow of potential rain. Being on the coast was something Finn enjoyed immensely and lamented that his normal duties and responsibilities to the crown precluded doing it more often.

Salem was a fantastic little coastal village with narrow streets and wonderful ambiance. It definitely banked on its 17th Century witch-trial cachet. The public line was they were killed by mass hysteria, a mania that seized the area due to a potent combination of puritanical religious fervor and a bad crop of rye. The truth was a great deal darker than that.

The Score of Martyrs rose in their power even as they and their families receded from 'normal' society, their offspring spreading far and wide and taking their Craft with them. But those descendants of the True Coven still returned here, the lands of their colonist ancestors, and it was interesting to Finn to see how they blended in with the tourists.

Shifters, Lupines and Felids especially, had a longstanding treaty with the True Coven of Twenty, due to some fairly significant overlap. They were known by their scent, a kind of sweet, intangible ether only available to the magically inclined, and here, it permeated everything. This was a town that felt like raw potential energy and it was noticeable even to the uninitiated.

Down a narrow, one-way side street, past the Orthodox church with the leaning cross on one of the blue roof domes and next door to the Ziggy and Sons bakery, was an unassuming royal blue colonial two-story with white trim and a red door. There was literally nothing remarkable at all about the place as she pulled down the alley next to it and up to a wooden gate locked with a code.

It wasn't until the metal gate, the whole fence was plated steel hidden behind slatted wooden fence painted the same white as the house trim, slid into place behind the car that he got an inkling that all was not as it appeared. The curtain over the back door fluttered as they got out and the door opened immediately.

A tall woman with close-cut white hair and glasses greeted them. Dressed in a floral blouse and dress pants, she could have been on her way to a garden party as she was at work. "Cora, Bob said to come on in and he'll meet you downstairs."

"Thanks, Miss Annie." Cora's hand never left his wrist as she led him past the lady who sealed the door behind them with both a deadbolt and a magical rune. Her wink as he passed her told him she knew who he was, but she never mentioned it.

"Where are we?" he whispered out of the side of his mouth as they stepped into a dinky elevator barely large enough to contain the two of them and his shoulders.

Cora crowded into his space as she reached around him as best she could to hit the button for the second basement. "Dr. Bauer is a good man. He'll get us fixed right up."

Finn wasn't sure what to make of the 'us' in that statement, but he opted to leave it alone, content to bask for a moment in her sensual citrusy-floral perfume underscored by calming pheromones.

When the doors opened to a giant gold ankh on the jet-black wall of a darkened hallway lit only by sparing red overhead bulbs, he froze, his mind hitting a blue screen and not rebooting well. *Yep, definitely losing a kidney today.*

"It's alright," she murmured with her free hand petting his forearm as if she could feel his tension spiking again. Her other hand in his with fingers laced tightly, she led him to the end of the corridor, each sealed room with blackened windows in the doors and some with a sliver of light underneath as the only indication of their presence. The only open room was the one at the end of the hall, a literal light at the end of the tunnel.

Dr. Bauer's office was sandstone-looking walls decorated with colorful Egyptian hieroglyphics and depictions of a bare-breasted lion woman with a green face, brown skin, and a red disc over her head. In the center of the room was an unassuming man in a white button-down shirt with a pale aquamarine-colored tie under a white lab coat. He was tall, thin, tan, with sharp features and a comforting smile and glasses that hid whiskey brown eyes that appear to have seen everything at least once.

For the first time since they walked in the place, Cora stepped away from Finn. "Thank you so much for seeing us, Dr. Bauer."

"I always make time for my best customer," he replied with a wink and a broad grin. He certainly didn't present like a man who was here to relieve him of his internal organs. To Finn, he offered a hand. "Dr. Bob Bauer, internist, among other things."

Firm handshake, assured. He smelled Leonine, which went with the whole casually regal air about him. It actually put him even more at ease. "Good to meet you, Doctor. I'm—"

The doc cut him off immediately with a hand up. "No names! This is not that kind of place."

What followed was a detailed explanation of the tests he would be performing on Finn's blood, with the understanding that with anonymity came an additional level of security. Cora remained by his side the whole time, a silent sentinel watching the proceedings with a practiced eye. The blood test was two vials, only a few ounces, that the doctor pulled himself, and then Finn was led back down the hallway to the room next door with a sliver of light under the door.

The door opened to reveal a much larger space than anticipated, dominated by a huge machine made mostly of a metal ring.

"What the hell do I need a CT for?"

CORA

Finn had been doing remarkably well, considering. He actually was a lot less freaked out than she'd anticipated given that she'd spirited him out of the palace without his guards, taken him upstate a bit, to a shifter-sanctioned mafia doctor in a Witch-controlled town. For royalty, he was slipping between worlds almost as easily as she did normally.

His sharp question made her sigh, but only because they were so close to being done, any stopping now was simply frustrating. "He's checking to see if you have glass in your intestines.

"I need to know if your GI tract is compromised," Dr. Bauer followed up calmly. "Any kind of perforation can lead to life threatening consequences."

Finn's blue eyes got large and he linked his hands with hers immediately. "So... will this make me glow in the dark?"

"Only if we're lucky."

She waited in Dr. Bauer's office for him, the lead-lined walls shielding her from the X-rays. She knew it wouldn't take long, and before she could even finish her crossword puzzle on her phone, Dr. Bauer was escorting Finn back to sit next to her.

The good doctor leaned against the desk between them with his arms crossed and his glasses pulled down to the end of his nose.

"Looked good for the most part. There was a bit of glass that I could see, but it appears to be a recent exposure. Anything else I know will have to wait for the blood tests."

"But we're cool otherwise?" she clarified. Now was not the time to take anything for granted.

"Well..." Dr. Bauer grinned, his expression just a bit cheeky. "I mean, he's a remarkable specimen. You're a lucky woman, if that's what you wanna know."

Holy. Fuck. He did not. If he didn't do such quality work for her on such short notice, she'd have to give thought to killing an old lion. "It's... um... yeah." She inhaled sharply through her nose to center herself around the blast furnace blush that had taken over her head. "It's not like that."

The doctor's open snickering was more wheeze than anything else. "Uh huh."

"You all know I'm right here, right?" One look at Finn's face said he was in no better shape than she was, blush-wise.

The doctor flicked away Finn's feeble protestations as he stepped away from the desk and took both her hands as she came to her feet. "Any more questions? No? Excellent. Cora," his smile felt like a hug, "always good to see you, kiddo."

"Thanks, Doc. Usual rate, usual location?" She didn't want to talk money in front Finn, but there was a certain protocol to this type of interaction. Cash at a dead drop was pretty standard fare if she didn't bring it with her.

"That'd be fine. Annie has something for you at the front desk, and would you ask her to send in my next patient on your way out, please?" He was already getting situated behind his desk again and looking over papers.

Hopefully it was more of her glamour, because there was no telling how long this job would go and there was no harm in stockpiling. "Will do, thank you again."

"Sekhmet bless and keep you. I have a feeling you're going to need her."

Cora's eyes flashed gold, revealing all the hidden glyphs in the room and on his desk. It wasn't like him to offer such things to her. Theirs was a cordial professional relationship and while he knew she was a Corvid, in the same way she knew he was Leonine, their varying religions weren't something either of them discussed. "I appreciate your and *her* concern. Thank you. See ya around, Doc."

Finn was silent as they left his office and in fact didn't speak until they got in the car and had left the gated lot. "Sekhmet, huh?"

She nodded. Something about the very mention of the Goddess troubled her. It wasn't like Dr. Bauer to say something like that and he didn't strike her as a guy who did anything without a reason. A part of her would like to think that Sehkmet and the Morrigan would fight side by side, but neither one could she see invoking unless left with no other options. The unsettled feeling that had enveloped her side of the car was broken by Finn's hum of discovery. "You say something?"

Reading from his phone, he stroked his beard and marveled, "'She Before Whom Evil Trembles.'" The title was followed by a long, heated look slipping down her body that was punctuated by him biting his lip before meeting her eyes again. "I could see it."

Cora watched him out of the corner of her eye, giving him a sly grin but otherwise not speaking. She didn't trust her words right then. It was so damn easy to fall into this pattern with him, this artificial closeness that felt like it could be so much more. It wasn't fair to either of them, but it truly wasn't fair of her to want more from him. There were too many strictures, too many reasons not to say anything to darken his prospects with something as useless and tawdry as her desires. They were who they were, products of their circumstances and experiences, next to each other physically but oceans apart in all other respects.

Music from the radio spilled out of the speakers as a dreamy, steady pace, notes and nostalgia winding around between the two of them until the passive agitation she felt from him reached the point of spilling over into words. "Why didn't you tell me?"

A part of her wanted to ignore it outright, even though she knew it was wrong to treat him that way. And she wouldn't disrespect them both by pretending she didn't know what he was asking. "I *couldn't* tell you."

"Contractual obligation?"

"Fuck no." She huffed in annoyance, her hands tightening and flexing on the leather of the steering wheel. "It would have been easier if it was."

"It *was* easy, though," he countered, shifting in the seat to face her, blue eyes full of hurt and anxiety. "I can't get past all those times you *could* have said something. At the bar, on the way to your place, on your couch before we... or after." He shook his head as he stared at the roof of her car. "You said you didn't do it for money."

"I didn't." She hoped her immediate answer would be enough to reassure him. Of the few times he'd made it into the news for negative press was from a woman who'd sold intimate photos of her and him together to the tabloids in an attempt to fashion that into a potential reality gig. After that, his public appearances with women in his company who weren't related were few and far between. As if she didn't feel bad enough, the guilt of feeling like she'd brought back all that trauma for him was sharp in her chest. "The reasons I picked you up had nothing to do with the job and everything to do with me, personally."

"So then tell me why. I deserve to know."

"You remember..." she sighed as she gathered her wits, doing her best to quell the butterflies in her stomach and not give in to the urge to floor the accelerator so this was over faster. "Back in high school...."

"This goes back to high school?"

"Eh, kind of. Your brother—"

"You were into *my brother*?" He exhaled a pouty growl, crossing his arms. "Of course you were. Every girl wanted Brendan. He was—"

The car jerked as she tapped the brakes in annoyance. "Not the subject of this conversation. May I continue?" He gestured for her to carry on and she stretched her neck, shifting in the seat to get more comfortable. "Your brother was dating my sister. We spent a lot of time together around that time, just because she dragged me with her so she could see him. Remember?"

"Right?" The way he drew the word out told her he had no idea where she was going with this, which, while disheartening, wasn't unexpected.

"Reading comics, talking, drawing..."

"I remember."

"Teenaged me had a massive, truly epic crush on teenage you." It was a great deal heavier than a crush, but this was not the time or place for that. The undying heart eyes of a fourteen-year-old girl were nothing to scoff at.

"What? No. Me? Really? Why...?" His mouth worked as he attempted to cram in a few more questions, finally settling on, "Why didn't you say anything? Do anything?"

"And what would you have said exactly? Done? My sisters were the amazing ones, and I was just the mousy little tagalong who barely had any feathers and couldn't even fly." The bile that rose in the back of her throat took a minute to settle back down before she could continue. This was the past, the distant past that she'd overcome a long damn time ago, or so she'd thought. Didn't matter that she was a decorated veteran or could kill a man fifteen ways with a hair comb and a grudge, nope. Here she would always be the shadow, the departed, the discarded. This, right here, was why you could never go home again.

At this point she owed it to both of them to finish, just to have this last secret between them laid to rest. "I got with you for me. Because I wanted to. Because I could. The job afforded me the opportunity and I'm the terrible human being who took it. Was I paid for the job? Yes. Was I paid to sleep with you? No." She couldn't even look at him now, her whole body was burning from the inside out, the shame of her lack of professionalism was so heavy and real. She wouldn't blame him for bolting the moment she stopped the car. Why would he possibly trust she could keep him safe when he couldn't even trust her to control herself around him? "Being a hooker would be preferable to being an adult nursing a seventeen-year-old crush. On someone I'm paid to protect, for fuck's sake. It's unseemly."

"Unseemly is not the word I'd use," he muttered to the window glass as he shrank back into the passenger seat.

Mortification at critical mass, Cora thumbed the volume button for the radio on the steering wheel. "You'll pardon me if I'm not interested in your semantic opinions right now." When he reached for the radio knob to turn it down again, she smacked his hand, her eyes never leaving the road. "Leave it alone. We're done talking. You wanted to know, now you do. That conversation is closed."

CHAPTER NINE

FINN

As answers went, it was definitely not what he'd expected from Cora. In a million years, he would have never imagined her motivated by anything other than an acquisitive desire for whatever it was that got her up in the morning. Her deeply personal response to him was paradoxically exactly what he wanted to know and yet didn't answer anything really. It definitely wasn't the pound of flesh he'd anticipated.

The bitch of it was he had more questions. Why did she still want him after all this time? Did she regret it? Would she do it again? Please? Gods, he was terrible. He knew he shouldn't want her still, and yet... fuck.

Honestly, it would have been easier to abandon his attraction to her if it had just been an act of mercenary drive or expediency. Instead it was the vulnerabilities of a frail, if incredibly dangerous, shifter woman who sometimes made mistakes too. The humanity of it was what drew him in. She wasn't some bulletproof paragon of righteousness or justice or unflinching secret agent coolness. She was… sweet, in her own way. Loyal, brave, a transplant to a world he could scarcely understand. Maybe a little nuts. And mute, apparently, because the entire rest of the car ride back to the palace was solely filled with nineties music and nary a peep from the driver's seat.

When she pulled the car into the spot where they'd left outside the drainage culvert, she pulled out her cell phone and fired off a few messages. The silence was so pressing it may as well have been an additional passenger.

"When we get to the library, you'll go first and I'll follow a few minutes later," she murmured, still not looking at him.

"Won't people see us?"

"Eh." Cora rolled a shoulder as a show of indifference as she got out of the car and headed toward the secret entryway. "At worst, people will assume we had a torrid assignation among the volumes."

Finn's sudden bark of laughter filled the tunnel and a tightness he'd had in his chest suddenly loosened. "What, are we in a Brontë novel? Did I miss something?"

Her sly grin gave her away. "Well… I was shooting for Jane Austen, but we make do with what we have."

"Fair." The walk back up to the house was conducted at a good clip, but in deference to her heels. A longer stride was not kind to someone on stilts, and he would never begrudge her the sexy footwear he secretly loved on her. It was part of her charm.

Hand on the release for the secret passage back into the library, Finn turned to face Cora. The light of her cell phone flashlight diffused off the stone around them wreathing her in shadows. There were so many things he wanted to say, to ask, but the biggest one he needed in that moment was, "Are we good?"

His heart clenched for a moment as her whole body heaved with a sigh. "I dunno. Are we?"

"Yeah." He nodded. "Yeah, I think so. I appreciate you telling me the truth."

Instead of acknowledging him, she gestured toward the door. "Go on, get. Before someone finds us here."

Tempted as he was to argue with her, he did as she told him and was back in the library with no one any the wiser. It was a blue bloody miracle the whole palace wasn't up in arms at his disappearing act. The fact Cora could affect such a flawless escape from the guards should have been point of concern, but mostly he was grateful that she was working on his side instead of for his enemies. She was not one he'd want to tangle with if he could help it.

Strolling around the room, he wandered over to the writing desk he used to use as a kid doing homework. Afternoons spent with Cora on one side of the desk and him on the other, working, telling stories, her drawing pictures to make him laugh. It was hard to reconcile the memory of the sweet smile and braids with the stone fox she was currently.

The main doors bursting open like someone had a federal warrant startled him out of his musings. "Aunt Gwen?"

"Finnegan, I have been looking everywhere for you!"

Gwendolyn Theodora Laurent, Dowager Duchess of Wolfingham (which included the Greater British Isles and Brittany, France, the ancestral homelands), was his father's sister and a major mother figure in Finn's life after the passing of his mother. If his mom had been disdainful of his very existence, prone to doting on Brendan, and otherwise lacking social niceties unless in the presence of company and foreign dignitaries. She was the Wicked Witch of the West in a crepe-de-chine Givenchy suit, though he would never in his life have the balls to say that out loud.

"Is something wrong?" He cast a nervous glance over at the shelf in front of the secret passage and hoped like hell that Cora could hear through it.

"Well, of course there is." She drew both the doors closed and leaned back against them like she intended to block his exit. "I stopped by your room and you weren't there. I'm told you've been sneaking out, is that true? Is it the influence of that Corvid?"

He blinked. There was so much to unpack there, the mind fairly boggled. "I left a 'Do Not Disturb' sign up on my room, Auntie. I left it on the door for a reason."

The older woman scoffed and casually strode to the writing desk he'd been admiring, taking a seat and looking like the most chic librarian in the history of ever as she crossed her legs. "That's for the *staff*, darling. Certainly not family. Do I look like staff to you?"

The way she said the word made him think of her as a 'staph' infection. His lips twitched but he kept his commentary to himself. "Of course not," he soothed. A lifetime of practice allowed him to slip into the role of placator-in-chief. It was always easier to deal with Aunt Gwen when she believed she was getting her way. The alternative was too loud and terrible to even consider. "I'm sorry that you've been looking for me. What can I do for you?"

"A little birdie told me you've been sneaking out without your retinue." She shook her head, mouth drawn into a tight moue of disappointment. "Aren't you a bit *old* for that?"

Of course Brendan sold him out. He was the favorite, after all. It was practically his duty. "It's nowhere near as bad as you've heard." What was intriguing, though, was the lack of information she was going on about. One would think she'd lead with the drive-by. It's not like Brendan didn't know unless that's information he doesn't want getting out. *Curious...*

"Your brother also tells me that you've been keeping company in secret with a woman well below your station. A Corvid." That one word almost glistened in the air between them dripping with contempt. "Have you introduced this," she paused like she had to think about it, "*woman* to your father yet?"

This time he smiled fondly, thinking back to the lunch the previous day, likely one of his father's last good days. "I have actually. He found her lovely."

"I... see." That news was met with The Eyebrow™, the indication of an incoming lecture regarding social standing, comportment, and whatever other princely duties or functions she felt he was not fulfilling to her exacting specifications. He was already exhausted from it and she hadn't even spoken yet. "I need you to understand, Finnegan—Finn," she peered at him with a serious expression in her slightly faded blue eyes, "you are the *Lupine* prince. We have a rich history dating back millennia."

"I'm aware, Auntie."

"Then you should also know that Corvids, while they have a debatable place at court, have absolutely no place at all in the royal wing of the palace. They are not now, nor have they ever been, marriage material. As such..." she trailed off, looking at him expectantly like she wanted him to finish the thought. When he stood before her, stone silent, she rolled her eyes and shoved to her feet, a surprisingly inelegant gesture from the woman before she stomped over and took both his hands. "You know you can't just keep company with an unmarried woman in the royal wing. It's tawdry, undignified. Certainly not befitting a prince of the house Lupine. You may not be the crown prince," he would have laughed at the smooth way she worked in the dig if he weren't so disgusted, "but once Brendan has ascended to the throne you will be and there will be expectations."

"Expectations," he repeated, rage in his veins stripping him of vocabulary beyond parroting.

"Surely, you understand, Finnegan. I know you think she's a fine girl, but she's not for you. Think of the children. We cannot have the potential bloodline of the throne contaminated so. Your brother understood this, I'm sure, in time, you will as well."

The sour taste in his mouth matched his disposition and while before he'd hoped Cora could hear into the room, it was long past the time when he truly hoped she could not. Dropping his aunt's hands as casually as possible, he took a deep breath, counting to ten, then twenty in his head before opening his mouth to allow the words boiling within him to flow out.

"I understand," he began, staring at her and making no bones about shifting both his eyes and his voice, "that you have a preference for the old ways."

"Finn, you must—"

"Oh no," he snarled, leaving her to close her mouth so quickly her teeth clicked, "you're done speaking. You said what you wanted to say and now you will hear what I have to say." He sat silently for a moment but for the seams of his suit shredding as he began his shift, challenging her to defy his order before continuing. "We have long passed the point where such antiquated rules are enforceable, nor are they even advisable. I'm not going to live like a relic because some old *fossil*," he couldn't even appreciate the way she flinched at his wording, he was beyond incensed, "has a problem with me seeing or marrying a Corvid. Cora is an incredible woman of character and principle, two things I'm not sure you've ever possessed honestly, and I will not—"

"I beg your pardon!"

"*I'm not finished*," he roared, loud enough that the din outside in the hallway fell away to the kind of quiet associated with a sepulcher. "I *will not* have her subjected to your base and frankly terrible inclinations and behavior. We are done here. Remove yourself from my presence, Duchess. We will not speak again. On this, or any other topic."

Pale now, his aunt reached for his hand, stopped short when he growled low in his chest. "Finn," she entreated softly, submissive whine coloring her tone. "My prince, you don't mean—"

"Leave me." He gestured to the doors, silver fur shimmering over his skin as he did everything possible to maintain his human form before he ripped her throat out. "Now!"

The quiet click of the door let him exhale, his hands shaking in fists at his sides as he counted the boxes on the coffered ceiling. Rage, waves of nauseating intense heat, the scent of blood and his aunt's terror in his nose, all of it welling up in him and leaving him helpless to fight it. His wolf burst forth, rending his suit to irreparable shreds of worsted wool.

When the door to the secret passage whispered open, he faced her not as the man she knew, but as the eight-foot-tall wolf he was. On his hind legs, in full silver fur, gold eyes, he watched her silently emerge into the room, head held high, jaw set and dark eyes diamond hard. He'd have believed she missed the terrible things his aunt had said if not for the brittle smile on her full lips as she passed him. Her hand slipped down his arm, a caress of his fur that swamped him with emotions.

He wanted... to hold her, to apologize, to forcibly call back every hateful word that woman had uttered in her direction and shield Cora from them. The feeling of helplessness felt worse than rage, and he knew there was no shifting back for him any time soon.

Cora's scent lingered at the door, wafting past him when she opened it. "Finn." He faced her, the glossy sheen of obsidian feathers visible on her skin, bright yellow eyes on full display. "Thank you."

Finn dipped his head, not trusting his words and very much desirous of physical contact she clearly did not want. He swallowed hard as she slipped the door silently shut behind her. That would be the last damn time she would experience such a thing. He'd make damn sure of it.

CORA

That she found herself in front of the Guard house directly outside of the palace after leaving Finn's company wasn't a surprise. She needed... familiar? ...structure? Something. Anything to clear the echoing words of him and his aunt's argument over her.

When she first heard the voice, Cora had been wary just because of their clandestine mission, but the more she'd heard, the more she really wanted to pop the old lady in the mouth. And then Finn stepped in.

All eight furry, growling feet of him. In what was left of an Armani suit.

Never in her whole life had anyone stood up for her like that. Not even when she'd been married. He'd dressed down the duchess without a second thought, lifting Cora up with his words like it was nothing at all. Maybe he did it because he knew she was listening, but he still did it and she appreciated it.

Maybe a little too much.

It was easy to imagine more when Finn did things like that. That inherent kindness again making her soft on him when she truly should be all edges and fight as she defended him.

Walking into the Guard house was like any other Guard house in the realm, showing her approved-for-public ID card which showed her honorably discharged status to the two fresh-faced young men by the door.

The startled blinks and murmured, "Commander," as they both pulled up straighter, was something that never got old, though there was no sport in impressing the youngsters. A fingerprint scan and a smile and she was in. There was no point in staying away from them since she was no longer entirely in hiding, plus she had business with Xander and Devon.

She found the two Day Watch Commanders back in Xander's office, a room with one window occupied by a massive, and clearly well-tended, African violet and decorated in coordinating muted purple and cream hues to match. He was clearly an interesting dude.

They both got to their feet when she came into the room.

"Ma'am." Xander cocked his head to the side as he watched her, eyes clearly taking in every single millimeter of her person as they flashed bronze for a moment before returning to their normal blue. He wasn't welcoming but he wasn't exactly foreboding either.

"Commander, what can we do for you?" Devon's smile was friendly and his body language open, even if his eyes were wary as hell. These two together clearly played to each other's strengths.

"I'm retired... discharged, whatever. Same rank. You don't have to call me that." She chuckled self-consciously before sinking into a chair in front of the desk with a sigh. "I'm sorry. Today's kind of gone to shit."

"Are you okay?" Devon asked, taking the seat next to hers and mirroring her posture.

"I think it changes from minute to minute," she answered honestly.

"Is there something we can do for you, Commander?" Xander repeated, clearly not into sharing feelings.

"Man, it's 'Miss' if it's anything, damn." An insult about hawks being able to see for miles but unable to hear for shit was poised on her tongue, but she kept it back with a wan smile. "It's Cora, preferably, but you seem to insist on a title."

Devon snorted, a broad grin stretched over his lips. "Alright, Cora. What's going on?"

"My assistant forwarded you the emails with the lab's initial findings on Finn's food."

"Your assistant?"

"What's wrong with Finn's food?"

Both questions were asked at the same time, with both men looking at each other with wry grins. Clearly this wasn't their first rodeo. "Start with the second," Xander directed as he pulled up his email, signaling Devon to join him behind the desk. "Okay, what am I looking at?"

"Glass and copper? Explain, please." Devon's cocked head and narrowed eyes as he stared at her telegraphed his confusion.

"Heavy metal poisoning is slow usually. Builds up over time, causes liver damage, kidney damage, neurological issues. It's actually pretty easy to do accidentally if you don't know any better."

Xander leaned back in his chair and crossed his arms, clearly still unconvinced. "And what makes you think this is deliberate versus accidental?"

"Couple things. First, your kitchen staff would know not to cook acidic foods in copper pots. That's the way this normally happens. Marinara in a copper pan or way too many Moscow Mules with limes. Occasionally shit happens, but that's not the case here." She paused because this was the part she truly needed them to appreciate. "That brings me to the glass. Hidden in the salt, you're not going to see it and you're going to eat it, and it's going to cause microtears in your intestines and you'll end up with a lot more copper in your body than you would otherwise have. This is deliberate and happening inside the palace."

Devon sighed and nodded grimly. "Has Vasily seen this?"

"He got a copy too."

Xander squeezed his eyes shut and dropped his head back

before rubbing the back of his neck. "I'll call him," he told Devon. "We're gonna get this figured out, Cora. I promise."

She appreciated his assurances. "Sooner rather than later. I'd rather not deal with a hungry wolf if I don't have to."

Xander's lips twitched into an almost smile. "There's a Duran Duran song in there somewhere, isn't there?"

"Yeah, yeah. Laugh it up, birdbrain. It's all fun and games until you look like chicken."

"Methinks the lady doth protest," he informed Devon with a sage nod.

"Oh, it's like that?" his partner inquired glancing at her with a wicked grin and eyes that glinted with mischief.

He snickered. "What? I have eyes."

Cora coughed deeply as his comment and accompanying unrepentant grin made her choke on her spit. "Yes, eyes that have been on parts of me that I would prefer you not think about right now. What is wrong with you?"

Devon thumped the blond on the back of his head with a disapproving glare. "Ignore him. He's touched."

This felt good, this easy camaraderie, this brothers-in-arms feeling she'd apparently been seeking by showing up on their doorstep. Xander's phone went off then, and when he looked at it, he slid directly from giggles to a glower.

"Something wrong?" Cora asked, rising from the chair and ready to move out if he said so.

"As much fun as this has been," he looked over to Devon who was already on his feet and buttoning his blazer, "I'm sorry, but we have to go."

"Go where?"

"The King's making a speech with the royal family and we need to be there." The dark-eyed man took a couple steps and then stopped, turning back to her. "You should come too."

"Me? Why?" It was a reasonable question even as she moved to follow both men through the Guards' entrance to the palace.

Devon's smile was not unkind. "I think the prince would appreciate you being there," he informed her softly.

"Uh... no. We're not public. More importantly, *I* can't be public," she objected, shaking her head vehemently. Cameras, she could handle; her glamour would take care of that without issue. Her relationship with the prince, however, was still very much under wraps, and without an official announcement, there was no way in hell she wanted to challenge that. The case was too important to rush or screw that kind of thing. Nope with a capital Hell No.

"See, I've been thinking about that," Xander placed his hand on the small of her back as they boarded the elevator to the second floor, "And I have a plan."

CHAPTER TEN

FINN

One of the benefits of being the third in line to the shifter throne was that stalking through the palace fully wolfed out wasn't something that merited scrutiny. In fact, staring was generally frowned upon, though thankfully no longer punishable by lashings or worse.

The suit was a total loss, which was a pity because it had been one of his favorites. He could take that out on his aunt too, but there wasn't a point to it, really, because she would never change. His whole life, she treated him as a spare part in a model kit, there if needed, but fuck off otherwise.

What he really wanted though was to reach out to Cora. Her face when she left him was burned in his brain, a welt that pained him every time he thought about it. He wanted to talk to her, to hear her voice. In his mind he knew that she was okay, that she was tougher than some hateful, hurtful diatribe from his aunt, but his heart could definitely do with some more convincing.

The peace and tranquility that came with returning to the sanctified quiet of his room allowed him to shift back fairly quickly. There was only the momentary spike of ire when he saw the 'Do Not Disturb' sign on the door and remembered his aunt's commentary. Taking advantage of the rare moment of downtime, he hopped in the shower to clean up a bit and shake off the vestiges of rage that were still clinging to him while he mentally prepared for whatever pronouncement his father was going to make that required his presence.

No amount of loin-girding, though, prepared him for seeing Cora in the throne room. Off to the side and under a portable light stand that all but obscured her features, she was at the front of the press corps, phone out like she intended to record the proceedings. His cheeks heated at the slight tilt of her chin and knowing wink, but otherwise they didn't interact as he took his place next to his brother behind their father. Aunt Gwen was there as well, but wisely kept to the other side of Brendan and gave him a wide berth.

It was a public announcement of the date of abdication and Brendan's formal coronation, both of which would be the next full moon which was less than three weeks away. Combine that with his birthday gala the following night and he could almost taste his stress level. The ever-present pit of anxiety and despair flared in his stomach, but he managed to keep his face impassive. Living with the constant scrutiny of vultures—both literal and figurative—had taught him many things, but that was definitely one of the most important.

The moment the presser was done, his desire to stand and take questions from reporters was nonexistent, so he turned to disappear back into the warren of hallways that eventually led to the royal residences. Blissful quiet embraced him as the mic'd up horde swarmed his brother. That was one benefit of not being the heir apparent.

His brother wasn't ready to rule. Anyone with eyes knew that. Even though he was the older of the two, he had never really recovered from their mother's death, drowning his pain in any number of intoxicants, both chemical and sexual. Still, if Finn couldn't convince him to back down, which was highly likely, he hoped he could help steer the transition by giving his brother counsel and support, while he worked on a new plan. He would never torch the kingdom just to advance his agenda. That was more Brendan's style than his, anyway.

The door to the throne room popped open then, startling him from his thoughts. The din of so many people and their differing agendas had died down to only a few voices and the sound of equipment being moved. Brendan slipped through with a quick glance over his shoulder and came to a screeching halt in front of Finn. With his long hair pulled back into a half ponytail and his emerald green tie, he looked like a well-dressed wraith, everything about him thin and rangy, too ethereal to be real and too sharp an edge not to be.

His blue eyes widened for a moment, fright plain on his features before he regained his composure. "Finnegan," he acknowledged him with a dip of his chin as he attempted to brush past him.

"Bren." Finn loosely snagged his wrist as he passed, hoping that the thinner man wouldn't swing on him. Last thing either of them needed was a fistfight with the press so nearby.

For a long moment everything is still between them, silent and motionless like the world was standing still waiting on them to make a decision as to how this was going to go.

The crown prince shook off Finn's hand with a flick of the wrist, looking very put out at the physical contact. "What do you want, Brother?"

"I want to let you know that I'm here to support you if you need me."

"You, support me?" The mocking tone reeked of contempt. "Do tell."

Blinking away his initial acerbic reply, Finn exhaled deeply. "Everything leading to this has been... difficult. Arduous." To say the very least. "And as much as I know these last few years haven't been kind to any of us—"

"You think?"

He continued on like Brendan hadn't just lanced into him with his tongue. "I want you to know that we're still brothers and you can count—"

"If you finish that sentence, I will disembowel you right here and claim Lunacy." Lunacy, by its very definition, was a werewolf-specific charge that fell somewhere between 'crime of passion' and 'they had it coming', and not one leveled lightly, especially among the House Lupine.

"You're welcome to try." He'd like to think he was channeling Cora's brand of chilling menace but knew that was probably a lot to hope for. Just because he truly did not want to fight did not mean he wouldn't if pushed.

"Look at you," Brendan purred condescendingly as he circled him slowly. "All big and bad with your righteous anger and your upright morals. The saint, they call you. The *Humanitarian*," he hissed the word like it was an epithet. "You're no better than me. Your only claim to fame is you're better at hiding it. But I know you."

Dammit, he came to offer support, not pick a damn fight with the man. Maybe lack of food was allowing his hangry impulses to drive. No more though. "It doesn't have to be like this."

"Like this? Like you're mocking me, like you, and every single other shifter in the kingdom, don't find me unfit for the throne? Don't think I don't know what's said. Whispered about in the halls, writ large in the headlines." He snarled and paced away a few steps, every heaving breath popping seams as he fought against his shift. Apparently, suits were a dime a dozen in the kingdom tonight.

"Then change it." Against his better judgement, Finn followed him down the hall, yanking him to a halt. When Brendan rounded on him, he held up both hands and took a step back to show his lack of aggressive intent. "Surprise them and be better than they expect. Be great and let them talk about that. Their opinion of you does not have to be static. Give them a reason to see something else."

For a moment, just a fleeting instant, the dark clouds parted and Brendan's face relaxed, jaw unclenched, vein in his forehead receded. And then the lightning struck. "It's amazing to me how incredibly naive you are. How you've lived so long with your Pollyanna worldview and your delicate sensibilities I'll never know. Your compassion and empathy are wasted on me, Finnegan." He snorted. "Offering me your support like you give a damn about me. Like you've ever given a damn about me."

"You're my brother."

"A mistake of bloodline only, I assure you." Not even allowing him to reply, he stalked off down the hall, snarling at the staff as he passed them, seeming to delight in the collection of cowering employees left in his wake.

Finn remained in the hallway outside the throne room for a moment, collecting himself so he didn't repeat his brother's atrocious behavior. Each deep, cleansing breath, though, was tinged with the faint scent of steak and his stomach growled loud enough that a passing maid stopped and eyed him with askance. A hungry wolf was not the kind of thing you turned your back on.

"Sorry," he offered her as he ducked his head in shame and scurried back to his quarters. He hoped to have Cora come as well, and as soon as he was out of his suit and relaxed, he'd call her.

The sight, and smells, that greeted him upon opening this bedroom door stopped him in his tracks. Cora sat on his couch reading from her phone, legs outstretched across the cushions and crossed at the ankles, feet bare, looking for all the world like she belonged there. In front of her on one of the serving carts was two silver domes as per usual, and a large, handled paper bag on the floor facing him.

"I—how?"

"Hey." She smiled warmly as she rose from the couch. It was incredible to him how much her smile eased his mind. Like all the turmoil with Brendan receded just a bit and let him breathe.

He was struck full on by her unreasonable beauty as she approached him with a glass of red wine in hand. She moved like a predator, all sleek lines and focus. Her dark skin and draped gray dress gave her a kind of sculptural quality, breathtaking sexiness in motion, right down to her delicately painted toes. He knew he shouldn't think of her in those terms, but damn if he could help it.

"Miss Westgate, I don't remember you being a member of the press corps," he teased. The tiny smile that tugged at his lips showed itself despite his best efforts at remaining serious.

Her dimples only made her more beautiful to him. "I took the 'if you can't beat 'em, join 'em' approach. Truthfully though, I didn't think you wanted to answer questions about us, no?"

Finn nodded vehemently as she handed him the half full chalice. "There's a whole lot I'd rather not discuss right now."

"Can't say as I blame you, really."

His stomach growled as the scent of steak wafted past him again and Cora giggled. "What? I'm starving," he grumbled as he approached the cart and lifted one of the silver domes. A bracingly rare steak, possibly the largest one he'd ever seen, lay on a serving platter, accompanied by a pile of garlic smashed potatoes and a forest of prosciutto wrapped asparagus grilled. He could have wept for joy. An engraved calling card rested just under the edge of his plate.

D'Antonio's has been run by the same family since 1887, a family of tightknit Bubalines who took their Michelin star rating very, *very* seriously. Asking for takeout could get you banned. It just wasn't done, and yet....

"Emilio," he blinked at her, agog at her obvious display of power and will, "doesn't do takeout."

She primly took her seat and lay the napkin across her lap. "He does whatever I ask of him for enough money and for me not to have his horns ripped out."

Her tone was so casual, phrasing so very exact, it was hard to tell if she was joking or not. Probably best not to know either way. Finn wasted no time diving into his massive porterhouse steak that had to be all of seventy-six ounces and asparagus. He moaned on the first bite, "You are a goddess and should be worshipped accordingly."

She scoffed and ducked her head, but her dimples gave her amusement away as she carved up her own rare meat. "And you've only seen me naked once."

"Twice-ish."

"Who's counting?" she asked around a mouthful of steak.

He took a few more bites of his food before leaning back to sip his wine. "I can't believe you'd do this for me. Thank you."

Cora looked up from her mashed potatoes. "Don't thank me; it was self-preservation. You missed lunch, and these legs," she used her fork to draw his eyes to her long, perfectly statuesque gams crossed next to the table, "ain't made of chicken. Feathers notwithstanding."

Finn huffed a quick laugh over his plate. "Noted. Though I will say, they do look quite edible." He didn't miss the hitch in her breath, or the growl she used to cover it, pleased that he could affect her so.

"That was smooth, Highness. Inappropriate, but smooth."

Her use of his title brought him up short, like she was distancing herself from him. "I feel like I should apologize." For this, and *so* many other transgressions, large and small.

Wiping her mouth with her napkin, she sat back, eyes assessing his every move. "That's not necessary."

"It kinda is, though." Sensing that he probably wouldn't get a better opening, he dropped his napkin and moved his chair around to be next to her, taking her hand in both of his. "I know you heard what my aunt said—"

"You don't have to apologize for her," she interjected with dark eyes like smoldering embers. "You don't owe me shit where she's concerned."

"I do, though. I didn't stop her soon enough. Didn't react—"

"You went full wolf on her," she reminded him dryly, sounding suddenly exhausted. "How much more reaction did you need?"

"Still, with everything you're doing protecting me, putting yourself in a position to face the family who abandoned you, you don't deserve to deal with that, too." Eyes closed, he sighed deeply before pulling her hand to his lips and brushing a kiss across her knuckles.

"It's not about deserving," she murmured as she stared at their joined hands. "I appreciate the thought, though. And as much as you'd like it to, it's never gonna change. You're a prince, not a god."

"That you know of," he whispered conspiratorially with a wink and a giggle. Damn, but he just wanted to make her smile, and felt his whole body relax a bit as she returned his grin with one of her own. Leaning as he was into her space, the kiss was almost inevitable, like the polar attraction of magnets, so too were his lips drawn to hers. It was inevitable, this kiss, this first amongst many he hoped, with no secrets between them. The tiny whimper when he cupped her cheek damn near broke him, his inner wolf now fully in the driver's seat. She tasted of wine and wanting, something dark and forbidden, something he knew he shouldn't want and yet refused to give up.

Growling, he gathered her into his lap as she reached for him, twining her arms around his shoulders. It was difficult to reconcile her delicate softness with the razor-sharp focused intensity he normally associated with her, but the way she melted into him... in that moment he's king of the world. The citrusy scent of her perfume filled his head as her sighs filled his ears. This was better than the kiss at the luncheon because they were alone, and he could take his time to sample each and every moan that fell from her lips.

Cora's great heaving breath as she pulled back from his kiss made him smile. Finn's addiction to her kisses was quite plain and clearly reciprocated. "You're dangerous," she exhaled softly, her voice rough velvet against his ears.

"Me? How so?" he teased as he brushed her nose with his.

"You..." She sighed, the slight curl to her lips taking on a sad cast. "You make me forget... make me wish—" A loud banging on the bedroom door cut into her thoughts and startled them apart. They had but a moment before Vasily would come bursting in, mad as a boiled hornet.

"What do you wish?" Finn inquired as he dabbed her lipstick from his mouth and straightened his clothes. He understood whatever she asked for, he would give her, without question, whether she knew it or not.

"Oh good, you're both together," the Night Watch Commander began as he stormed through the door clutching paper copies of the test results she'd sent him. "Saves on the yelling."

"So?" the prince prompted her again.

Sighing, Cora filled her wine glass and moved from the table to the couch, preparing for what would surely be a lengthy browbeating by his best friend. "I sometimes wish things were different."

CHAPTER ELEVEN

VASILY

"I'm going to assume," he hissed as he stalked over to where Cora sat with her legs crossed and holding her wine glass, "since you somehow managed to go to *fucking Salem*, without any of the Day Watch Guards being aware, you knew you were in the wrong." He stared at her, with her Giaconde smile and her arms crossed as she held her glass, "You appreciate why that's not fucking okay, right? Why that's not kosher? Do you—" he turned to face Finn who was methodically working through the last pieces of his steak, "do you have any idea how many treaties you two violated in your little jaunt? Hell, it's practically the prelude to an International Incident, capital I's on both."

The judgmental curl to Cora's lips as she sipped her drink incensed him. "You think this is funny? Am I a fucking joke to you?"

"You don't want an answer to that," she offered blandly as she moved to stretch out in the corner of the sofa, and he was struck, again, with the urge to cheerfully strangle her.

"You know what—"

"Vasi," Finn barked, startling him into silence. "Have a seat before you have a stroke, damn."

"This? Right here?" She gestured with her wine glass in his general direction. "This is exactly why we didn't tell you."

"I swear on my mother's wings..." Seeing that neither of them was taking him seriously, he took a seat on the far end of the sofa from her. "Overlooking that—"

"Oh, and I plan to," she assured him.

"Overlooking that," he sneered as he shooed her away focusing instead on his best friend, "How do you think this goes if something happens to you, Goddess forbid? In a witch town? Really?"

"It was fine. Everyone lived. It was a day trip."

Cora's dismissal of his concerns was both relentless and fucking annoying, so he continued appealing to what he hoped was left of Finn's better sense. "You are the Lupine prince, and you don't get to just go tromping into the territory of the True Coven without fucking announcing yourself prior. You wanna get cursed? Because that's a damn easy way to make that happen."

"We've been at peace with them since the Seven Years War," she asserted, sounding bored with the whole proceeding as she folded her legs daintily off the side of the couch. "It was a quick in and out and nothing was harmed."

"That you know of." Vasi turned to face her, over her shit and beyond too through. "Goddammit Cora, he's not a soldier or a spy and *you can't treat him like one*. He's not even a regular civilian. There are rules in place for a reason. Now, I know *he* won't tell you otherwise, because he's always one to overlook his own interests in favor of everyone else's, but if you're serving the crown, *his* interests are paramount. You cannot forget that."

"I'm sitting right here," Finn reminded them, but clearly that was as little of a concern to her as it was to Vasi in that moment.

"His interests are my only priority," she snarled, leaning forward to face him. "Part of that is finding out who wants to kill him and taking care of that, but believe me when I say, I would not be here if I wasn't going to look after his interests." Draining her wine glass, she set it on the floor by her bare foot. Only a fool would think she looked relaxed and disarming, regardless of the front she put on.

Sensing he needed a different approach, Vasily held up a conciliatory hand. "And I appreciate that. We're on the same side," as much as it pained him to admit. "This investigation has been tough on everyone, and I just need you to be more careful in the future. And no more kidnappings. Please." It was as close to a moratorium as they were going to get tonight.

"It hardly constituted a kidnapping. I didn't even use a hood," she muttered under her breath, jaw still clenched. The stare down lasted a few moments longer, then she crossed her arms and pouted, but nodded once. "Fine."

"Fine." He could do without her snotty tone, but at least she wasn't arguing anymore. "How's your investigation going? Have your people turned up anything useful?"

"Not yet," Cora growled softly. "You know, for as dirtbag as we know him to be, he's exceptionally good at covering his tracks. People who have knowledge and might talk are terrified of him, and people who actually might talk have an alarming habit of going 'missing'. All the usual suspects are accounted for, and miraculously, no one has seen or heard anything. Nary a knocked up or knocked down barmaid to be found. It's weird."

As much as he wanted to know more about her definition of 'usual suspects', Vasi kept that question to himself. "Maybe it's not him," he offered, though just to goad her a little. He wasn't innocent enough to have hope.

"Oh, it's him." She nodded gravely. "At this point, I don't see how it could be anyone but."

"Alright, so say it is him. What then? You get proof and then what, force him to abdicate? Blackmail?"

"Forced abdication, yes, but not because of blackmail, but because of exposure. All his dirty dealings brought to the light.

And the Guard, but definitely public first. The kingdom deserves a trustworthy monarch, and neither of those words apply to the crown prince."

"That would kill him," Finn observed from the table, and surprisingly enough did not sound all that put out by the thought.

Cora shook her head. "No, it will keep him alive. There are very few acceptable outcomes for this that leave him alive."

Color him shocked that she drew the line at regicide. "You think your employer makes such distinctions?"

For the first time, he saw her look unsure, maybe even uncomfortable. That did not bode well. "Honestly, I doubt it. All I know is, absent a physical threat, I do."

Okay, he could appreciate that. She wasn't entirely amoral, just mercenary. He could work with that. "So, what are you prepared to do if this doesn't work?"

"Like a nuclear option?" Her phrasing had Finn sitting up and playing close attention to the conversation now.

Vasi winced. "I wouldn't call it that, but yeah."

"So what would you call it?" she asked suspiciously.

CORA

"Knocked up."

"I-I'm sorry?" she sputtered. One sentence and the little bit of dinner she'd eaten wanted to come back up. It took several deep breaths to regain both her composure and her control over her gag reflex. "Not this soon, no."

The Night Watch Commander closed his eyes and braced himself like he'd been struck, and she couldn't stifle her vicious little snicker. "Brain bleach," he murmured, then shook his head. "Okay, so real talk. Line of succession, that's what you think the motive is, right?

Keeping Finn from threatening Brendan's place on the throne?"

"I do."

"Then we need to test that theory."

"By getting pregnant."

"By *faking* a pregnancy," the owl corrected, smoothing his bangs out of his face.

"I'm not following."

"Okay, so Brendan is the presumptive heir, the crown prince. But he's unmarried and has no girlfriend, no heirs. What if, and just go with me on this, you come up pregnant before he ascends to the throne?"

"I fail to see how providing an heir to the spare, no offence," she looked to Finn as sincerely as possible. They'd come too far for a flippant turn of phrase to screw them over now.

His lips twitched even as his eyes crinkled at the edges. Gods but she was gone over him. "None taken."

"I fail to see how having Finn's child is going to affect anything."

"The King is the second born."

She felt her whole face pucker in confusion. "Wait, I thought that was just because of outdated, chauvinistic rules."

"No, surprisingly. Lady Gwen, Duchess of Wolfingham is the older sibling but Finn's father was the one quicker on the draw, child-wise, before the abdication. Brendan is the whole reason we have a King and not a Queen. The one with the child jumps the line of succession since the crown prince's job, aside from seeing to the welfare of all of Therantia, is to ensure the continuance of the line."

"Even though the child won't be fully Lupine?"

Vasi shook his head. "I'd have to do more research, but I'm pretty sure. You should be in the clear."

"Oh damn," she breathed as she got the lay of the land. "We... tell the king I'm pregnant. Tell the *world* I'm pregnant. All to force their hand." Even as she said it, her mind went to planning and logistics, judging the feasibility and workability of his idea.

Vasi nodded. "Pretty much."

Just thinking about it had the air smelling like copper with every inhale and she hoped to the gods she did not pop a nosebleed right then, or more awkwardly, a beak. Closing her eyes, she focused on pulling back her raging heartbeat and calming her breathing so she could think.

If Brendan thought she was knocked up, he'd think she was vulnerable. He'd be confined because of the media frenzy, but he'd be on a clock, too. This was Venus Flytrap levels of aggression on her part, lure and hopefully demolish.

"Okay." She walked over to stand by Finn so they could present a united front. "Say I do this, then what?" His lips twitched as she tossed his words right back to him.

"What do you mean?"

"I mean, say I get knocked up by Finn—" The man in question began choking on air. "*Hypothetically*," she emphasized while rubbing a circle on his back. "How does this work? We have a quickie marriage? We have a full royal to-do and then I miscarry, and we get divorced? But it won't matter because you'll be on the throne? What does success look like here?"

"It won't get to that. This is just a stall—"

"That's a helluva thing to call my sex life!" Cora snorted at Finn's mortified squawk but watched his best friend intently.

"*This is just a stall*," Vasi repeated through gritted teeth, "while we draw out who wants to kill Finn. If it's Brendan, then this is problem solved."

"And if it isn't?"

"You're doubting yourself *now*?" He smirked, but it wasn't nearly as antagonistic as it had been in the past.

"No, but there's no harm in having contingency plans and in this case lots of them."

"*If* Brendan is innocent..." Vasi stared out into the middle distance as he trailed off, jaw clenching and unclenching as he thought about it. Finally, he said, "If he's innocent, then the culprit will be caught, you'll be on the throne, Cora will be queen, and we will work the rest out from there. Best case scenario."

There were holes in Vasi's thinking, she knew. Assumptions that Brendan would take Finn's usurpation of the throne in stride. Like this wouldn't cause a war that hadn't been seen since the Yorks and Lancasters or worse, the ongoing skirmish between the Winter and Summer Courts of the Fae. Of course, there was always another option, an extinction-level option as it were, but she didn't want to bring it up until she had to. She could and would protect herself and Finn if she had to, by whatever means available. "Alright."

A warm hand in hers pulled her from her musings as Finn stood in front of her, blue eyes full of sincerity and affection. "You don't have to do this."

"There are many worse fates in this world than being your consort," she replied softly, petting his hand with her thumb, and meaning every single word. "This'll force their hand in a major way. The blowback will be immense, but they won't be able to hide, and they will have to act quickly."

"I'm sure whatever you're being paid, it doesn't cover this." He spoke in the direction of their toes as he seemed focused on their joined hands.

Tilting his chin up, she gazed at him, hoping to impart some of the growing confidence she felt in the situation. Unorthodox, yes, but this was exactly the kind of job at which she excelled. "I'm paid to keep you safe, however that looks."

"What we're proposing is treason."

"Only if we get caught." She couldn't resist her cheeky grin at his dire expression. "Eh, at best, it's fraud."

Brows drawn down in a scowl, he captured her hand in both of his to keep her still. "The punishment for which, in this case, would very likely involve a quick drop and a sudden stop."

Cora favored Finn with a fond smile as she cupped his bearded cheek in her hand. "I'm aware of the stakes, and I'm gonna do it anyway."

"I can't—*won't* ask you to do this for me." His tone was nothing short of pleading, that he backed up with some luminously blue weapons' grade puppy-dog eyes.

"I appreciate that, but I need you to understand something." Her eyes fell to his lips, like they often did, and it was hard not to imagine sampling them right then, especially as he worried over them with his tongue and teeth. There was nothing in the world she wanted more in that moment than to comfort him and ease his mind. "I wouldn't do this for anyone else."

CHAPTER TWELVE

VASI

Maybe it was what she said. Maybe it was the way she said it. Maybe it was the way he looked at her like she was first ray of warm sunshine after a long, cold winter. Regardless, Vasi suddenly felt like he was intruding on something extremely intimate. They startled apart when he cleared his throat, and he was grateful for the reprieve.

"The first thing we need is a doctor willing to sign off on this charade." He looked directly at Cora, who smirked as she poured her coffee.

"Doctor is handled. What's next?"

"Need to inform the king."

"Privately and with his advisors," Finn supplied. "Preferably before the next full moon."

"And you'll need to pass more than just a blood test, but a scent test, too. A room full of wolves will be difficult to fool."

Her confident grin was reassuring as she twisted her hair up into a bun and secured it with a sharpened, silver chopstick she produced from who the hell knew where. "Don't worry about me. Let's walk through the political fallout, physical stuff will be handled on my end."

The mood lightened considerably as they hammered out the finer points of the drastic contingency plan. None of them expected it to get that far, but it was a good play to have just in case. That was the kind of thing that almost always ensured it would not be needed.

Turning back to Finn, he sighed. "I read the email. You doin' alright?"

"Much as I can be." Nodding in Cora's direction with a puckish grin, he added, "She promised I'd glow in the dark, so I'm sorely disappointed on that score."

She rolled her eyes. "Bitch, bitch, bitch. You got to keep both your kidneys, damn. I don't know what more you want."

Vasi looked between them, staunchly ignoring the blood-pressure-related twitch in his eyelid. Leaving these two alone together had clearly been a terrible idea. Temples suddenly aching, he asked, "Were you dropped on your head as a chick? Is that what your problem is? Just kicked out of the nest and landed on what passes for your brain?"

"Is he always this grouchy, or is this just a reaction to me?"

"*Duceţi-va dracului,* to both of you assholes." He was on his feet, unable to decide if he was going to punch Finn for being so goddamn cavalier about his safety or take a shot at Cora and see who bled out on the Persian rug first. He was saved, though, by his phone buzzing in his pocket and a message that he was needed at the Guard house regarding some unaccounted-for staff members. "I have neither the time, not the inclination to fight with you two right now. I'll be back in the morning and hopefully by then we can have an actual conversation that doesn't sound like you've been marinating in pinot."

CORA

Watching the door to the antechamber shut, she sighed deeply. She hated that Vasi was right, but she had been more than a little heedless with Finn's health and wellbeing. He was not built for her world and she had ignored that because it was inconvenient to getting the job done. She just wanted him with her as she worked the case and didn't think of the consequences. Because when looking out for only herself, the consequences would be fairly minimal, or at least manageable. Once affairs of state get involved, however...

From the corner of her eye, she watched as Finn rose from his seat and headed to the closet. He returned moments later stripped of his social armor of coat, jacket and tie, his strong and chiseled frame deliciously displayed by his A-shirt and trousers that cost probably as much as her car. It was like her eyes abandoned any semblance of decorum as they slipped over his artfully messy hair to his mischievous blue eyes and perfectly groomed beard all the way down to his surprisingly cute bare feet. He was made for a good time and damn if she didn't want to indulge a little. She wouldn't, of course, but she definitely wanted to.

After pouring more wine for both of them, she retreated to her corner of the couch. "Better?"

"Much," he agreed as he moved over to the other end of the couch, far enough away to be proper but almost close enough for her feet to touch his unreasonably muscular thigh.

The intent, unflinching way he watched her as he sipped his drink gave her ideas, of the sweaty, naked variety. *That I am going to ignore,* she reminded herself. "What?" she demanded when the silence failed to provide her the barrier she'd hoped for.

His voice was soft as he stared at the wine swirling in his glass. "You said something earlier and I'm curious."

"About?"

She was snared in his gaze as he watched her over the rim of his glass. "What would you change if you could? About all this. What do you wish were different?"

Cora tittered nervously, and her eye roll should have registered on the Richter scale, but even that wasn't enough to fully quash the smile that was currently holding her lips and dimples hostage. The man was a menace and it was hard to be a badass when he made her want to bat her lashes at him and pout like a damn schoolgirl. "Goddess..."

"Well?" he prompted, nudging her feet with his knee.

If he'd been anyone else, if this had been any other job, if, if, if... "Doesn't matter, does it? I mean, if wishes were horses then beggars would ride."

"What does that even mean?" He laughed and drained his glass, immediately pouring more for both of them.

Her answering smile felt hollow and forced, but she gave it to him just the same as she accepted her glass. "Means that you can't always get what you want."

"Your family?"

She shook her head, unable to catch her smile before it fell completely from her face, hoping she could hide its absence behind her wine glass. "No, not at all," she answered softly. "I was never gonna be what they wanted."

"Your marriage then?"

She snorted, drank more wine. "Fuck no." It had been a mistake, but she treated it as a learning opportunity. Most of the time. That was not a conversation she wanted to get into at the moment.

"That bad, huh?"

Cora rolled her shoulder and took another healthy draught of her wine, draining her glass and setting it on the floor in front of the couch. "Another in a long series of disappointments."

"Like me?"

The question, so gently posed, kinda snuck up on her. Much like the questioner. She'd desired him for so long from afar, content to live her life with just another in a line of celebrity crushes, and then she tossed her professionalism out the window and slept with him. And now, when he looked at her? Like she designed and hung the moon and stars solely for his benefit? Her chest hurt at little at the strength of her desire to give him the world.

"No," she replied, eyes closed to shield her from the man in front of her, knowing that if she looked, like Perseus to Medusa, she would be forever damned. "I'm mad about that, actually. Life would be a lot easier if I found you disappointing." She swung her legs over the side to sit on the couch properly rather than run the risk of facing him.

"I'm sorry?" he offered with a tentative grin that made his eyes crinkle at the edges.

Gods, she was tempted....

"You should be, dammit," she grumped, crossing her arms and affecting the most pronounced pout she could muster.

"Be that as it may," Finn nudged her with his shoulder, "you still haven't answered the question." She sat there silently, likely out of spite as much as melancholy, and only looked down at him when he laid his hand over hers on her knee. "All right, then. How about I answer for you?"

He turned on the couch to face her, using his free hand to bring her eyes to his when she refused to look at him. It was torture staring into the face of the sun, all perfect searing heat that brought life and killed with equal measure. "Go on, then," she challenged, her voice barely above a whisper.

"I wished that night, you know. The one we met? Well, re-met. Whatever." He shook his head before getting back on track. "I wished I was just a regular guy who picked up a beautiful woman and maybe stayed the night and bought her breakfast." The pink tinge to his cheeks and the way he kept glancing at their hands broadcast his reticence to share this info with her.

"Guess that didn't work out so well." She chuckled self-consciously at his unspoken compliment, eyes falling to her lap.

"I don't know," he ducked his head until he regained the eye contact and straightened back up, "this hasn't been so bad."

Cora's eyebrows made a break for her hairline and the sheer audacity of his statement had reduced her to a squeak of disbelief and mild outrage.

Finn threw back his head with a loud bark of laughter, shifting his whole body until his leg from the knee down pressed along the outside of her thigh. It was intimate but not overbearing, and she loved that he did such things for her seemingly unconsciously. "In some respects," he emphasized. "But without that, I would have never reconnected with you, and it hasn't been very long, but I'm kinda partial."

The look of soft affection in his eyes was almost more difficult to see than just his smile. He wrecked her, and he'd barely laid a finger on her. She was pretty sure this was the textbook definition of 'emotionally compromised'. If this were an op, she would have been pulled from the field and sent for a fitness for duty exam. Deep blue with oblique facets of emeralds, she found her heart losing traction to their pull.

"I wish I'd known this side of you sooner," he whispered, his fingers framing her jaw before winding in her braids and his thumb light on her cheek. "I wish our paths aligned when we were younger. I wish..." he sighed, licked his lips, leaving them shiny and so damn inviting.

"Yeah?" she prompted as she leaned toward him, toes curling in anticipation as he did the same. The urge to lick her lips as he watched them was unbearable.

"I wish you'd let me kiss you," he growled, his lips swallowing her moan as she surged against him. The soft heat of his mouth against hers touched off a wave that broke over her slowly, rolling through her and leaving her arching into his touch.

Her awkward sideways angle kept her from fully reaching him, their only connection their lips and her hands on his face, until he came to his knees, strong arms wrapping around her and pulling her to him. It was a few seconds later that he was stretched out on the couch with her draped on top of him like she weighed no more

142 ~~   Alexis D. Craig

than a blanket.

Finn's hand in hers as he held her to his chest made her feel so safe, wanted. His kisses unhurried, like there was nothing else he planned to do, ever. The hand that rested on her hip meandered slowly from her shoulder blades down to her ass and back, leaving a mellow buzz that raced across her skin, almost aroused but so very relaxed. Like the day was melting away completely.

"How's your wish going?" she asked against his neck, her lips and tongue lovingly teasing the spot just below his ear and lobe, leaving him a trembling mess beneath her. He smelled so good, like bergamot and cedar and wolf and she buried her face in the crook of his neck for a closer sniff and maybe a taste test or two.

"Almost perfect," he exhaled on a shuddering breath, his fingers digging into the flesh of her ass cheek through the silk of her dress.

"Only almost?" Cora looked at him askance as she used his shoulders to leverage herself over him. Unable to decide if she was incredulous or offended more, she was sure her tone reflected the conundrum.

His laugh was silent but heralded by the shaking of his chest as he looked at her, truly happy for the first time she'd seen him. "You're amazing, you know that? I'm so damn unworthy of even just your smile and you grace me with it anyway." He hugged her closer, his arm around her waist subtly shifting her up his body until she was all but sprawled over his chest, lips brushing his as he gazed up at her. "This is us," each word a nip of her upper or lower lip, "no lies, no deceptions, and—if they know what's good for them—no interruptions."

Her giggles died on her lips, wilted under the heat of his mouth slotted against hers, a perfect fit. Her tongue found his in a tangle, the growl he gave underneath her giving her gooseflesh. A shimmering unease, a restlessness that danced across her nerves, left her skin feeling too tight and was too warm in her less than substantial dress.

Finn's clever fingers, found the zipper on her side, finding more than one ticklish spot that had her bracing her hands on his broad shoulders to yell at him. Any reprimand she had faltered under the look on his face, pure, focused *want*. The sheer single-minded intensity in his eyes gave the blue a golden cast and sent a shiver down her spine that curled her toes.

"Tell me you want this." His words a rumble in his chest that teased her fingertips. "Say the words." Even though she was the one on top, he was very much in control.

Cora sighed at the way he bit his lip, a shuddering broken sound just this side of an audible whimper. As if she could ever deny him anything. "I want this," she relented, each breath feeling like too much and yet not enough. "Please."

Finn made quick work of her zipper, her dress peeled back like a banana skin, before flipping her to her back beneath him. The warm leather was soft against her back as he settled between her legs. His tank top had disintegrated at some point, leaving him in a pair of gray trousers she planned to ruin, at least a little bit by grinding up against him. The hard ridge of his cock nestled against her softness left her squirming as he leisurely explored her mouth.

His big hands framing her face, he kissed her like he needed it, like it was more important than air. His lips were so soft, the brush of his beard a tantalizing counterpoint, the touch so loving even as he demanded her responses, it wasn't long before Cora was actively rubbing her pussy against him in search of friction or some blessed sweet relief. Her nipples grew stiff and sensitive, abraded by his chest hair as they moved against one another.

"I wanted to go slow," he lamented as he bit and then laved a spot on her neck before doing the same to her collarbone as she whined underneath him and sank her claws into the meat of his shoulders. That beard would be the death of her, and she had no problems imagining how it would feel on other parts of her body as he returned his attentions to her mouth.

"Next time," she panted against his swollen lips, because right at that moment, she wanted nothing more than to feel him inside her with her, all of him. "You have anything?"

Finn stilled as he thought about her question before hopping up from the couch. "Have gun, will travel," he chuckled as he scooped her up and carried her naked-but-for-her-panties clad form to the bed with her squawking and protesting the whole way until he dumped her onto the bouncy mattress.

"You coulda warned me!" she groused as she moved to sprawl herself out in the center across his pillows wanting to look like the sexiest porn centerfold he'd ever seen.

"No fun in that," he muttered as he kicked his way out of his trousers and pawed through his nightstand for a condom. The look of pleased and stunned shock when he turned back to the bed was worth it, though.

"Oh, I can show you fun," she purred, drawing her fingertips over her thigh and up her belly to cup her breast. "If you're interested."

"Oh yeah?"

It was almost impossible to keep still as he stalked her up the bed, her heart damn near pounding out of her chest as he let some of his predator instincts out to play. Before her eyes, the sweet, gentle man she'd come to know receded to reveal the wolf she knew him to be. He was all slow blinks and sinewy movements and then suddenly he was on her, his teeth in the skin of her neck and his hips grinding into hers as the pillows behind her yielded to the onslaught.

"Fuck, you taste so good," he growled into her neck as she explored the muscles of his back and shoulders with her nails. She would not be the only one with marks tonight. His fingers teased and tickled her sides as he positioned her thighs to wrap around his waist. "So fucking soft."

The head of his cock brushed back and forth over her clit as his hardness made itself at home in her slippery folds, sending a cascade of sparks through her as she arched into him. "You gonna tease or you gonna go to work?" she groaned, knowing full well that she was goading a dangerous beast.

His answering dark chuckle trailed down her collarbone to her nipple, his beard making her obscenely hot as it tickled and teased and otherwise made her a whimpering, squirming mess. "Cora," he breathed, pausing all his movements until she was able to focus her eyes on him, and only then did he slide into her, filling and stretching her around his thick shaft with his name a breathless moan on her lips.

"So fucking perfect," he marveled, his face a mix of wonder and straight arousal. His fingertips tracing down her nose and over her cheekbones, the moment more intimate than any she'd had in the past. Like he was seeing her for her, and honestly, it was a little too close for her comfort.

She rolled her hips, her whole body an undulating wave that ended in his panted warning growl. "You gotta move, Finn. I need it. I need..." her words left her as he did exactly what she asked by grinding down on her and abusing her sensitive little clit in the best possible way.

"Oh I got what you need, baby," he boasted, then immediately burst into quiet giggles she shared with him. "Sorry, I had to," he breathed as he pulled almost all the way out of her body, a whine of displeasure on her lips.

A wrenching gasp was punched out of her as he slid all the way back in, bottoming out against her with a little shimmy of his hips. He took his time with long, slow strokes that had her embedding her claws in his arms or his shoulders, strong thighs clenching around him. His name on her lips was a plea, the filthiest wish she could have ever asked for, fulfilled in so many ways and the feelings of heat and desire that had been pooling in her belly since that very first kiss broke over her in wave after wave of sparkling perfect pleasure.

FINN

Finn purred with pride as he felt her walls flutter around his cock, barely hanging on as he had been since they started. Fucking Cora was a life-altering event and deserved the utmost reverence. He stilled for a moment both to give himself a quick breather and to let her come back to herself. "Is this real?" he gasped, feeling a little lightheaded and delirious as he looked down over her glorious nakedness.

"Goddess, I hope so, or my batteries are gonna run out."

His wheezing laugh quickly melted into a moan as he moved within her. "Was that alright?"

"I don't know, are you done?" she punctuated her question with her body tightening its unbearably perfect grip around him.

"Not by a long shot," he replied, rubbing his thumb in tiny circles over her still swollen bundle of nerves.

"Mmmm..." She closed her eyes as her hips rose to meet his touch. "Then we'll discuss it afterwards."

"Yes, ma'am."

The moment he began again, sliding all the way out only to push back in just as slowly, he reveled in this sting of her claws on his skin, the way her breath hitched when he hit bottom and rubbed up against her clit. The pressure was intense, a heat that started low in his back and spread through his balls as he moved until he wasn't able to deny the throbbing pleasure that overtook him, gripping her hips tight enough that she would likely bruise as he emptied his soul into her.

Coming back to this plane of existence, the first thing Finn became aware of was the pleasantly ticklish feeling of her fingers running up and down his back, lightly shaping over each muscle group before moving on to another. It was comforting, sweet. Next was her lips, warm and slightly damp, as she pressed tiny kisses along his clavicle that were just this side of ticklish.

"I'm officially taking you hostage," Cora mumbled sleepily between nips as she briefly squeezed her legs around his thighs and wriggled underneath him.

Finn snickered weakly and hummed in pleasure as he nuzzled her cheek. He could think of few better fates. "As if family gatherings aren't awkward enough."

She made a noncommittal sound as she brushed a kiss over his temple. "Ask me how much I care."

Her quiet giggles followed him into the bathroom while he dealt with the condom and then waited as she returned from her sojourn as well. He was unsurprised when she returned to his side and moved to sleep on the side of the bed closest to the door. It was probably best he didn't think too hard about what she kept under her pillow.

She murmured something as he spooned up behind her and pulled her back against him with his hand splayed across her belly, her words barely audible even to his wolf's ears.

He purred an interrogatory noise into her shoulder as he reveled in the feel of her soft skin against his lips. "I missed that," he prompted as he reached over and extinguished the light, bathing them in strips of moonlight from the massive windows.

Cora's soft voice sliced through the darkness, trembling even as her tone was sure. "You know this isn't just another op for me, right?"

And there it was. The admission he didn't know he'd been waiting for, hoping for. In his wildest fantasies, he would have never imagined that he'd hear those words from her lips voluntarily, and surely not under torture. This was her, giving as much of herself to him as she could in that moment, and he treasured it more than anything else in the whole kingdom. "Good. Because it's not for me, either." After tonight, it would never be again.

CHAPTER THIRTEEN

CORA

Early mornings were for assholes and suckers, and for the moment, at least until she got some coffee in her, she worried that she was dancing on the edge of matching both of those descriptions. Actually, that wasn't wholly true, since she awoke, without an alarm, under the warm and comfortable weight of Finn's arm wrapped around her and his breath on her nape and down her back.

The day before was kind of a blur, a compilation of hot mess, adventure, and back to hot mess. It seemed the castle was a hotbed for the mess. She did not, however, expect to end the day in Finn's arms. Again. At this point, she had no choice but to call it what it was, a mutual infatuation that would, in all likelihood, lead to both of them going to jail or the morgue. Obviously, she would work to prevent both those outcomes, but there was no percentage in being unrealistic about it.

Finn snuffled against her neck, reminding her of a rooting puppy, his lips against the spot just behind her ear that made her shiver and punctuated with still-sleepy snores. She knew she'd need to get up to pee soon, but she put it off for as long as she could in order to remain snuggled up with the prince. She stretched and wiggled, wakefulness flowing through her slowly like chilled honey, and he moved with her, his legs tangling with hers like they were in some sort of dance. It was cute, and endearing, and more than a little obvious that he was more awake than he was letting on by the feel of the stiffness grinding against her ass just enough to be noticeable.

"Morning," he growled, his voice rough from disuse. Fuck if that alone didn't send a bolt of heat through her straight to her core.

"Hey," she breathed, snuggling back into the enveloping warmth of his broad chest, fitting her body to his. "This is a helluva way to wake up."

"You complaining?"

"Not in the slightest." She turned over in his arms, loving the feel of the soft fur on his chest against her nipples and the firmness of his muscles beneath her fingertips. For a guy so gentle, his incredibly chiseled form was an embarrassment of riches and she could not stop touching. The warmth of his skin on hers was positively addictive. "So, what's on the agenda today?"

Finn sighed as his hand progressed down her back to grab a handful of her ass possessively before pulling her leg over his hip. Cora snorted in amusement at the new and highly intimate arrangement. The light brush of his fingers up the inside of her thigh left very little to the imagination. "Oh I see."

Anything else she might have said died on her lips as he sealed them with his, a deep carnal kiss that left her breathless and confused when her view changed from the door of the room to the ceiling beneath him. "Neat trick," she huffed, dragging her fingers from his wrists up to his shoulders and slowly back down again.

He winked. "You ain't seen nothing yet, gorgeous," he rasped as he divebombed her neck, covering her delicate skin with kisses and glorious beard burn.

"Finn! Cora! You decent?" The question was accompanied by

the kind of fierce pounding on the door that only came from law enforcement training.

"Are you fucking kidding—"

Finn's hand slapped over her mouth smothered the rest of her indignant yelling as he snarled toward the door. "You better have fucking coffee."

There was a pause, a hesitation, followed by a soft sigh. "I have a cart out here with me."

Cora's dark eyes promised murder above his hand. The moment he turned her loose, she was putting three bullets in Vasily and that was all there was to it. If she was feeling charitable, she might let him live. Emphasis on *might*.

"No killing before caffeine," the prince warned her as he gently removed his hand like she might bite him. And she contemplated it out of spite. He moved off her, backing away like he didn't trust her not to make a mad dash for her pistol and take out his best friend.

"No promises." Sweeping from the bed and dragging the sheet draped around her like a toga with a train, she stalked over to the door and threw it wide with a welcoming arm. "By all means, Commander Cockblock. Come on in."

Finn snickered behind her, his giggles moving toward the closet and the bathroom. "I'll be back in a moment. Please keep in mind this room is filled with priceless antiques that would not do well with bloodstains and/or direct impacts."

She grunted petulantly as he closed the door behind him, leaving her to turn her full attention to Vasi. "Well?"

At least he had the good sense to look chagrined as he came through the door bearing food and the all-important life elixir in a bigass box from Starbucks. "My apologies for the early hour, but this couldn't wait."

"I sure as hell hope so," she grumbled as she set out coffee cups and began attending to their morning ritual. "This is the second time you've interrupted our time alone. Next time I'm just going to open with gunfire and sort it out later." She turned to face him with a delicate porcelain cup and saucer in her hands, making sure to keep her threats short and her smile frightening. "Sugar?"

The Night Watch Commander blinked a few times, his eyes flicking over her shoulder to the closed bathroom door, but his attention clearly still focused on her. "Yes, please. Two." As they waited for Finn, he unpacked the bags of breakfast food he'd brought with him and smuggled in under the domes. She appreciated that he was taking her recommendations about the prince's food seriously until they worked this out.

"Ah, good. Everyone's still alive." Finn emerged from the bathroom dressed, refreshed, in another impeccable suit and waistcoat combo that made her curse Vasi all over again. He smiled brightly, blue eyes shining and making her heart melt as he accepted his coffee cup from her with a kiss. "Thank you, angel."

"Angel?" Vasi asked the question on the tip of her tongue as he took a seat at the table. "Wrong color wings for that."

Cora smacked him in the arm as she took her own seat. "You talk a lot of shit for a man who expects to live through breakfast."

Finn blanched, Vasily snorted in amusement and pushed the cream cheese tub in her direction and all was okay in her world for the moment.

FINN

As much as he thought he'd prefer his best friend and Cora get along, actually witnessing them agree to some kind of ceasefire was kind of terrifying. She sat perched on her chair attending to her bagel and lox, braids down, looking like a combination of Nefertiti and Juno with the perfectly wrapped sheet that did not at all look like she just rolled out of bed deliciously naked. Her ability to go from rumpled to resplendent was ridiculous.

Shaking his head, he withdrew from those thoughts as she looked up at him with a raised eyebrow and a smirk. "So, what brings you by that couldn't wait?"

Still chewing on his bagel, Vasi got some more coffee from the vat. "We had a missing persons case come to our attention."

"Those are your purview?" she questioned, skepticism plain in her voice as she chewed and eyeballed him.

"They are when they're palace employees and were last seen in the palace."

"Fuck me." He set his cup down at the same time as Cora all their attention on his best friend.

"Who was it?" He needed to make sure whoever it was, their family was seen to. Some members of his family didn't interact with the palace staff in any way other than in a professional capacity. He was not like that. These people took care of him and his family daily, since forever, and the least he could do was to look after theirs.

"Kitchen steward, Hircine. Young girl, early twenties." He slid his phone across the table to show them her picture. She was short, with a forest of long, dark brown curly hair, mahogany skin just a bit darker than Cora's, gray eyes and a sassy smile. In the picture she was wearing shorts, flipflops, and a t-shirt proclaiming 'Sarcasm: Now Served All Day'. She was the epitome of carefree youth and just seeing her innocence made his heart hurt.

He swallowed hard. "I've seen her, but I don't know exactly who she is. Do you have any leads?"

Vasi shook his head and swept his free range bangs behind his ear. Normally he wore it in a bun at the base of his skull, but by this time of day, he's usually abandoned that pretense. "Not really. It's still pretty early, though. Driscoll's leading a team to run down her timeline and relevant encounters, but I don't have word yet."

"Let me know what I can do," she offered as she put aside her folded napkin and rose from the table. Both men were on their feet in an instant, and she leaned over to kiss his cheek. "I'm gonna go get cleaned up and I'll be back out shortly. Commander." She nodded as Vasily as she swept from the room to the closet.

"Cora."

Finn watched her leave, the smile on his lips involuntary at best.

He definitely enjoyed watching her walk away.

"So that's new." Vasi's tone was light as he poured more coffee, his bright blue eyes dancing as he sipped. "You take 'sleeping with the enemy' quite seriously I see."

Finn snorted and rolled his eyes. "Yeah, yeah, yeah. I think I liked this better when you two weren't getting along."

His best friend just smiled wickedly and raised his cup. "And here I thought I was doing you a solid."

Watching the closet for her reemergence, he sighed deeply. "This thing with Cora is complicated. I like it, it works for us, so let's just leave it there, okay?"

Vasi's hum indicated he wasn't convinced. "Not sure about how well it works but I'll trust you for the moment."

Finn sighed. "I appreciate the vote of confidence."

He smirked. "I do what I can."

CORA

While waiting for the delivery from D'Antonio's the night before, Cora had gone to the room assigned to her and collected her belongings. There was no reason to sleep there so long as she and Finn were getting along. Not that she'd planned to seduce him by any means, but she figured it was easier for her to look after him if they were in the same place. This morning as she showered using her face and body washes, she applauded her foresight.

She'd wanted a minute to reflect on this new situation, the changing parameters of the job, how far it had bled into her personal life. Because this thing between her and Finn? It was pretty damn personal, despite her intentions to the contrary. If this had been any other client, any other protectee, any other person, this wouldn't even be a question. Finn was worth breaking all the rules, she knew that in her soul. As to how that would affect the case going forward, however... that was the question.

Her phone beeped, a check in from her handler that she answered as she draped herself in touchably soft cashmere cowl-neck sweater, a houndstooth pencil skirt that clung to every single inch between her waist and her knees, and knee-high black patent leather boots with a convenient-but-subtle knife holster in the top of each. It was her go-to 'I'll fuck you up, but I'll be warm doing it' attire. Added bonus was it made her tits and ass look incroyable, and for reasons she'd like not to examine too closely, she felt like showing off a bit for the prince.

She told him that the personality conflicts of the previous day had been resolved, and if she didn't happen to mention how, that wasn't her problem. There was no way in hell she was telling him about this recent change in status.

All appeared well as she emerged from the walk-in closet, refreshed and ready to take on the day. With Brendan's birthday gala that evening, she needed to go out and make arrangements for her attire. "So, what's the plan, gentlemen?" she asked as they got to their feet.

Finn grinned broadly as he wrapped an arm around her waist and buried his nose in her neck for a moment with a pleased hum. "I'm headed into the office to receive my brother's obscenely large birthday donation to the charity in a televised event I can't get out of."

"I'm headed back to the office to keep working the missing persons case, Xander and Dev are setting up the security detail for the gala tonight." The hollow shadows under Vasi's eyes whispered of exhaustion, but the rest of him appeared resolute.

"Speaking of, I need a dress. I'll be going into the city to acquire one. Maybe some shoes."

"New shoes are the last thing you need," Vasi snapped, though his playful smile conveyed his teasing intent. "Speaking of, how's that gonna work?"

"What, the dress? No idea, I'll know when I see it."

"I meant your face. I can't imagine Marius LeStrange not recognizing his own daughter."

Oh that. "Miss Annie is a solitary member of the Coven home office, skilled in the old ways. Her glamour is topnotch, family-proof. It interferes with the person's visual interpretation of me. I look… like me, but sexier. Like my fraternal twin or cousin. Just far enough removed that if there are questions, they can be easily dismissed."

"I'm not sure my heart can take you looking any sexier," Finn murmured into her neck as he nipped at her earlobe.

She shivered at the brush of his beard against her sensitive skin. "I'm sure I'll find something to bring you back to life. Any requests?"

Licking his lips, his grin turned downright wicked. "Bright blue and easy to remove."

"Oh, I do love how you think," she purred.

When she slipped her arms around his neck and snuggled in closer as Finn flagrantly palmed an ass cheek, Vasi was struck with an intense coughing fit. "Alright. Great. So… I'll have Driscoll and one of the guys drive you to… wherever. Away from here."

Cora frowned. Vasi was a damn fine tactician, and absolutely lived up to his billing. His ability to interrupt a romantic moment was going to get him killed if he kept it up. "That's not necessary. I'm not an invalid."

Vasi shrugged at her complaint and set the domes back on the food. "Nope, you're the prince's girlfriend, currently living in the palace. You get a security detail. Just how that works." He pushed the cart to the door, holding it open as they preceded him into the corridor. "Not that I'm really worried. Anyone who kidnapped you would return you right away for being a pain in the ass, but it's protocol."

A part of her wanted to argue, just because dammit, she was neither fragile nor helpless, but Finn apparently sensed it. A finger under her chin, he tipped her face up for a quick kiss, a look of sheer affection and adoration in his baby blues. "For me. Would you do it for me?"

Cora grimaced, scowling darkly at the request before finally relenting with an exaggerated huff. "For you."

"Thank you." With a quick kiss to the tip of her nose and the sunniest smile she'd ever seen, he stepped away and followed Vasi down the hall. "I'll see you this afternoon!"

"The car will meet you downstairs," the Strigian called over his shoulder.

"Yeah, yeah." Watching the two men leave, she shifted mental gears to the dress. She was not shopping for herself, per se, but for the persona. What that would look like was anyone's guess, but the guess would start at Chanel. Or Marchesa. Or Valentino.

Driscoll met her at the front door and handed her into the back of the waiting Range Rover like he did it all day long. He didn't say much, but she could feel him scrutinizing her every move from his position in the passenger seat. She recognized the Corvid driving as a cousin—first, second, whatever, but fortunately for her, the glamour held nicely, and he didn't have any probing questions for her.

"I'm sorry you got stuck on this detail," she murmured as she stared out the window at the passing scenery. She meant it, too. He'd been up all night and the last thing he needed was to chase after her.

The vulture's head popped up like her words had woken him from an unintentional nap. "I don't mind, just a little tired." His head dipped again like the snooze had caught up with him. Shaking it off, he shifted in his seat and rolled his shoulders. "We'll hit a Starbucks inside if that's alright with you, ma'am."

"Of course. And you can call me Cora."

The vulture's toothy grin was infectious. "Even if you weren't the prince's paramour, you're still a superior officer. So, if it's all the same to you, *ma'am*..." he trailed off as they pulled up in front of Bergdorf Goodman.

"I'm retired, but fine," she grumbled as he handed her out of the car. "But I'm buying your coffee."

He snorted and held the door for her. "No arguments there, ma'am."

"'Paramore'? Seriously?"

The afternoon went quickly from there, three cups of coffee, two scones, three pairs of Louboutins, and one show-stopping Chanel dress that was going to require tape and an engineering degree later. Driscoll was a sweet kid, from Oklahoma, more siblings than she had and parents that still loved him. By the time he'd deposited her back at Finn's suite, they were almost buddies.

"Get your nap in, because you know tonight's going to be nuts," she admonished him. She'd watched as he'd taken no less than six calls regarding coordination of the night's security.

"Will do, ma'am. See you this evening."

When she walked in the interior antechamber door, Cora was greeted by a sight that made her giggle even as she appreciated the view. Standing on the coffee table, Finn posed there as three Trochilidine flitted around, hemming his pants legs and attending to the length of his tux cuffs.

"No one ever told you not to put your feet on the furniture?" she teased as she dropped her bag of shoes by one of the armchairs and draped her garment bag over the back.

One of the hummingbirds looked up at her voice. "Miss Westgate, yes?" She was bright eyed, green-haired, and could not have been older than twenty-five. She was armed with a pincushion wristlet and a utility belt that looked menacing in its sewing content.

"I am," she answered cautiously.

The girl smiled and offered a forthright hand. "I was told to expect you. You have your dress? I'm here to assist in your styling."

At her silent blinking, Finn barked a laugh but didn't move. "It's easier to just give in to them, they'll just outrun you and outlast you."

Cora sighed, already over the night and it hadn't even started yet. "Good to know." Taking the young woman's hand, Cora smiled. "Nice to meet you, the dress is in the bag. Do you have any tape?"

Finn looked vexed. "Tape?" and all the women in the room just snickered.

Okay, so this wouldn't be quite *so* bad.

FINN

The benefit of living in the palace was that he didn't have far to go to get to the gala in a timely fashion. And he didn't have to run the paparazzi gauntlet if he didn't want to. Finn truly never wanted to.

However, it was also less time for him to get used to Cora in that mind-bending, religion-altering dress that sure as hell deserved all the press coverage it could get. To be fair, the press coverage would be more coverage than the whole dress itself, and he wasn't even a little bit upset. She was his, dammit, and he wasn't worried about a damn thing.

When she'd walked in the door, he had no idea what to expect from her garment bag from Chanel. When she'd put the floor length sapphire blue silk dress on, Finn's lungs took a powder. The soft-looking, shiny fabric gathered on one shoulder with a jeweled neckline cut to the waist across her chest in a teasingly serpentine angle and then opened to a slit that started midthigh and cascaded down to the trumpeted hem, artfully draped open back, and shrink wrapped so closely to every single, solitary curve that she required both tape and a lack of underwear. She was a fucking vision coming and going and he'd needed to take a moment to learn about breathing again. Even then, he wasn't especially good at it.

Cora was on his arm, all that sexy brown skin on display with that walk that could crush empires, and Finn could not have been happier if there were three of him. Instead he walked the red carpet. Talked to the select few reporters who'd been tasked to cover the event. Cora deserved to be shown off, and he was happy to let her have the limelight.

She was in fine form, completely at ease with foreign officials and celebrities alike. Her ability to blend in and mimic the tone and vibe of the room was amazing to see up close and that was with him knowing about the glamour. To the outside world, she was just this ridiculously sexy socialite he happened to be dating, making him the envy of damn near every man and several of the women in the room.

"That dress is going to haunt my dreams for weeks," he rumbled in her ear as he held her chair at the head table.

Ever the tease, Cora lightly trailed her fingernails down his neck to his chest, the barest hint of sensation leaving him tense and on edge. "Then I should make it memorable, no?" She shimmied, a reminder that she was one good deep breath and poorly applied piece of tape away from a wardrobe malfunction and in its own perverse way, it turned him on like nothing else. He'd never seen himself as a public sex kind of guy, but tonight her very presence was making him reconsider.

Brendan was announced and the whole room applauded the crown prince, as was his due. He almost tripped as he walked past Cora and she curtsied, giving him a view to die for, though to his credit he held up, his cheeks a bit flushed as he took his seat next to a supremely salty-looking Aunt Gwen. Part one of the event was finished with all was proceeding without incident.

The food was catered from an outside vendor, thankfully, meaning that they could eat without fear of contamination or poisoning, though he made sure she signed off on it before he did so. Last thing he needed was to keel over in such a public venue. Not that he anticipated his brother being so brazen, but it was best to expect the worst where he was concerned.

"How long do you want to be here?" she whispered as the salad course was taken away. So far, Brendan had only made one strafing run to the bar and everything appeared to be going well.

"Long enough to speak to enough people that we can honestly say we were here, and then I can get you back to the room and learn the intricacies of that dress." He cleared his throat and sipped his wine as he smiled blandly at the former governor of Massachusetts and current Liaison of Shifter and Human Relations for the European Union.

Her snort of amusement next to him was music to his ears. "As you wish, Highness."

CORA

The dress wasn't exactly comfortable, but there wasn't enough of it there to qualify for discomfort exactly, so she'd call it even. There'd been no shortage of men eager to make her acquaintance, to Finn's amusement, and more than a couple women had complimented her and asked about the engineering. It was a girl thing.

Her preliminary tour of the room found her introduced to several heads of state, their spouses, and while she didn't get a formal introduction, there were the heads and leg-breakers of several crime families also in attendance to celebrate with the crown prince. Quite the interesting mix of guests.

Her sisters were in attendance. She'd seen them off on the fringes across the room with their spouses. It probably should have bothered her that she couldn't think of their last names or ranks, but it was whatever. She hadn't felt a need to seek them out but knowing where they were was a matter of both personal and operational security. Every once in a while, she'd catch the eye of Vasily or Driscoll, making the rounds even as she monitored the entrances for anything untoward.

When presented to Marius LeStrange, or as she knew him, Dear Old Dad, it had been little more than a quick introduction to him and her mother, Terese. In his tux with his chain of office as the king's Chief Advisor, he looked almost regal himself with his towering height and faint dusting of silver hair. Her mother was in a shimmering lace and satin gown that showed off her youthful figure even with the white streak through her jet black french rolled updo, secure, of course, by the LeStrange tiara.

"She could be Dominic's daughter, couldn't she?" she'd said when Finn presented Cora, her heavily bejeweled hand on her husband's arm as she smiled right in Cora's face. Dominic was Cora's uncle, her father's brother, and as painful as it was, it meant the ruse was holding fast.

His smile actually turned her stomach. It was... pleasant. The kind of smile he gave to her sisters and she'd never once seen directed at her. "She could. A nice Corvid girl like you, how did you two meet?"

Finn seemed to sense her growing distress because he excused them a moment later. "I'm sorry, Your Grace, but it appears my father is retiring for the evening and I need to speak with him."

They nodded and he guided her away from them, across the ballroom, and to the furthest table in the corner. "I will be right back." He snagged a glass of whiskey from a passing waiter's tray and set it in front of her. "I'm not leaving, but I do actually need to speak to my father."

Cora nodded and sipped her drink, feeling all the anxiety and anger boiling through her with every unintentional clink of ice in the glass.

"Fancy meeting you here."

The voice was familiar, more than familiar, *familial.* Swiveling the seat to face the voice, she smiled coyly at the tall, dark-skinned man with razor-sharp features and eyes that could lay you open, bleeding and raw, like obsidian. "I'm sorry, have we met?"

It was the only play available to her, really, that wouldn't cause him to make a scene. Even still, there was no reason to think he wouldn't raise hell if she didn't get out of there, and soon.

"Nicodimos LeStrange, but my friends call me Mos." He offered her his hand, which she rose and shook to be polite.

Nicodimos 'Mos' LeStrange, was technically the Baron Westravna, formerly a region in Bohemia, now part of Poland and the Czech Revar, a courtesy title from their father's side. He was smart, had sharp instincts, and somehow managed to see through her glamour with no trouble at all. Last she knew, he was a data analyst in her father's administration, learning the ropes from the ground up. In a midnight blue velvet jacket over a black shirt and tie, Cora's brother was at once touchable and mysterious. That was edge upon which he thrived.

"Any relation to Marius?" she simpered, doing her best to appear as the vapid society chippee until Finn returned. This could get dicey, quickly.

His toothy grin sent a chill straight through her soul. "I should certainly hope so, Coretta. Otherwise this would be terribly awkward."

It was definitely that. For the first time that night, she wished she'd worn more dress. "How the hell did you find me? How did you know it was me, anyway?"

His whole face pursed in a familiar look of disappointment. "Considering I'm the one footing the bill." Her brother looked her up and down appraisingly. "Really, Chanel?"

"Can't sell a honeypot if it's empty, sweet cheeks." She patted his face with the most condescending grin she could muster, at least until she processed the rest of that sentence with dawning horror. "I... you! The fuck do you mean you're footing the bill?" she hissed through clenched teeth.

"Who do you think you've been talking to on the phone, genius? Seems like an unusual oversight for you. Should I be worried?"

"We hadn't spoken in most of a decade. I'll thank you to fuck off." The room began to smell of ozone and she knew she was not going to keep a hold of her temper or her shift if this went on much longer.

Dark eyes flashed to dead yellow as a faint sheen of feathers glistened across his skin. "You're being paid to keep him safe and alive, not fuck him."

Unable to resist a worthy target, Cora smiled, feeling her hands shift to talons. "Yeah, about that—"

"Is everything alright, Angel?"

And just like that, the burgeoning bubble of rage and inappropriate behavior receded at just the sound of Finn's voice. She turned to him as he slipped his arm possessively around her waist, her hand on his chest feeling his barely restrained growl when he pulled her to his side.

"We're fine. Baron LeStrange was just leaving." She smiled sweetly up at her brother and though she knew they'd have to speak soon about the case, for now, this was neither the venue nor the time. "Another time, perhaps?"

"Of course." Ever the smart man, Mos simply smiled back and bowed slightly to her. "Highness, Miss Westgate."

"Baron." He waited until his back was turned. The way he could take two steps and melt back into a room was equal parts impressive and frightening. "Do I wanna know what that was about?" he murmured out of the side of his mouth as they slowly meandered around the edge of the dance floor to the exit.

"Not here," she offered with a smile and giggle when Brendan looked their way. Finn nodded and they made small talk until they were in the clear, outside of the ballroom and stalking the deserted corridors of the empty royal wing. She had a lot to think about and the venue left a great deal to be desired.

Chapter Fourteen

FINN

The moment they were clear of security, he pulled her into a side room off the corridor. It was a small study not far from the ballroom with dark wood bookshelves, a small desk and chair, and a more comfortable leather armchair positioned by the window with a view of the gardens. The only light was the half-moon shining through the glass casting everything in stark shadows. It was the best he could do on short notice.

The door closing behind them sealed in the finality of the moment. They were finally alone for the first time since that morning and of all the things he wanted, talking was the last of them. He knew it wasn't the most mature idea, or even the best one, but the honeyed-citrus scent of her in his head all night, and that fucking dress, holy shit that dress, and he was done for.

Cora leaned back against the door, hands behind her with a

tiny smirk curling the corners of her lips. "I suddenly don't feel like talking."

Finn stepped closer, watching her dark eyes glitter to gold and back as her plush bottom lip slipped wet and glistening from between her teeth. The angel on his shoulder spoke of responsibility and duty and the devil, well... he was the one reaching out to tilt her chin up into his kiss to silence them both.

She tasted like whiskey and sounded like heaven with each little whimpered exhalation as he licked into her mouth. Inching closer, he backed her into the door until he was pressed against her from shoulder to knee with one hand on her hip, and his thumb tracing down the underside of her jaw to her throat.

No panties. Skimming over the soft, clinging fabric his mind could suddenly focus on nothing else. Finn groaned deep in his chest as his hand scaled the outside of her bare thigh only to meet not even a hint of underwear. "All fucking night," he whispered against her lips as he massaged her naked hip, "all I could think about was you sitting there looking all refined and put together... with no panties on. I'm surprised I didn't embarrass myself in front of the Court."

The evidence of his desire for her was rubbing against her stomach, separated by mere millimeters of fabric.

"I admire your restraint," she purred, wrapping her leg around his hip and pulling him even closer between her legs. She leaned up and whispered in his ear, "But I can assure you, it's no longer necessary." Finishing her declaration with a nip at his earlobe touched off a flurry of action with his jacket hitting the floor, his tie left hanging undone from his opened shirt and his trousers shucked to his knees.

His hands were practically shaking as he fought to reign in his urge to claim her as he traced a finger down the delicate neckline of her dress. The way she shivered and trembled at his touch made his inner wolf test the bounds of his restraint. Peeling the dress from her skin like a candy wrapper from a red licorice vine he left her naked but for her heels standing in a puddle of discarded silk.

"I have been waiting all night to see that," he growled as the last tethers on his veneer of civility snapped. His mouth went straight to her neck, with licks and bites that left her squeaking in surprise and squirming in his arms as one hand braced against the door and the other slipped down her chest to cup her breast.

Cora gasped, her breath catching as he pinched and plucked at her nipple, until it stood firm before he moved on, sending ticklish shivers down her spine as he teased her ribs and scraped his claws barely against the tender flesh of her belly. Gods, she was so vulnerable to him in that moment, so open and free and he felt so fucking privileged…

Finding the silken flesh of her pussy wet was not a surprise, she was always so responsive for him. Something he adored about her, the way she reacted to him, melting around his fingers and tongue. His forehead against hers, he watched as her folds parted for him and glistened in the muted darkness.

"I don't have time," he murmured as his finger rubbed tiny circles over her clit, "to eat you like I want. Properly. To show you just how bad the big, bad wolf can be." He hissed as she moaned when he slipped two fingers inside her, testing his resolve once more even as the feel of her juices dripping down his hand made his cock throb. "But believe me, I *will* make that up to you."

Her dark eyes were glassy as they stared into his, lips wet and swollen from his kisses as she panted and moaned riding the sensations his hands were pulling from her. It was nothing at all to have her grinding down on his fingers, his thumb dedicated to tormenting her clit. The feeling of her claws in his bicep and behind his neck told him when she was close, and he stopped, leaning in to cover her wail of protest with his lips.

"I was right there," she gritted out as he licked his fingers clean. Her scent and taste were imprinted on his brain and there was no finer flavor for his tongue to find.

"I know, baby," he commiserated as he drew both hands down her back to rest on her perfect, round ass. "And you will be again."

He hiked her legs around his waist, loving the way her body immediately cradled him, and how light she was relative to her size. "So many possibilities," he whispered before ducking his head to take first one nipple into his mouth and then the other. His boxer briefs shimmied down his legs as he kept her on edge and otherwise occupied.

The bite of her nails in his shoulder and scalp spurred him on, and he pulled back to stare into the endless pools of her eyes. "I need you," he whispered, his member grinding against the slippery folds of her pussy. It was perfect, it was torture. "Please, Cora. I need you."

Then, in what he could only think of as a moment of the goddesses' divine providence, she smiled. "Then have me."

Rolling his hips, he slipped into her tight, wet, heat, his soft groan more a broken breath against her lips as he bottomed out inside her. The feeling of closeness, intimacy beyond merely physical, swelling through him as he pulled back and rocked into her again, making her gasp his name.

"Yes, baby," he encouraged as he took his time with long slow strokes that were so incredible in both their pleasure and torment, he felt his fingers sink into the muscles of her pump ass. "Fuck me, angel. Give me everything you got."

Legs locked around him, Cora strained against him, the intense friction spurring him to faster and harder strokes until the door was softly knocking against the frame and her tits bounced with the motion. Her creamy pussy hotter and wetter the longer this went on, feeling her juices drip down his balls as the room filled with the sexy obscenities of wet flesh smacking against flesh as he filled her cunt again and again.

"'It's so good, baby. I'm so close," she breathed as she threw her head back against the door, arching her back and offering him her breasts to suck on as he slipped a hand down between them.

"Oh! Yes! Fuck!" she practically howled as her eyes came open and she met his gaze. He smiled around his mouthful of her nipple as his fingers rubbed against both sides of her clit.

Her body clenched all at once around him, everything going taut for a moment as time stalled and he saw her at her most perfect and beautiful. Neck and back arched away from the door, her hands on his shoulders as her body held him inside her so fucking tightly.

Finn lost it, his strokes losing their rhythm until finally he filled her one last time, his ball sack contracting as wave after wave of release burned through him. His whole body throbbing, mind just on fire as he slowly came back to himself. His breath warm and wet against her skin as he sighed against her shoulder and rubbed his face against the crook of her neck.

For a few moments, the world consisted of solely them two, their desires, their breaths as they both came down from their highs.

"I should probably move," he groaned softly against her skin. He would gladly die in this spot and regret not a damn thing, but alas...

Cora snickered weakly. "Yeah, probably. I'm not sure I can feel my legs."

"That makes two of us." He huffed a quiet laugh to cover the surge of pride that went through him at her admission. "Come on, I'll hold you up."

She unwound her legs from behind his back, and he waited until she was steady on her feet before readjusting his clothing, unceremoniously stuffing his softening cock back into his boxer briefs and pants. For her part, she stood staring at the husk of discarded silk forlornly.

"This is going to be a pain," she predicted as he fastened his pants, already mostly put back together.

And she was right, so very right as none of the tape worked anymore and they couldn't get the folds to lay correctly, the neckline gaping obscenely leaving one of her breasts exposed. It was wrong how hot he found that but getting hard for her again would only pose more problems, not fewer. She didn't give up, though, trying to press the tape back into place to no avail. At some point they had to concede that the dress would never again resemble the outfit she'd spent the night dazzling the glitterati of the shifter kingdom.

"It's alright," he soothed as she hiked the one shoulder of the dress up with a huff.

"Really?" she scoffed bitterly. "You're okay with me walking the halls with my tits out?"

"No, I never said that," he chuckled and took the jacket of his tuxedo and held it up for her to slide her arms through.

She purred at the warmth, the weight of the jacket seeming to ease her distress immediately. "It even smells like you," she preened happily as she buried her face in the shawl collar.

Seeing her in his clothes did something to him, not that his wolf needed any help in the possessiveness department where she was concerned, but goddamn. Seeing her in his clothes was almost as arousing to him as seeing her in only her heels. He marveled again at her beauty, how perfect she was to him. Maybe even for him.

That line of thinking though came with its own problems as the events of the night intruded into his mind. He sighed as he looked around the room to ensure they'd leave nothing behind when they made their escape.

Seeming to sense the change in his mood, she smiled ruefully. "I guess we should talk about it, huh?"

He nodded. "I think we've avoided it long enough." She sighed next to him but didn't say anything else. "I'm sorry about your parents."

She shook her head immediately. "Don't be. I'm not." Even as she said he could hear the remnants of bitterness in her voice. "They lost me a long time ago. It just became official a few years ago, but I was of no use to them long before then."

He knew that was a damned lie, but he wasn't going to poke a wound that had been so recently reopened. Unable to think of anything else to do, he wrapped his arm around her waist, tucking her into his side and resting his cheek on her head. "I'm so sorry."

"Don't be. It's not your fault," she reassured him.

"Okay," he agreed because there was nothing else he could do.

She let him hold her a moment longer before she looked up at him. "We should probably go."

He snorted. "Yeah, we probably should."

Cora stepped away from him and stretched her arms over her head with a lusty purr. "Thank you for this. I clearly needed it."

"Me too, apparently."

She laced her fingers with his as he opened the door, checking the hallway before leading her outside.

"So that was your brother, huh?" he asked after looking around to make sure they were truly by themselves.

CORA

The click of her heels seemed to echo through the empty marble halls. She paused long enough to lean against him to remove her heels so she could be blissfully barefoot on the soothingly cool marble floor as they kept walking. "Yeah. Yeah, it was."

"He was hitting on you? That had to be both awkward and unpleasant." He chuckled a little but looked concerned when she didn't share in his mirth.

"He wasn't hitting on me." It was still so much to take in. He was the one bankrolling her mission to keep Finn safe. He was the one who sought her out. *Her*, the family outcast. Was he alone? Did her father know? Was he involved? What was the real endgame now? How was this all supposed to work now?

Finn, smarty-pants that he was, arrived at the conclusion all by himself. "Your handler!"

"Keep your voice down," she growled, yanking at his arm in agitation. This was not a conversation she wanted to have outside of his suite where she could monitor for listening devices.

"What the hell, Cora? What else aren't you telling me?" He had the audacity to sound pissed off like she hadn't just found out herself.

She held up a single finger as they neared his chambers. "We will discuss this shortly, but not here."

"Oh, we're going to discuss it."

Her snarky retort was cut short by a scream, a younger feminine scream, coming from the end of the hallway. It was loud and quick, and they both took off in that direction. Finn and Cora arrived just in time to see a young woman fall from the upstairs landing and come to an abrupt stop in midair, dangling from what appeared to be a bedsheet or curtain around her neck.

She was dead, whoever she was, not even really twitching and it was beyond surreal. Driscoll came barreling around the corner, wide-eyed and frightened looking. "I heard a scream. Highness, Cora, are you alright?"

She didn't know how to answer, unable to look away from the horrible sight in front of her.

The vulture followed her line of sight upwards until he, too, gasped. "Holy shit!" Fumbling with his radio, he summoned backup and a medic. That done, he immediately began tending to them. "Highness, you can't be here. Cora, please come with me," as he herded them into a sitting room at the other end of the hall. The one they'd just left.

CHAPTER FIFTEEN

FINN

They didn't really have time to process the levels of awkward in being together in the room in which they'd just fucked, because almost as soon as they sat down, Driscoll was back and leading Finn away to keep the witnesses separated. It was protocol, she'd assured him, even though her eyes looked concerned.

He hadn't expected that it would be several hours before he'd be allowed to see her again. By the time he and Cora were allowed to go back to his quarters, the sun had long been up and all he wanted to do was fall over and collapse.

There was a cart waiting for them in the room with silver domes and a carafe of coffee, which drew Cora like a moth to a flame with a moan of gratitude. Despite the tension between them, he smiled.

"You keep making noises like that, we won't get to the coffee," he joked as he sank down onto the couch with a sigh.

"Uh huh." Her lips twitched. "First order of business, though, has gotta be getting out of this damn dress." She laid his jacket carefully on the side of the bed before dropping the blue dress from her shoulder with barely a shimmy. Bold and unashamed, she walked across the room and collected her pajamas, clearly aware of Finn's eyes on her. Finn didn't even attempt to hide it, unabashedly enjoying the show as he poured them both a cup of coffee.

CORA

With the clothes on, she was a bit more hesitant, maybe a little more inclined to pay attention to the unresolved tension and anxiety between them. She took his jacket from the bed and traded him for a steaming mug.

"Looked better on you than it ever did on me," he murmured as he rose from the couch and took it from her. He moved over to the closet as she sat, treating him to the same level of scrutiny. Damn but he was pretty, it was unreasonable, brain-melting even, the muscular lines of his back as he changed out of his tux, his squeezably muscular ass. He didn't bother with his shirt, just threw on some sleep pants and headed back to the couch.

She couldn't be expected to concentrate on breakfast, or the niceties of conversation when he was dressed like that, right? Her eyes skipped down the ridged landscape of his chest, over the dips and swells of his abs to the hint of v-line just above the loose waistband of his pants. Jesus.

They picked at the bowls of fruit that had been left for them, drinking black coffee, wary of the condiments again. His cheeks looked a little hollow, she noticed, and the lack of regular meals was becoming a concern. Last thing she wanted was a starving wolf on her hands.

"I told them we were together," she informed him over her second cup of life-giving elixir. "When they asked about what led up to us finding the girl, I told them I was with you."

He nodded. "I did, too. Did you tell them what we were doing?" His wicked little smirk sent a shiver through her at the memory.

"I said we were talking." At his scoffing exaggerated cough, she giggled so hard her nose wrinkled. "What? I told them I was in your jacket because of the way the dress was held up."

Finn blinked, incredulity plain across his face. "And they believed that?"

Cora rolled her eyes. "They didn't say otherwise. Why, what did you say?"

"I told them we were talking and taking a late-night stroll together, which is how we ended up on the scene."

"Not entirely inaccurate." She nodded, they could work with that. So long as neither of them lied outright, just didn't come up off the entire truth, they could dance in the gray area for as long as they needed to. "So long as we're on the same page, we're good."

He set his mug down and laced his fingers across his belly as he crossed his ankles with his feet on the coffee table. "At least about that anyway."

"Meaning?"

She absolutely was not ogling the way his biceps bunched up as he crossed his arms over his firm pecs. "You weren't going to tell me your brother was bankrolling your mission?"

Cora exhaled sharply and pushed to her feet. She hadn't really had time to process that yet and didn't know how she felt about it. It was somewhere at the intersection on the Venn diagram of 'pissed off', 'used', and 'betrayed'. "I found out just before you did, trust me." She collected their coffee cups and cleaned up their breakfasts, leaving the cart in the hall. When she returned, she flounced down on her corner of the couch with an annoyed harrumph. "I don't know how, or why. Or for whom, honestly."

He sat up at that, bracing his elbows on his knees. "You don't think he's the leader?"

She closed her eyes as she thought about it, rubbing the spot between her eyes to stave off a burgeoning headache as she mentally ran through the information they had. "I think he's the face, but I don't think he's the final word. He doesn't have that kind of money but apparently makes a damn good middleman." She wasn't comfortable running spy craft past Finn and the Night Watch Commander's warning to her played over in her mind. "We need to talk to Vasi."

Thankfully, he didn't fight her. "Agreed."

Just then, a knock at the interior antechamber door sounded. "Finn! It's me."

"Speak of the devil," she muttered. Cora got up and let him in, looking him over from head to toe. "You don't look like you have horns."

His blue eyes narrowed. "Do I even want to know what that means?" He looked wrung out, worn, his gray suit, normally perfectly pressed and put together now limp and wrinkled. His hair had long come out of its bun at the base of his neck and was now tied back in a half-assed ponytail that left his bangs free to drape around his face and angular jaw.

"Have you seen the news today?" he asked, sounding almost as serious as when he had his gun on her and thought she was a gold digger.

Cora shook her head and got up to grab her clutch from the night before. She hadn't even thought about her phone since the evening before. "Not yet. Something we should be aware of?"

Vasily growled and drove his fingers through his hair in irritation, frowning when they got hung up on the hair tie. Once he got that sorted, he stared at Finn critically. "Look, I *know* you didn't do this."

"Of course not," Cora snapped, growing more and more annoyed as she scrolled through her news feed and read the increasingly breathless and lurid allegations.

"The fact this got out so quickly, with so many salient details from an 'anonymous source close to the palace,'" he held up the air quotes, "tells me someone's out to get you."

"Out to get me how?" Finn asked as he reached for her phone. Cora held it just out of reach because he didn't need the stress of seeing everything she did. He bared his teeth at her, but still she didn't give in until he sat back in a huff. "Fine. What does it say?"

Scrolling back down, she frowned. "Not much of anything substantive. A lot of intimations, supposition, and conjecture, but not a lot in the way of actual fact. It does lead the reader to draw some unsavory conclusions, though."

Finn cradled his head in his hands, fingers tangled tightly in the golden blond strands. "Shit."

"I know," she soothed, rubbing soft circles on his back. "Don't worry yet, though."

"How can I not worry?"

"You didn't do it. We weren't even on the same side of the building and got there just after the fact." She looked to Vasi to confirm and only got a cringe in response.

"And then there's the matter of the note."

Both Finn and Cora blinked at him. "What note?" she demanded.

"She had a note in her pocket." He dug through his pocket and produced his own cell phone.

"That said," she prompted when he trailed off.

Scrolling as he read, he quoted, "That said she couldn't go on. She was having an affair with a royal, and since he planned to leave her, she wanted to assassinate him by poisoning his food."

"An affair?" He sounded offended at the very idea. "Did the note say who?"

"Clearly, it wasn't you." Vasi blinked at him meaningfully and she couldn't help her snort. "The letter didn't say but..."

"Well, since we know Finn's been with me, that leaves only two other male royals. And one of those," her eyes cut to the prince briefly, "hasn't exactly been able to hoist a mainsail in quite some time."

Finn's hands went to his eyes to rub vigorously. "Oh my God."

Vasi blanched, echoing his best friend's horrified expression. "Please do not ever, *ever* say that again."

She sighed impatiently. "Delicate sensibilities aside, you have to admit, this all seems… convenient. Like overly so, no?"

Vasily shook off his disgust and threw open the two couple buttons of his black dress shirt after loosening his tie. "Ain't it just?"

Cora was quiet for a little while, eyes gone to the middle distance as she turned these new pieces of the puzzle over in her head. "It's beautiful," she concluded, raking her upper lip with her teeth.

"I know, right?"

FINN

"What's beautiful?" Finn asked, looking between the two of them with growing concern.

"It's neat," she repeated, her dark eyes clearing and flashing over to gold.

Vasily nodded, dipped his chin once, his eyes now hard and cold, yellow, maybe orange. "Too neat," he agreed.

"I'm assuming you have handwriting analysis on it, yes?"

His best friend nodded again. "It's protocol and it's got a rush on it. We'll know more soon."

Finn growled as he lost all patience with the two soldiers. "I'm gonna need you two to stop sharing a brain and start sharing with the rest of the class."

Cora took his hand, lacing their fingers together and petting down his arm with an expression of sincerity on her face that gave him pause. "Somebody's doing a bang-up job in making it look like you had a hand in this."

He blanched as he blinked at her, suddenly exceptionally

nauseated. "I'm sorry, what?"

Vasi put his phone away and steepled his hands as he continued to stare, unfocused into the distance. "By intimating the affair, the letter hits all those tabloid titillation buttons that's gonna have the paparazzi all over you and your brother. They're gonna want dirt, and if they don't get it, they'll make it up. You know how that goes."

"Provided it's real." She looked far too serious and stoked his anxiety that much more.

"Yes, provided it's real," Vasi confirmed.

Picking up his thought, Cora continued, "The threat of regicide makes this extra messy. Was she working by herself? On someone's behalf? To what end? Either way, with the coronation coming up, it casts your brother in a sympathetic light."

"And me, not so much, right?"

"You *do* have the most to gain if he dies," she reminded him gently. It wasn't a fact he wanted to think about, but it was certainly unavoidable.

The implications bloomed and unspooled in front of him spreading out like some acid-tripping fractal painting. "Holy shit."

"Yeah," she agreed, looking far too serious for his comfort.

"What are we going to do?" He looked from her to his best friend and back. The idea that this could happen, that someone would do this to him for no reason he could think of other than his proximity to the throne, sickened him.

"I don't know yet." The look on Vasi's face made him fear for his coworkers' lives honestly.

"We need a plan!" he asserted, feeling all of the anxiety bubbling out of him and his hackles fighting to come up.

"We need sleep," she countered, still watching him carefully.

"You expect me to sleep after this?" Had she lost her mind?

Cora nodded. "At least a couple hours, we'll plan everything after that, okay? You too, Vasi?"

"No dice. I have to take care of this. I can't just leave this on

Driscoll's shoulders." He sighed and pushed to his feet, rubbing his palms on his thighs in agitation. "You're my best friend, I can't let this go."

Finn got up and hugged the other man before stepping back. "Thank you. For everything." He could barely think, his mind so cluttered with all this new information.

Cora's hand on his arm was cool, the temperature change a brief distraction. "We'll be here. Let us know if you need anything."

Vasi nodded and was out the door, leaving them alone in a roomful of thoughts, worries, and potential accusations.

"C'mon," she cajoled, leading him to the bed and all but forcing him flat. She pulled the sheet over them as she laid her head on his shoulder and threw an arm over his waist. The silence stretched on between them, thoughts and things left unsaid settling down like rain around them as neither one of them slept. And then she spoke, soft, strong, with lethal levels of promise. "I don't know how yet, but I will protect you from this too. Believe that."

CHAPTER SIXTEEN

CORA

It was two days of hell that followed. The paparazzi descended like a swarm of starving mosquitos, dogging Finn's every step off the palace grounds. For her part, she did what she could to stay anonymous in the background, but of course, pictures from the gala had been publicized and now everyone wanted to know about the new 'it' girl on the arm of the Lupine prince.

Her contacts on both sides of the law had damn little for her in the way of enlightening information, and Mos... Hell, the longer she went without speaking to her brother, the better as far as she was concerned.

By Wednesday morning, she'd put her foot down about Finn leaving the house. He was extra jumpy and hostile and having people constantly on his ass, asking invasive, personal, and frankly inappropriate questions was tiring, and he hadn't slept enough to keep his temper in check. Cora felt he was one overzealous paparazzo away from a public mauling the likes of which hasn't been seen since the thirteenth century. Thankfully, he listened.

She yawned and stretched as she sat up, the room filled with the wispy remnants of late morning sunshine. One look at her phone said that they'd slept through breakfast. No idea when she'd passed out, but honestly, she could do with more.

Finn grumbled at a knock at the door, pulling the pillow over his face and she smiled despite the circumstances. He was so fucking cute, and she truly wanted nothing more than for him to rest before he dealt with any more body blows.

Throwing open the door, she prepared to snarl at whomever was on the other side. Vasi, however, looked even more haggard than he had when he'd left two days before with hollow shadows below his eyes and an unnaturally large refillable coffee mug. "You look like shit."

"Fuck off," he muttered but there was no heat behind it, as he stalked into the room past her.

"Keep your voice down." Cora closed the door and looked to the bed, relieved that Finn was still asleep. "You have news, I take it?"

"As such." He cut his eyes to the bed, seeing what she did, and moved closer to the sitting area. "We can prove you and Finn weren't on that side of the palace when she died."

"Do tell." She took a seat on the couch and held out her hand to bid him to do the same, but he kept shifting restlessly from foot to foot.

"Timestamped video outside of the ballroom. Shows you and Finn leaving and also entering that sitting room for," he cleared his throat as he fluttered his lashes at her, "quite some time."

"There's no camera in that hallway." It wasn't a denial, there was no point, and she wasn't ashamed, but the idea that she missed a camera was... concerning. Her handler had given her a layout of the palace security system in case some of her more finite skills were needed. She still avoided cameras on principle, even if they weren't.

"There is when I have half the shifter leaders from the Western

Hemisphere, in the building. We had double patrols and several extra guards besides."

Ignoring the implications about Vasi seeing her half naked and sneaking around the palace, she focused on the investigation. "Makes me wonder how she managed to get through the palace unseen to kill herself."

He hummed and took a long sip of his drink. "She was seen. We have time stamps that show her on the other side of the palace at the same time you and Finnegan were... indisposed."

"Excellent, so then what's the problem?"

"It appears she was running from someone. Looking over her shoulder as she ran down the hall, the camera didn't catch anyone else, though. And the autopsy..." he drew his hands through his hair, taking down his bun and shaking out his shoulder-length curls. "She had perimortem blunt force trauma to the back of her skull."

Cora sat up straight at that. 'Hit in the head and thrown off a balcony with a makeshift noose' made this a whole new ballgame. "Homicide?"

"Suspicious death and leaning that way, yes." They both grimaced, thoughts on prior cases and prior deaths. It was never easy. "It gets worse, though," the owl volunteered.

"Worse for whom?" she inquired carefully. The phrasing raised her hackles something fierce.

"She was knocked up."

Well, that was certainly motive. Growling, Cora pushed to her feet and stalked to the window, an eye toward the bed and the unmoving body of the prince. This was the very last thing he needed, close to the edge as he was. She came back to the couch, working very hard at both keeping her voice down and also not exploding in a ball of incendiary rage. "How far along was she?"

"Ten weeks, give or take." He looked as disgusted as she felt about the whole situation.

"And the father?"

Vasi shook his head. "Preliminary tissue tests show wolf DNA in addition to goat. I have rush in on further testing. Late tonight, tomorrow morning at the latest?" He held up his phone. "This is the first time I've had a moment's peace in days."

"Cherish it," she snickered. She didn't envy him, but she definitely saw how seriously he took his responsibility to both the crown and Finn himself. "What do you know about her?"

"Sweet girl, by all accounts. Worked in the kitchen for a couple years with her mother and her brother. I believe you've met him. Finn's attendant, Francis?"

Shit, the one she'd pulled her gun on. "She was the little Hircine kid's sister?"

"Their poor mother, she must be heartbroken." Finn gave up the pretense of staying in bed to join them in the sitting area, rubbing his eye with his fist. "Obviously, we'll take care of her family. It's the least we can do."

Vasi rubbed the back of his neck, looking like he was fighting a cringe. "I'd hold off on that, if I were you."

"What? Why?"

"The news… they've been going out of their way to insinuate and fabricate connections and the girl, even going so far as suggesting it's a failed lover's tryst between you and her. Some kind of pact to off your brother to put you on the throne and make her queen. Offering her family money or any kind of compensation right now would only add to that story."

"Fucking hell!" Finn shot to his feet and stalked into the closet and back out, holding a fresh shirt in his hands. "How the fu—I don't even unders—"

Vasi held his hands up in a physical demonstration of his lack of malice. "I know, and I'm sorry. I wish I had better news."

Cora walked over and wrapped her arms around his waist. "On the upside, all evidence puts you in the clear, so there's that."

"Cold comfort for Francis' family."

"Finnegan, we'll do press on it to dispel as many of the rumors as we can. But we need to get ahead of this media storm before the court of public opinion puts a rope around your neck."

The prince stomped over and collapsed into his armchair like a puppet with cut strings. Even though he'd just gotten up, he looked so, so tired. "I'm listening if you have suggestions."

CHAPTER SEVENTEEN

BRENDAN

It would not be unreasonable to expect him to be pissed. Extravagant birthday gala interrupted by something as tawdry as a suicide, and of a member of the household staff, even. And yet Brendan could not be more pleased than if he had a crown. Sure, the young woman's death was inconvenient, but it was *necessary*, and that was what was truly important.

"You're in a good mood." His dearest Auntie Gwen sat across the table from him, eating her burnt toast and coffee as black as her soul. Even though she'd long retired from public life, the Dowager Duchess was dressed to the nines in an Hèrmes turtleneck and skirt, ready for her closeup at a moment's notice.

"Why wouldn't I be? Seeing my saintly brother's good name being dragged through the muck in the media puts a bright spin on any day." He popped half of a hulled strawberry in his mouth and grinned cheerfully.

"That was a cunning bit of work on your part."

"Thank you," he preened smugly.

"How *did* you manage it? With the girl, I mean."

"Timing, mostly. And a few well-placed and loyal staff willing to curry favor with the crown prince." She was a nuisance, a dalliance who forgot her place. That type of thing had consequences.

"It's perfect, honestly," he gloated as he delicately punctured the egg yolk of his breakfast, over easy. "I'm in the clear, seen by all and sundry on the other side of the palace. But Finn, on the other hand..." he trailed off as his kitchen steward poured him more coffee. "Well, I don't know where he was, do we?"

"Off with that Corvid tramp, I suppose," Aunt Gwen sulked. Ever since the failed drive-by and Cora moving into the palace, however temporarily, there was no appeasing her. The whiff of impropriety proximal to the throne sent her into paroxysms of righteous—and relentless—indignation. "Did you see that dress? I mean *honestly*, who wears that to court?"

Brendan looked down at his ramekin, barely able to squelch his smirk. Cora, for all that she was an obstacle to him dealing with his brother directly, was a beautiful woman and he would absolutely *kill* for the opportunity to have her at his side. And maybe he would.

"Regardless, it seems my brother's sterling reputation is not quite as shiny as it once was." He hummed in pleasure as the creamy custard coated his tongue. "And all it took was one dead girl and some well-placed people with some interesting speculations."

"Thank the goddess for the twenty-four hour news cycle." She smiled as a servant poured more coffee into her cup. "He'll be so busy chasing his tail, he won't have time to worry about much of anything else."

Brendan's grin was accented with sharp fangs as he raised his cup to her. "And that is distinctly to our benefit."

"Hear, hear."

FINN

Everything he'd worked for, everything he ever stood for, was flaming around him. All of the goodwill his foundation had, had been on his back and now? Gods, how could he even face his employees, much less his donors or the board of directors. Would he be removed? Or given the opportunity to step aside?

Vasi's cell phone going off startled him out of his thoughts. He stepped into the antechamber to take the call while Cora remained at his side, thumbs flying as she texted at light speed. Every once in a while, she'd reach over and pat his knee or gently squeeze his thigh.

The owl blew back in the room with a broad grin that gave Finn a measure of cautious hope. "Finnegan," he said in his best Maury Povich voice, "you are *not* the father!"

Even though it had never been a question, the relief he felt was palpable as his shoulders relaxed a bit and his jaw unclenched. "Of course not, so what now?"

"Now, we get the results independently verified just for the sake of paperwork, but I'm comfortable with both your history and your alibi and, more importantly, everyone else will be, too."

"What he's saying is he's gonna clear your name, right?"

Finn smiled at her fierce expression and the way she moved even closer to him like she would physically shield him if necessary. And just like that, there was a light at the end of the long, dark tunnel. This one, at least.

"And what does that look like, exactly?"

Vasily sat in the armchair and rested his forearms on his knees phone clasped in his hands. "I'm texting with the public information officer to set up the press conference now. Should be set up in a couple hours."

"That soon?" Finn couldn't decide if he was grateful for that or concerned.

"The faster we get your name off the list, the faster we shift the investigation to hunt for the real killer."

"Is that gonna be enough?" Cora's gaze was firm, unwavering and not nearly as hopeful as he'd prefer.

"What do you mean?"

He caught her quick look out of the corner of her eye before she continued interrogating Vasily. "I mean, is there a plan in place to get him off the front page? And quickly?"

The Commander sat back with a thoughtful expression. "You got something in mind?"

The devious curl of her lips sent a chill through his soul. "Well, the only way to shelve a scandal is to make an even bigger scandal. Preferably during the evening news cycle."

The slightly feral look in her eye made him vaguely nauseated. "I don't like where this is going."

Vasi clearly had no such issues as he sat forward with a curious grin. "Keep talking..."

CORA

"...and we can state definitively that Prince Finnegan of the House Lupine was not involved in any way with the death of Bedelia Fielding. The investigation is still ongoing..."

Cora disconnected the call she'd been on as Finn pulled up the live broadcast on his phone. Everything that was about to happen would take split second timing, but she wasn't worried.

Devon's smooth delivery at the press conference just inside the Guard house roll call room, backed up by a glowering Vasily, was the perfect backdrop. Darkening sky in the window behind him reflecting back the bright white lights of the cameras, the click-whirr of still frame cameras, dour-faced detectives in suits. "This'll do nicely."

Her phone chirped in her hand, the message exactly what she'd wanted to hear. There was a reason she was the best at this. All it took was twisting the right arms and bending the right ears.

Petting Finn's arm, she grinned as she watched Devon wind his way to his closing. "And here we go."

"What—?" She silenced him with a delicate finger over his lips.

"We'll now be taking questions..." he didn't get to finish the phrase before the reporters drowned out his voice with their first salvo.

"Are you looking at other suspects?"

"Have you ruled out suicide?"

"What was the evidence that cleared the prince?"

So far, so good. Exactly what she'd expected, and from whom, even. They were nothing if not predictable. Especially as it got closer to the end of Sweeps month, more often than not, the local stations wanted to finish with a bang, and today, she was happy to oblige.

Devon was the picture of competence, unbothered by the rapid fire interrogation by the press. This is what he did, and really, better him than Xander. He was barely civil on a good day so far as she could tell. Very little in the way of home training, that one.

"Do you have any further on the autopsy?"

"Right on cue," she purred, wriggling in her seat as the plan proceeded to the letter.

"Are you sticking with suicide as the cause of death?"

"Wait for it..."

"Is there any truth that she was pregnant before she died? Do you know who the father is?"

There was a moment, a clarion moment of silence right before the first shockwaves of the bomb rippled through the air as it exploded. What happened next would have been charitably called a 'feeding frenzy' if all parties involved had been of the fishy persuasion. Question after question, demand after demand, practically leaping over and clawing at one another to get out their inquiries, it was perfectly orchestrated bedlam and went down exactly as intended.

A redacted copy of a copy of the autopsy report, with the important part revealed, was handed off to Mookie and Samson, who then couriered it to her media contacts, et voila. Instant scandal just add fetus. So long as people remained predictable, she'd remain employed.

Finn closed the news app and stared at her for a long time, blue eyes cautious, wary. "You're scary as hell, you know that?"

To be fair, she was paid damn good money to be scary. Keeping her clients out of the news or at least off the front page and out of trouble was exactly her current skill set, minus some of the more hands-on aspects. "Only to those who oppose me."

"Not comforting, Angel."

She hummed to acknowledge him, not interested in his judgment, especially considering her play worked like a charm. #WhosTheDaddy, #DaddyorZaddy, #LupineSupine were all trending on social media, with Brendan coming under increasing scrutiny and fire, which was also exactly as intended. The royal twitter account was under siege, and so were Insta and Facebook.

People started questioning Brendan's fitness to succeed King Niall on the throne in under an hour. And sure, maybe she had some of her employees steer that conversation a wee bit, but it took hold like wildfire. Finn's name was officially second-rate news, getting cleared not nearly as titillating as the possibility that Miss Fielding had been killed carrying an heir to the crown. This suddenly became a Big Damn Deal, and Finn was almost completely out of the blast radius. Sure, there were some who wouldn't be convinced, but they were outliers, and so long as she controlled the loudest narrative, they were good to go.

CHAPTER EIGHTEEN

BRENDAN

"**A**re you fucking kidding me?" he all but roared as he read the alert on his phone. The Soricine page in front of him knelt, face bloodied from his claws and smelled like a midnight snack.

This had been his story to tell, his tale to control, and now his phone would not stop ringing with requests for him to comment. Somehow his sainted brother had skated by yet again. Everyone was always so quick to grant him the benefit of the doubt and in the same breath believe him to be an unspeakable monster. It wasn't fair. It wasn't like he was the one to actually kill the girl.

He felt the shift in the air of his quarters, like the gates of hell were opening on visitor's day, before he heard her voice. "I taught you better."

With a sigh so deep it could have been a well, he turned to face her. "I have no need or use for your 'I told you so's."

"'Failure to plan is planning to fail,'" she remarked as she perched in a chair at the dining room table. "Did you know?"

"That she was pregnant? Of course. You couldn't miss the change in her scent."

"And so you killed her? With no other plan in place?" Her disappointment was a separate presence in the room.

"I did nothing of the sort," he bristled. "I told her to take care of it, gave her the money to do so, and when she back out, I had it sorted out accordingly." He'd always planned to kill her, to have her serve this glorious purpose of casting his brother into doubt, and securing his place as the rightful, if unwanted, heir. Why could nothing, literally *nothing*, go to plan for him? Just the once?

"Apparently not," she sniffed.

CORA

Content to let her little op run on its own now, Cora stood and stretched. Finn wilted back against the couch cushions. The prince looked tired, though she knew he'd slept, and his cheekbones were a little more pronounced. He was starting to get that ultra-chiseled Michelangelo's David look to him. Lovely on the statue, worrisome as hell on a wolf. "Have you eaten?"

Finn closed his eyes and shook his head. "Not since yesterday."

His listlessness was cause for concern, but the real issue came in the form of a ravenous wolf. Ravening was a canid-specific sickness, like Lunacy, but driven by extreme hunger. It wasn't illegal, exactly, but definitely frowned upon, especially in House Lupine. Staying fed was a personal responsibility and the fact he wasn't and didn't seem to care about it was starting to scare her.

"I'm gonna have Driscoll bring us a few steaks, okay?"

FINN

He nodded and then headed on back to bed. Everything about the days since his brother's birthday party had left him hollow and devoid of anything other than worry and concern. How would the Society of Angels go on? Who would look after their father once Brendan became king? Who was tending to Francis's family in their time of need? At least now, he could release his worry that he was going to prison for a crime he didn't commit. And now the SoA would likely settle down and return to normal as well.

And that was thanks, in large part, to Cora. He watched her pace around the room as she texted, looking over at him with a fond smile every now and then. She had ridden to his rescue again, this time wearing little more than a bathrobe and armed only with a cell phone. She was his brown-skinned goddess, his raven, and so he would let her feed him, even though it wasn't necessary. If she enjoyed looking after him, who was he to deny her? Besides, even if he did, she'd do it anyway.

That night, Finn lay in bed with his belly full of meat and his arms full of raven and for a moment, he felt like he could find peace. Her sweet scent of amber and oranges sending him off to the land of dreams quietly and without complaint for the first time in months.

The alarm that woke him wasn't his normal morning wake up call. In fact, it wasn't an alarm at all but an urgent notification from his father's press secretary that a press conference was called for eight o'clock, sharp.

"Is this your doing?" At Cora's half-asleep, interrogatory grunt, he put the screen in front of her face. "The presser. Is this you?"

"No." She shook her head and nestled back against him more firmly with her face turned toward the pillow, like she planned to go back to sleep. He could tell the moment the information had sunk in when she stiffened, then growled low. "We should be there."

It wasn't a question and she kicked her legs out from under the blankets to head into the bathroom. "Give me ten and I'll be good to go."

Smart man that he was, Finn had a cart with coffee brought up and waiting on her when she emerged from the bathroom looking like a damn runway model. In her gray and pink striped sweater, pale pink skirt, gray tights and heels, she looked so soft and sweet and he wanted nothing more than to pull down her demure bun and ruffle her up as much as possible. She made soft and delicate look sharp and sexy as all hell.

"I love you," she muttered as she made a beeline for the caffeine. "You are the only thing that matters to me."

The unexpected exclamation left him a bit flat-footed. "I... um... that is—"

"I was talking to the coffee," she admonished around her sips of boiling life-juice.

"Right. Of course." Cheeks now on fire, he strategically retreated to the en suite bathroom to hide and get ready for the day. And if he heard her soft giggles behind his back, well…. It was too early in the morning to pick that fight.

CORA

By the time they made it down to the throne room, the press were already jockeying for positions, setting up cameras and lights and chatting amongst themselves. There were several from national media outlets outside of the shifter community, and just seeing the number of people there gave Cora a very bad feeling. Whatever he was going to say was going to be huge, and likely life-altering for all involved.

Brendan stood off to the side, a rangy wolf who looked both hungry and impatient in a flawless navy-blue suit, with an equally cranky looking Aunt Gwen at his side. Evidently her coffin opened too early for her pleasantness to make an appearance. She wasn't even pretending, with her lips pressed into a line so thin they looked drawn on in crayon.

King Niall walked out and a hush fell over the room. He was in a suit, slate gray and slim cut, though as thin as he was now, it still hung awkwardly on him. His attendant was at his elbow, but the frail monarch was moving under his own power for the moment. The sick feeling in her stomach began doing backflips as Finn gripped her arm in alarm.

With a quiet, shuddery breath, the King leaned against the podium in front of him and adjusted the mic. "Thank you for coming out on such short notice. I know it's early, so I'll get straight to the point. Due to the terrible circumstances surrounding the death of Miss Fielding, I will be postponing the coronation until the end of the investigation. I do not wish for there to be questions or accusations outstanding when my son assumes the throne." He paused, looking like each word he uttered cost him dearly, but then he soldiered on. "As your king, I have endeavored to serve you with honor and integrity. You, as my subjects, deserve nothing less from me, and whomever succeeds me on the throne. To that end, I will continue to serve you until my very last breath. Thank you."

Cora's eyes went to Brendan as the king spoke, watching his face as each word sealed his fate in stone. There was no missing the careful omission of his name, or the fact this was brought about by the glaring light of the investigation she'd shone on his slithery, slimy self. Other than a jaw so tense she feared for his teeth, he was remarkably expressionless. The same, however, could not be said of her prince.

Finn blinked next to her and out of the corner of her eye she saw the blood drain from his face and down beyond the collar of his shirt. This was what the ongoing debacles of his brother hath wrought. Their father, disinclined to pass the crown to his eldest and unable to skip the line of succession without cause, left stranded on his throne as his body failed around him.

They watched in amazement as the king, having made it out there on his own, turned on his heel to return from whence he came, only to get is feet tangled at the last second and crumble before their eyes. Finn was at his side in an instant, cameras rolling press in an uproar, Guards pouring in like army ants, clearing the way for the royal doctor to come retrieve him.

And through it all, Brendan watched off to the side, removed from the scene like he was watching a play, or CSPAN. As much as she wanted to examine that further, Xander appeared in front of her.

"Commander, I need you with him," he murmured in her ear as he directed her to Finn's side. "He's going to need someone if this goes bad."

Hell, if this went bad, the whole shifter kingdom was going to need someone, and it wasn't going to be just Finn.

CHAPTER NINETEEN

BRENDAN

"How perfect was that?" The moment he was away from the cameras, he practically danced down the hallway in giddy delight. "He may have postponed the coronation, but if he doesn't wake up..."

Gwen's smile was all teeth, razor-sharp and diamond bright. "Then all the news conferences in the world won't matter at all."

"Exactly." Brendan nodded as he held the door for her to precede him into his quarters. "And if he has help in that department..."

Gwen took a seat in his armchair and pulled out her cell phone, a devious smile curling her lips. "Then long live the king."

FINN

Cora was able to coax him away from his father's bedside at the hospital late that night, and that was only with the promise of food and the threat of bringing Vasily in. News of the king's collapse had gone worldwide in an instant with varying relatives calling in, far-flung members of the royal family poking around for updates on his condition and tidbits of information on him and his brother. She'd confiscated his phone after it beeped almost nonstop for five solid minutes, and he'd let her, or it was going to get ground to dust in his hands. Shockproof and waterproof were still not wolf proof.

Xander and Devon escorted them back to the palace with the understanding they'd be headed back the following morning. There was nothing more they could do, as the ailing monarch was not due to wake until the following day at the earliest anyway.

If he was going to wake up at all, but Finn didn't need her pessimism.

She'd just stepped out of her shoes when Vasily came barreling into the room without knocking. The owl was wide-eyed and emitting a level of tension that had her claws out in just on general principle.

VASI

"Regent," he huffed, practically falling into the armchair. He ran all the way to the quarters from the Guard house and normally would not be winded, but it was damn cold outside, and he may or may not have gone flailing down the marble staircase due to a freshly waxed floor and slushy boots.

"Hello to you, too." Finn emerged from the closet barefoot and stripped down to his undershirt and trousers, moving slow like exhaustion was pumping through his veins instead of blood. He slumped down in the corner of the couch, and was immediately joined by Cora, who snuggled up against him like that was a totally normal thing for them.

The Night Watch Commander held up a hand. "Your brother," he huffed. "Brendan is setting things in motion to become the regent. He's been in meetings all day arranging it so when the king is officially declared incapacitated, he will become the regent."

"But the press conference—"

"Doesn't mean shit if the king is not able to rule." He trusted Cora knew he wasn't trying to be overly harsh, but those were the stakes and it was better that everyone got on the same page, and quickly.

His faith in her pragmatism was well-founded. "Okay, so then is there a plan?"

"Not unless you have some magic you haven't shared with us." He knew that would be in violation of several treaties and laws on the books governing shifter/witch interactions and magic usages. There were certain immortals, sure, but the ones that were mortal had to stay that way, too. At this point, he was willing to try anything.

"Not for that, no." She shook her head sadly. "Say the word, though…"

Tempting as it as, Vasi shook his head. "I appreciate the offer, but even I can't risk inciting a war over this." The last shifter/witch conflict left lasting scars on both sides as well as a fair amount of treaties and case law. He didn't tangle with witches if he didn't have to.

"May be a little late for that," Finn muttered, and Cora nodded in agreement. If it came down to it Vasi had no idea how a factionally divided court would work, or even if it would work without copious bloodshed. Brendan was the rightful heir, the crown prince presumptive, but Finn's inherent compassion and humanitarianism, not to mention his popularity with the public, shifter and human alike, made him the better choice. And then there was Cora.

Finn's Corvid was firmly at his side. He imagined her employers would have something to say about the order of succession, too.

Likely at gunpoint. As it was, he figured she was just one more botched assassination attempt from going full Morrigan on Brendan by herself, and no one wanted that. "Hopefully it won't come to that. We need the king to want to come back. He needs something to live for."

"And the kingdom and the lives of his sons aren't cutting it?"

"Clearly."

"He needs something to fight for."

"Like...?" Cora rose from the couch. "Hold that thought. I'll be right back; my bra is in attack mode."

Vasi recoiled. "Eww! I didn't need to know that."

His best friend smiled serenely. "I could stand to hear more."

Her throaty giggle and wink followed here out of the room. She was gone but a moment when she stuck her head back in. "I'd kick a toddler for some food. Would one of you get that called in and maybe have one of the guys bring it up?"

"I got it, Coretta. Go ahead and do what you need to do."

After a moment of silence and tolerating is friend's dopey grin, Vasily snarked, "I still maintain that's too much car for you."

"And I do not care."

FINN

The next morning came too damn soon for his liking. They were up, dressed, and out the door to the hospital before coffee even arrived at his quarters. It was unconscionable. Thank goodness for the Starbucks in the hospital. They didn't dispense by the gallon, but at least they had some food he could eat without being concerned about being poisoned.

It was almost second nature to him now, watching Cora examine the food and find it acceptable or not. It was a level of trust he couldn't even put a name too, but easily as close as family. She remained by his side all day, through doctors' visits, changes in the nurses' shifts, the Day Watch Guards trading out with the Night Watch. They were in the VIP section of the hospital, but that didn't make the waiting any easier, just in more comfortable chairs.

Didn't matter if he stood or sat, Finn couldn't get comfortable enough to calm down. All he could think about was his father's deteriorating condition what they were going to do if he died and holy shit. He blew out a deep breath and tugged at his cuffs. Anxiety was a living, breathing organism, wearing him as a skin suit.

Bruises dark on his exposed arms, one hand was taped up with an IV, an oxygen mask obscuring his face, Finn could not get past how small he looked. Fragile. That was not a work he associated with his father generally, but these days, it definitely applied.

The antiseptic scents of the room and the varying murmurs beyond the doors stirred echoes in his mind. Memories of sitting here, in this exact same hospital with his mother as the life slipped away from her, from them. To be honest, he wasn't sure if he could do it again, grieving a loss alone. At least when his mother died, he has his father and brother to lean on, but now?

Cora's warm hand was soft as it slipped into his. She didn't speak but he felt her comfort, nonetheless. In her cream-colored sweater and jeans, she reminded him of the night they met. So much had happened since that fateful meeting in the bar, it was ridiculous to contemplate, and yet now he took solace from her very presence.

"Finnegan?" his father's voice was weak, faint, and he had to sniffle back tears the moment he heard it.

Scooting his chair closer to the bed, he clasped his hand in both of this. "Da! Good to have you back. You scared us. Do you remember what happened?"

Eyes still closed, his lips curled as he hummed softly in response. "I had no idea the floor was so affectionate."

Finn's laugh was a strangled wheeze, the joy and relief competing to steal his breath as the doctor walked in the room, led by Cora. "Dr. Moallem," he acknowledged clambering to his feet.

His father's personal physician of many years, Dr. Mo, as he liked to be called, was the essence of no-nonsense. He was a tall, reed-thin Ibidine, who was damn good at the job and didn't need to boast about it. "May I have the room please? Now that His Majesty is awake, I need to run some tests."

Cora slipped right up to his side, wrapping an arm around his waist. "We're gonna go grab a cup of coffee, and we'll be right back."

"Thank you, Miss." The tall Ibis flashed her a quick grin as they ducked out the door.

"But—" Finn protested on the way to the elevators to head down to the lobby.

"They need a minute," his raven informed him. "And so do you." The doors slid shut behind them and she enveloped him in a tight hug. Even though she was shorter than him, it felt so restorative to have her arms around him his around her, like a piece of him he hadn't noticed had gone missing. Her hands were warm on his back, petting him and soothing his frayed nerves.

They didn't speak again until they both had a large mug of caffeinated lifeblood and a panini. It wasn't much but it would get them through.

"I heard the nurses talking, the human nurses," she whispered as they took over a table in the private waiting room. Their associated Guards remained outside, but the potential for leaks was an ever-present thought. "They still don't know what's wrong with him. They're treating symptoms because that's all that's left to them."

It wasn't exactly news. His father's sickness had been as elusive as it was effective, taking the man he loved and admired one bite at a time, but still it hurt to think about how close to the end they were. "He'll get through this," he replied with a great deal more conviction than he felt. They'd gotten lucky this time, but that would not always be the case.

"Of course," she reassured him. They finished their dinner in almost tense silence before returning to the room.

King Niall was sitting up in the bed, his mask exchanged for a canula in his nose and with a bit more color in his cheeks. "Finn." He waved him over to sit in the chair the doctor abandoned. "They tell me you've scarcely left my side."

"I didn't like the idea of you waking up alone." Not that he would have been alone, with his guards and personal nurse there, but still, family was paramount.

The smile on his father's face stretched wide and crinkled the edges of his eyes. "You've always been so compassionate. I have no idea how we managed to give you all of the heart of this family, but you use it with great skill and purpose."

And just like that, tears were rolling down his cheeks unabated. In the absence of his mother's love, that was truly all he wanted was his father's approval. "Thank you." Cora's hand appeared on his shoulder, a delicate tissue between her fingers, and his gratitude was amplified.

"And you, Cora." Their monarch took her hand in his and kissed the back of her fingers. "You take such good care of my Finnegan. Thank you. I see a lot of Angela in you."

"It's no hardship, Your Majesty." She smiled down at him fondly. "He brings joy to my life and that's a gift." Her reply did nothing to help him fix his face.

The old man chuckled softly. "So it is."

"Da, the doctors told me you were awake?"

Brendan didn't wait to be bid to enter, coming through the hospital room door at a good clip, like he barely paused. Clearly this was a regular occurrence at the palace, irrespective of their father's privacy. He was still trussed up in his suit, minus the jacket, looking flawless in his waistcoat with his long black curls gathered into a ponytail at the base of his neck. A line of Night Watch Guards crowded in behind him as well.

"Father, have you seen—oh!" If he had brakes, they'd be smoking as fast as he came to a halt in the room. The moment his green eyes fell upon Cora, he dropped seamlessly into his most cloyingly solicitous and charming persona. "I beg your pardon. I had no idea you had visitors."

"Brendan," Cora murmured as she rose to her feet, a smile on her face that looked more like a warning to Finn than an expression of happiness as he followed her to his feet. She brushed kisses over both of his cheeks that he returned. "How wonderful to see you again. Would you join us?" She paused, blinking as if she'd just thought about it, then turned to their father. "With Your Majesty's permission, of course."

King Niall's smile, on anyone else, would look completely smitten. Finn could relate. "Of course, my dear."

Brendan's thin lips approximated a grin, though his sudden pallor was a bit concerning. "Oh, but I couldn't."

Their father, however, was having none of it. "Nonsense! Your brother and his lovely girlfriend were just entertaining me. This hospital stay has been dreadfully dull so far." He signaled to one of the Guards. "Another chair, if you would." The younger kestrel standing next to Finn, pulled up straight as a board and clicked his heels.

"Oh! No, really. It's not necessary." Brendan was backing out of the room now, clearly not prepared for Cora's lethally subtle frontal assault. "I am terribly sorry to have disturbed you. Father, I will speak with you later. Cora, a pleasure, as always."

His omission of Finn was quite telling.

"Bye Brendan," she purred as she resumed her seat. Turning to Finn with a wink, her grin could have slit throats. "Your Majesty, would you like me to get you some ice water?"

CHAPTER TWENTY

BRENDAN

"**W**hat do you mean 'you don't know'? What am I fucking paying you for?" he snarled into the burner phone as he stalked back to his suite of rooms. It was unconscionable that his brother would be in there with his little chippee, taking advantage of their poor father's ailing health. He tugged on his tie as he entered his antechamber, snarling viciously as it went to tatters in his hands.

"He's been at the hospital almost every waking moment since the king's collapse. I'm not sure what you were expecting otherwise."

"And you didn't think to mention Cora was there with him?"

"And seem unduly interested in the prince's girlfriend? No, thank you. You want me around to report to you and creeping on her would likely land me a cushy desk job in northern Alaska."

He snarled in disgruntlement but couldn't argue with the logic.

So long as Brețcu was in charge, his second in command, while well placed, still answered to him. And if Cora complained about the Guard, Brendan had no doubt that Lt. Cmdr. Driscoll would be dealt with. Which would complicate his plans immensely. "Fine, but next time, think ahead and find a way to get me the information I need. I can't keep track of him if I don't know what he's up to."

"Understood, Highness."

FINN

"I didn't mean to frighten him off," Cora observed once they were alone in the room again, sipping her coffee like the delicate flower she was not. He knew damn well she did, and it was a sight to behold, his brother on the run from a gorgeous woman.

"Beautiful thing like you, I'm sure you didn't scare him off. He's a busy man, you know. Getting ready for his upcoming coronation."

Cora grinned triumphantly at Finn. "See? Someone appreciates my charms."

King Niall cackled, laughing himself into a cough that had Finn by his side in an instant. The deep wracking sound was excruciating to hear, and he could only imagine how painful it was to experience. When he finally caught his breath, he replied, "If I were a much younger man, this one here would have competition." He made a point of looking her up and down with a cheeky grin as he dabbed his eyes, still watering from the cough. "Though in all honesty, I like how happy you make my Finnegan."

"I'm glad. You raised a wonderful man. I'm very fond." The soft, genuine curl to her lips made his breath catch in his chest as he took his seat again. When she blindly reached for his hand, he took it and laced their fingers without a single complaint.

"I cannot tell you how much joy and peace comes from finding the one you love and spending the rest of your life with them.

Especially once you have kids." His misty blue eyes got a faraway look in them, seemingly lost in a memory that seemed to bring him a measure of peace and comfort.

Shaking it off, he continued, looking at Cora directly. "So is there any chance I'll get to see at least one of my sons married and settled before I pass? I mean, one on the throne and one happily married would be a wonderful legacy." He wasn't subtle, their king. Nope, not subtle at all.

Finn flinched, sensing the precipice they'd reached. Her subtle nod was all the impetus he needed to go forward. "So... about that..." he trailed off, staring at Cora meaningfully.

CORA

Sitting up straight with her hands folded in her lap, she took the hit. "We... kind of put the cart before the horse there."

Eyes narrowed in a shrewd glare, the king glanced between her and Finn and back. "You're..."

"Pregnant." Finn's voice was full of carefully banked apprehension, no doubt worried about how his father would take the news and if he'd managed to sell the lie.

The leader of the whole shifter kingdom went deathly still. He didn't even appear to be breathing, which was more than a little concerning. Especially when he dropped his chin to his chest and curled in on himself. Finn knelt next to him, calling his name but to no avail.

She was halfway out of the room to summon a nurse when the king barked a single command from his sickbed. "Wait."

When she turned around, the look on the old man's face was a mix of joy, awe, and strangely enough, gratitude. "Your Majesty?"

He reached old, beckoning her to his bedside next to Finn.

Holding both of their hands, his blue eyes shone bright with unshed tears. "I've wished for this day, waited for this day. Hoped..." he trailed off with a sad tremulous smile. "Your mother was amazing, and the joy and fulfillment she brought to my life was incalculable. I cannot tell you how it does my heart good to see you so happy."

Finn's free hand wrapped around her waist like it was a perfectly normal thing for them to do. "Da, your blessing means everything to me, to us."

Running his thumb across her knuckles, he paused when he passed over her ring finger, frowning. "You appear to be missing some hardware, Miss," he teased looking from her to his son expectantly.

Finn's bright blue eyes were wide with alarm as they cut to hers. "I... we... that is..."

"We wanted to wait for your approval," she filled in smoothly. "It's a lot to take in, and we didn't want to presume anything." Finn practically melted in relief at her quick save.

"The royal jeweler, you'll see him in the morning to select a ring. And then my son will propose to you properly," he promised her. To his son, he chided, "She's the mother of your child and you didn't get her a ring? Who raised you?"

His cheeks above his beard were apple red as he grinned wryly. "It will be fixed in the morning."

"Damn right it will." The old man nodded decisively, looking even more alive than he had just a few minutes prior. "I'm gonna be a grampa!" If her heart hurt a little bit at the elation on his face, well, that was between her and the Goddess. Morrigan would appreciate her motivations if not the methods.

Cora and Finn remained at his bedside well into the night until finally, King Niall was too tired to continue. With promises to return the following day, they rode the private elevator down to the waiting SUV.

"We're out of options. It's the right play," she assured him as the doors opened in front of them.

"I hope you know what you're doing," Finn murmured as he

helped her into the back of the vehicle.

"That makes two of us."

FINN

He'd gone to work the next morning, checking in on the office before heading to the royal jeweler, as per his father's demand. She'd left him with her ring size and the assurance that he'd make a good decision. It was an impressive level of trust on her part, even if this was just an elaborate ruse for the most part.

From there he went to the hospital. They'd gone their separate ways where he attended to his father and Cora... well, he wasn't quite clear on what she planned to do. She'd told them, when they'd initially discuss the nuclear option, the doctor stuff was handled, but the vague possibilities of what she meant by that were scary as hell.

Not that he didn't trust her, by any means. Between her and Vasily, there was no one he trusted more. He just wished he knew what she was planning to do or that he could help her in some way. The idea of her doing even more heavy lifting for him on this case did not sit well, at all. Finn appreciated it was her job to keep him safe, but the risks were so much greater now...

CORA

It was hard not to squirm as she sat across the desk from Dr. Bauer. He looked over her charts and was preparing to aid and abet her in committing treason. That's the kind of thing you'd want to double-check the paperwork, a couple times. Not that he wouldn't do it, she was paying a lot, whole-house-and-a-boat money if she was being honest, to set up this ruse. This was for all the marbles and would either result in a resounding success or her death.

"You know," he rumbled as he read over the chart, not looking up at her, "I always pegged you for a little reckless, maybe a little crazy, but I never would have thought you were suicidal."

"I'm not."

The older man looked up at her over his glasses, not raising his head. "Really."

"You said you could do this."

"I can do this," he scoffed, clearly offended at the insinuation to the contrary.

"Then, with all the love in my heart for you and Miss Annie, I'm not paying you to care."

He hummed his disapproval but didn't comment further. Not that she needed him to. She was getting ready to submit to some heavy medical shit, both magical and not, to facilitate this plan. 'In too deep' was miles in her rearview, and she had nowhere to go but forward.

Finally, after what seemed like forever, he signed the affidavit attesting to her pregnancy as well as the associated and accompanying DNA test she knew would be the very next question on their lips. Between her and Vasi, this was run down to the tiniest detail, because that's where you got fucked up, more often than not.

"Okay, so the shots I'm going to give you are going to mimic pregnancy in every meaningful way. And I do mean every."

"Shots, plural? And what sort of ways are we talking about? Morning sickness? Cravings? Tears at the drop of a hat?"

He nodded as he herded her over to the examination table and had her put her generous cowl neck sweater to good use, baring one shoulder. "Among others. This is not going to be a walk in the park for you, but it will absolutely pass even the most stringent scrutiny they throw at you."

"Even a sniff test?" Because, really, she had no doubt in her mind that the moment they announced her pregnancy his aunt and her uptight snout would be all up in her business.

"But of course. You pay for top notch, and that is what you get." The doctor nodded and pushed up his glasses, pulling out a zipped case with a set of prepared syringes in it. The material inside was a disconcertingly iridescent pink.

"Whatcha got there, Doc?" she eyed him warily as he prepped her arm with an alcohol swab and grabbed the first syringe.

"This," he exhaled, and the ultrafine need slipped into her skin with little more than a hiss from her. "Is a cocktail that Annie and I cooked up. We went to work right after you reached out. She's got magic older than this country in her books and she knew exactly what we needed on that end. My science side was making sure the DNA matched up and that it was safe for a Corvid."

"Thanks for thinking of me, Doc." She smiled as he prepped her arm again and grabbed a second syringe.

Eight shots in all, and after about the fourth or fifth one, the whole room began to feel unbearably hot and smell of burning rosemary.

"I smell fire," she murmured as she closed her eyes against a wave of vertigo and nausea.

Seeming to sense her wooziness, he helped her recline on the exam table while he finished the shots in both arms and applied a hormone patch. "That's the *lupus mithridatus*. That's what the wolves will be looking for when you give them the good news. The patch is to help everything blend better with your own makeup. If anyone asks, it's to help with the nausea."

"Speaking of," she leaned over the side of the bed and was barely able to grab the nearest trash can before she lost her breakfast. Wiping her lips with the back of her hand, she frowned. "Sorry about that."

He waved away her apology and tied off the trash back. "To be expected. Now, lay there for the next half an hour. By then the worst of the nausea should be past and you can leave. See Annie on your way out. She has things for you. Vitamins and such."

Cora appreciated how well he looked after her. "Thank you, for all of this."

"You know, if I have to live out the rest of my life on a tropical island with no extradition, I'll likely blame you." At her startled expression, he winked with a broad grin. "From my hammock while drinking a pina colada."

"Jesus, man." She chuckled weakly and breathed a sigh of relief just as another wave of nausea hit her.

Dr. Bauer's hand was cool on her forehead and then on her wrist checking her pulse. When he looked back at her from his watch, his expression was very serious. "I know you're doing this for very good reasons, but have you thought about what happens if this fails? I mean, besides us fleeing the country and you getting hung for treason with your co-conspirators."

She blinked at him, unable to answer due to her teeth sweating as she fought the urge to release all the emptiness in her soul into the trash can again.

"If there's any question at all, my suggestion is you get pregnant for real." She snorted but he didn't look amused. "I mean it. I'm sending you home today with something that will make that happen if it comes down to it. Consider it a failsafe."

Her lips twitched but she didn't laugh, afraid that if she opened her mouth, her stomach might interpret it as permission. Cora took his hand in hers and squeezed, grateful that his nuclear option meant bringing life into the world, whereas hers had been to take it away. Of course, it was always nice to know that if desperate times came, there was more than one desperate measure available to her.

It took an hour for her body to stabilize and she hated every single minute of it. Dr. Bauer had Annie install an IV in her arm for hydration, but for a little while there it felt like hell was empty and the devils were all flowing out of her mouth at a high rate of speed. When she returned to the palace, Finn met her at the door.

"Are you okay? You didn't answer your texts, and I called." His eyes were wide, and his hair looked like he'd been finger-combing it. He'd dispensed with his suit coat down to his waistcoat which only emphasized how his strong, broad shoulders tapered down to that narrow waist. And the way those pants framed his perfect ass? It was a damn good look and if she felt better, she'd say something about it. The level of sheer, unbridled lust she was feeling for him was disconcerting as hell considering how sick she'd been only recently, but to be fair, he was pretty damn hot.

"I'm sorry, I was at the doctor's office." She held up the bag Annie had given her as proof.

"Okay, so then my original question stands." He crowded closer to her, something she enjoyed immensely as he smelled deliciously of bergamot and soft woods. Brows drawn with worry, he chewed on his full bottom lip as he searched her face. It was easy to forget that they were having this conversation in front of the Guards, though, really, that played well with the plan.

She took a breath and realized that her stomach wasn't through with its reign of terror. She managed to push him away just in time for her to dry heave right on the cobblestone. "Fuck," she breathed, face sweaty and feeling both too hot and too cool. Nothing came up, but that was a matter of her being dead empty, still hurt like a bitch though. She turned back to see three thoroughly horrified guards and was immediately overwhelmed by Prince Worrywart. "Highness, I am so sorry—"

He shook his head, cutting her off as he herded her inside the palace and down the corridor with a firm and protective arm around her waist. "Absolutely not. C'mon, let's get you to bed. I thought you went to the doctor to get well. They let you go like this?"

"It's more complicated than that," she panted, each step heavier than the one before. "I'm actually fine."

Finn's face was the last thing she remembered seeing before she went down.

FINN

"I swear to the gods, if he poisoned her, I'll kill him myself."

Vasi rolled his eyes at his best friend as he paced and tugged at his cufflinks to roll up his sleeves. "She's fine, she fainted. That shit happens. When she wakes up, she'll tell us about it, and we'll go from there."

"You didn't see it. You don't know." Goddamn, he had no idea she could even be that pale, an ashen cast over her dark skin, and thankfully, he was able to catch her before her head hit the marble floor, but it was inarguably the scariest thing he'd ever seen. And that included the time his brother filled his bed with garden snakes when they were ten.

From the moment she'd gone down, he hauled her into the suite, setting her up on the bed in the biggest pile of pillows he could find. He'd summoned a doctor and Vasi, because he needed someone with a clear head because he was losing his damn mind with worry. The doctor had left just recently, with a comment to call him if she didn't awaken within the hour. Within the hour was not a good enough timeframe for him.

He smoothed a hand over her forehead, taking the time to appreciate how delicate and peaceful she was asleep, because she certainly was neither of those things when awake. "I mean it. I'll kill him and feel good about it." He folded her hand between both of his, content just to feel her warmth.

"Well, hopefully it won't come to that," his best friend reassured him as he stood and headed over to the liquor cabinet. He poured out two tumblers and set them on the coffee table, gesturing to Finn. "Hovering's not going to help."

"Oh, so you're a doctor now?" he replied acidly before closing his eyes and driving his fingers through his hair for what felt like the millionth time. "I'm sorry."

Vasi waited to reply until Finn had joined him on the couch. "Don't worry about me, we're fine." He handed him his drink and stared over at the bed. "She's gonna be fine, too. The Commander is made of tougher stuff than either of us."

"Stop calling me that," she groaned softly from the bed.

Finn was at her side in an instant, clambering onto the bed and curling around her to help her sit up. "You checked out on me." He didn't mean for it to come out like an accusation but couldn't stop himself.

"Not on purpose, I assure you." She blinked a few more times, her eyes much less glassy and her dark skin returning from its frightening ashen pallor. Yawning so hard he feared she'd pop her jaw, she smiled up at him sweetly. "I didn't mean to worry you."

"I wasn't worried at all," Vasi minced as he came to stand at her bedside with a smirk. "You're too mean for anything to do any really lasting damage."

"I'm not mean," she pouted. "Maybe it's just my reaction to your sparkling personality."

"Crow."

"Owlet."

"Carrion feeder."

"Plague carrier."

"Enough!" Finn's eyes bounced back and forth as Cora and Vasi nipped at each other. It was surprisingly playful for two predators. Turning back to her, he tucked her against his side as he snuggled down in the pillows. "What happened at the doctor's?"

Her wicked grin should have been the warning. "I don't know, what do I smell like?"

"The hell kinda question is that?" Vasi demanded with a grimace.

Cora blinked at him, with the desire to smack him writ clear across her face. "One I need *him* to answer."

Finn frowned and sniffed the air tentatively. "Sweet, soft... Really, really good." He took a deep breath and held it, staring at her the whole time. It was amazing, whatever it was, and somehow, the longer he looked at her, the more beautiful she became to him. "What... I don't understand. Are you... *glowing*?"

CORA

"You'd think so, right?" She beamed up at Vasi, whose look straddled the lines of concern and vaguely horrified.

"Holy shit! Did you go out and get *actually* knocked up?" The Night Watch Commander looked like he was on the verge of a hysterical freakout, and she knew he'd seen combat.

"No, but no one outside of this room knows that. I think if we keep it to the three of us—and Devon and Xander—we stand a better chance of pulling this off. It's not that I don't trust Driscoll, but we need seasoned operatives now and I don't have time to train up the FNG."

Vasi snorted and Finn asked, "FNG?"

"Fucking new guy. She means Driscoll." He looked both disappointed in her opinion and amused at the same time. He was a complicated man.

"He's sweet, but the stakes are way too high for him to cut his teeth." Cora shooed Finn away from the bedside and went to the table where he'd set her belongings. She laid out and explained each and every test, piece of paper, and the other associated elements of sealing this cover down tight. They were bulletproof for the moment.

Finn joined her on the couch, his thigh touching hers and his arm casually around her waist like he was cuddling her. "So you smell so delicious—"

The rumbling growl in his voice sent a shiver down her spine she had to work to hide. "To make my mate feel more attached and protective over me since I'm expecting. It's what your family will be looking for when we announce it to the world." She licked her lips, his blue eyes immediately falling to them as his pupils expanded. "Is it working?"

Finn's predatory grin was nothing short of scalding as he looked her over, even showing a little fang. His fingertips lightly traced the fine hair at her temple as he rumbled, "You have no idea."

She cooed and preened under his attention before focusing on the task at hand. "Just to be safe, I got a boost on the glamour as well."

Finn frowned, his look of desire melting into one of concern. "Is that why you got so sick?"

She nodded. "Doc said it was a side effect of both the hormones and the glamour. It should be fine by tomorrow for when your father gets sprung from the hospital."

His features softened considerably when she explained that. "Good, because you scared the hell out of me."

The kiss he pressed to her hair just above her ear warmed her from the inside out. It may have been a side effect of the hormones, but she really did enjoy his affection. "I'm sorry," she murmured as she admired the ridiculously defined muscles of his forearm under her palm.

Finn tipped her chin up, leaning in to kiss her, when Vasi cleared his throat loudly. "So... question."

She smoothly turned her attention to the scowling owl and did her best not to giggle at the disgruntled growl in her ear. "Yes."

"Will the prince be immune? To the new glamour, I mean. Obviously, the hormones are *quite* effective."

Cora hummed as she thought about it, paying no attention at all to the small circles Finn was rubbing on the divots at the base of her spine. "Should be, mostly. The glamour and all that were made using his DNA and mine, both, so in theory, we should both be immune. There may be some residual effects or something, but nothing serious. Certainly nothing that's going to blow my cover."

Vasi nodded but looked unsettled. "Alright, well, get some rest. Tomorrow is showtime."

Cora gave him a genuine grin. He was a pain in the ass, but he wasn't bad people. "Thank you, Commander." He nodded at Finn and took his leave, and then they were alone.

They'd been alone before, lots, but for some reason, now it felt different, closer. More intimate maybe. These hormones were a trip, and she damn sure did not want to allow them to make decisions on her behalf. The potential consequences were immense.

"Have you eaten?" she asked, casting about for a safe topic.

He shook his head. "I was too freaked out when you got sick. I can send for something. You have any requests?"

"Low key and bland is fine. I'm wanting cheese. Like swiss cheese. Is that weird?"

Finn blinked, looking her over speculatively as he reached for his phone. "Cravings, huh? You're *sure* you're not pregnant?"

He said it as a joke, but she heard the concern in his voice. "I'm good, I swear. I just want cheese."

"As you wish."

While he was up calling in their order, she went over to her bags and pulled out her pajamas. She wasn't going anywhere tonight and there was no reason at all not to be comfy. Except maybe his appreciative glance as she made her sleepwear selection.

The feelings before all this were already making this case much messier than normal, and now she was physically compromised in addition to emotionally. As mad as she wanted to be at herself, the fact was, she was in this voluntarily from jump. Foolhardy was a bad look, but stupid was worse. She knew better and now here she was, fucked, or rather, on the near side of 'probably should not be'.

Unable to linger longer in the en suite bathroom, she stepped out into the room in a giant, fluffy robe that hid her tank top and shorts. She was feeling vulnerable enough without adding to it with her clothing choices.

Finn quickly herded Cora back to the couch, making sure her feet were up, and she had a pillow behind her back. "I don't want you getting sick again."

"Thanks, but it's not necessary, I feel fine now."

"Uh huh. I had to carry you in here, you'll excuse me if I'm a little concerned."

He continued fussing over her until she laid a hand on his arm. "Finnegan. I'm okay. Really. Relax." His mouth was set in a mulish line, but he didn't argue. Cora let him pick up her feet and settle them in his lap, his huge hands warm and comforting as they rested on her ankles.

"I like taking care of you," he said simply, his thumb skating over the arch of her foot. His deep voice colored with sincerity. "You have done so much for me, you're *doing* so much for me, and..." He hummed in annoyance, frowning down at her feet. "I just want to look after you the way you've been looking after me, okay?"

Her heart stumbled over in her chest at his pained admission, but she had no illusions about this. At this point, since she couldn't tell what was the hormones talking and what was actually real, it was a safer bet to assume his outburst was entirely hormone based and go from there. "That's truly not necessary," she assured him.

Pulling her feet from his lap, she wrapped her arms around her knees, body language as closed as it could be without a lock. "I don't need you to take care of me. Really."

A knock at the interior antechamber door kept the argument from really getting traction. One of the kitchen staff, an older Hircine woman wheeled the cart in the moment he opened it. She kept her eyes locked on Cora like she expected her to sprout additional heads or attempt to eat her. Her reputation preceded her, she supposed, and felt marginally bad for it.

Finn wheeled the cart past her in the direction of the bed. "C'mon."

She watched as he pulled the cart around to her side of the bed, er, the side of the bed she'd been sleeping on, and set up their dinner. "I can't eat laying down."

The quirk of his eyebrow over his shoulder as he looked at her was clearly a challenge. "And you won't eat if you don't get your butt back in this bed. You need to rest. Hop to it."

Time stretched out between them as she remained on the couch, at this point out of spite more than anything else, and he sat on the side of the bed munching on... whatever he was munching on.

"Dammit," she grumbled as she left the couch and stomped back over to the bed. His triumphant little grin made her want to smack him. She had just pulled back the blankets when he grabbed her arm. "What?" His eyes dropped to her robe and she growled. "Oh for fuck's sake. You gonna tuck me in, too?"

He blinked slowly at her as his lips twitched. "Maybe. If you ever get your cute little ass under the blankets I will, yes."

"You think my ass is cute?" At this point, she was deliberately fucking with him as she handed him the robe and did as he asked. He had the dome off his food, a large stack of sandwich quarters and a steaming bowl of what smelled like tomato soup, both of which made her empty stomach growl.

"You still haven't eaten, I'd settle down if I were you." All the heat in his warning died when she saw the tiny smirk and twinkle in his eye. He stacked the pillows behind her and made sure everything was super fluffy and comfortable before she laid back. It was going to be hard to go back to her normal bed after this.

The moments the blankets were in place, he ran his hands down the outside of her thighs, making good on his promise to tuck her in. Then he revealed her dinner with a flourish, a plate of cheese cubes he placed on her lap, each skewered with a toothpick.

"Really?" she asked as she held one up, twirling it between her fingers.

Triangle of a grilled cheese sandwich in one hand, Finn took a toothpick and pressed the cheese cube to her full lips. "Shut up and eat your cheese. Calcium is good for the baby."

Tears leaked out of the corners of her eyes as she laughed at that. She would have fallen over but didn't want to get food everywhere. They ate in silence, with him sneaking the tiny sandwiches onto her plate in exchange for cheese cubes.

Belly full and finally settled, Cora nestled into the pillows and sighed contentedly. It had been the longest of long damn days and all she wanted to do was sleep for a week. That feeling was underscored when Finn dimmed the lights and grabbed his sleep pants and ducked into the ensuite.

"Thank you," she whispered as he finally extinguished all the lights and slipped under the blankets next to her.

"For what?" Finn scoffed as he shifted around to lay on his side facing her.

She turned her face toward his voice. "You know, taking care of me. Fragile flower that I am, falling at your feet 'n all." His blue eyes seemed to catch all of the faint light in the room, leaving them almost shimmering in the shadows.

"You'd be surprised how many women have tried that before." The wayward blanket slipped down the steep angle of his chest and pooled at his waist, and it was not fair that she got to sleep in bed with him and not really do anything about it.

"Great, now not only am I gravely embarrassed, I'm derivative." Blowing out a deep breath, she turned and faced the door as she'd done the night before, hopeful that the heat in her cheeks would dissipate quickly.

"Not hardly." His arm around her waist pulled her back to him, cradling her against his body as he spooned up behind her. "And you don't have to thank me. With everything you're doing for me, this is the very least I can do."

His soft, rolling growl and breath across her neck made her toes curl and her body ache with the desire to melt back into his warmth and enjoy all that his body had to offer. "Sleep well, Finn."

There was no point in feigning sleep because he could hear her heartbeat, so they lay there in silence with all the things she wanted to say left to die on her tongue. Responsible adulthood sucked and she wanted a refund.

He stilled behind her, and for a moment she wondered if she'd hurt his feelings or if he was going to turn away and go back to his side of the bed. Instead he simply sighed and kissed the back of her neck. "For the record, I'm not sure my heart can take you being any more beautiful."

CHAPTER TWENTY- ONE

CORA

Thankfully the heaviest parts of the previous day's shots had worn off, leaving her more or less in fighting form. Good thing, too, since she positively hated the whole hothouse flower routine, and she had shit to do.

Including shopping for a new dress before the king's release from the hospital. Though it hadn't been explicitly stated, she and Finn assumed this would be the date they debuted the engagement ring, his paternal grandmother's and purple was all he'd told her, and she knew those pictures would be shots seen around the world.

Accompanied by members of the Guard handpicked by Xander and Devon, she visited numerous salons and stores that specialized in couture in search of the perfect specimen.

"What does one wear when they commit treason?" she murmured to herself as she sat by herself in the salon and the clerk brought out yet another sheath dress.

"I'm sorry, ma'am?" The young lady who'd been so patient with her as she looked at and rejected all the selections. She wasn't normally this indecisive but prepping for her first official press conference with the royal family was a big damn deal. It was one thing for an impromptu luncheon. It's another entirely for a planned event, in front of the entire shifter kingdom, where it was likely she'd be announced as the fiancée of the newly installed crown prince.

A glance at her watch, a delicate, diamond Chopard affair her mother had gifted her when she graduated high school and worked perfectly for a cover like this, said she was running low on time if she was going to do her hair and makeup appropriately. "Shoes please."

"Of course, ma'am."

FINN

The butterflies in his stomach were rapidly transmuting into a squadron of angry hornets, the agitated buzz a vibration just under his skin.

For her part, though, Cora was the soul of cool. From the moment she'd returned from the atelier with her clothes, she'd dressed, and they were headed to the hospital, she was as pressed as a new suit, perfection walking. He would not want to play poker against her, because that poker face was professional grade and under other circumstances, more than a little frightening.

In the back of the SUV, he fumbled with the antique ring box, dropping the blemishless sterling silver cube in the footwell in front of her. "Fucking hell," he groused as he knelt down to get the box before pressing it into her hands. "Here."

He watched her trace the emblem on the lid, the engraved crest of House Lupine, her perfectly manicured nails following each line and whorl. When she opened it, she gasped, dark eyes big and round as she took in the three-and-a-half carat oval amethyst surrounded by twenty-eight seed pearls set in a gold ring nestled in obviously old blue velvet. It was Victorian, perfectly faceted, and absolutely breathtaking. Just like the woman holding it.

"Finn," she breathed, his name on her lips an exclamation as much as an exhalation.

"Well?" he prompted as he clambered back into his seat. "Put it on."

Cora reared back, brows down in confusion. "I'm sorry?"

"What? We needed an engagement ring to sell this, so there it is. You don't like it?"

She blinked at him a few times like she was trying to focus, mouth opening and closing like she had things to say but better angels kept intervening. "You... don't want to—you just want me to put it on?"

"Well, I—-" He swallowed hard as he felt a sudden heat burning in his cheeks and down his neck. "I just thought... that is, I thought because we—" he held out a hand gesturing vaguely, feeling helplessly mortified.

Slowly the warmth in her expression crystalized, hardening until it looked like she was happy, but he could feel in his soul that she was not, and he had no idea why. "Right. Of course. My bad." She took the ring and slipped it onto her finger with no preamble and no further commentary.

As she stared out the window, Finn felt the overwhelming urge to apologize. "Should I have—"

"No!" she cut him off decisively. "No, it's fine." Her gaze fell to the ring sitting perfectly on the third finger of her left hand. "Just kinda reminded me of my first marriage proposal."

The last part, said so softly only a wolf could hear it over the hum of road noise, broke his heart and told him exactly how badly he'd messed up. "I'm sorry—" he started, reaching for her hand.

"Should I tell your father it was glorious and romantic?" she pulled her hand just out of his reach and didn't even acknowledge his apology.

He huffed a laugh, as self-conscious and embarrassed as he'd ever been in front of her. "No need to lie to the man. You can tell him I bumbled my way through it like I do most things involving beautiful women. Badly."

"Women? Plural?" At his wide-eyed sputtering, she giggled and took his hand. "You do this type of thing often, do you?"

"Killing me outright would be kinder," he pouted as they pulled into the underground garage and headed to the private elevator.

"But not near as much fun." She kissed his cheek as they boarded the elevator, and from there, they were the picture of a happy couple. She floated next to him swathed in glorious purple silk that wrapped around her luscious curves to perfection and made her dark skin luminous, hair twisted up and into a bun that was in no way demure, showing off her long neck and her amethyst necklace and earrings that effortlessly matched her ring and his tie. Cora was a vision, and he was too wound up to appreciate it fully.

He was too busy focusing on the next crisis looming on the horizon: his father's press conference. Finn was under no delusion as to how this would proceed. The look on his father's face when they'd told him of the pregnancy all but sealed his fate, today he would become the crown prince. What happened from there was anyone's guess.

When they were announced at the door of his hospital room, she took his hand and smiled up at him, beaming like she really was his girlfriend and for a moment, he almost let himself believe it. Almost. And then he remembered they were here to commit treason on behalf of the kingdom and lying to a dying old man and he'd get all wound up again.

King Niall wanted to present a united front as a family to ease the worries of the shifter kingdom as a whole. It was part of the job, he'd say when he had to go on camera and reassure the people. Part of ruling was bringing calmness and surety to dark and insecure times. The impending death of a monarch didn't get much darker.

Finn squired Cora about, taking her first to his father, who embraced her in a hug after looking at her hand. His smile of approval and remarkable exuberance were shocking to the advisors in attendance including Marius LeStrange and his son Mos. If she felt concern over speaking with them again, she didn't show it. Again Finn couldn't help but marvel at her icy cool demeanor. She moved like she was bulletproof and knew it, and he absolutely believed she was.

Especially when his father casually mentioned Cora's status as expecting an heir to the throne.

Finn had never seen a roomful of people straighten up and fall mute so quickly. Astonishingly enough, Marius was the first to recover his composure, offering a hearty congratulations and a first handshake. The fact a Corvid would be consort to the king was not lost on him at all, Finn figured, and he was nothing if not a calculating man. Mos looked like he'd swallowed a porcupine, pointy end first, but was also congratulatory, nonetheless.

That was a conversation he hoped to be privy to.

He wondered how they'd feel when they saw the real her, knowing she was more than his fiancée but their estranged family as well. Well, Mos knew, but his opinions were still up in the air. Slipping an arm around her waist, he hugged her to his side, as much a show of possession as a show of solidarity for her. Regardless of everything else going on, he would support her, and needed her to know that.

After that, everyone in the room pretty much got onboard, with the press secretary finalizing spellings and pertinent information for the formal announcement from the palace, and even a first picture together as an officially sanctioned couple by the royal photographer. There were things that needed to be discussed, interviews with the media to coordinate, stories they wanted told versus ones they wanted to keep for themselves. It was incredibly surreal, and then Brendan arrived.

He should have been there when Finn and Cora arrived, but as it was, he in his funerary chic slid in the door with Aunt Gwen in tow immediately prior to their scheduled departure. The intent was to have the press conference on the steps of the hospital, and then leave the rest of the day to make preparations for coronation and now the royal wedding.

Of course, it would have been better to have a minute to speak with Brendan about this rather than just spring it on him, but Finn wasn't the one making the rules. Their father had never suffered lateness gladly.

The squall line of press gathered outside in the late afternoon chill was immense and just seeing that many people as witnesses to his deception made his stomach drop. Thankfully, Cora was right by his side with an affectionate squeeze at his waist and a beaming smile. He positioned himself next to Brendan, as it was the easiest way to keep at least one person between Aunt Gwen and Cora. He wasn't worried about the spy's ability not to start anything, but from experience, he could not say the same of his aunt.

Of course, he would have preferred to be on the other side of the planet than his brother, but he could suck it up and behave like an adult for their father's sake.

King Niall looked surprisingly spry as he stepped up to the bank of microphones in his long slate cashmere coat and scarf. He had always had an air of restrained refinement about him that had dimmed in the recent months as his illness accelerated. But now, it appeared to be making a comeback and it brought Finn's heart joy, even if the reason wasn't exactly kosher.

"Good afternoon. I'd like to thank the many people who reached out to my family to offer prayers and comfort these last couple days. Your ongoing support has been greatly appreciated. Rumors of my demise have been greatly exaggerated." He paused to catch his breath as a chuckle wound its way through the throng of reporters. "To that end, I have wonderful family news I'd like to share with you all. Miss Cora Westgate, of Philadelphia, has accepted a proposal of marriage made by Prince Finnegan of House Lupine, my youngest son. I would like to take this opportunity to formally welcome her to the family," he glanced over his shoulder at them with a mischievous twinkle in his eye, "and to announce a change in the order of succession."

The collective gasp that went through the crowd was drowned out by the sounds of both Aunt Gwen and Brendan choking on air. Questions burst forth in a torrent from the journalists, but all fell silent at his raised hand.

"In addition to announcing the crown prince's engagement, I

have permission from the family, to my great joy, that I am to be a grandfather. Under the rule of Primo Progenitor, the same rule that allowed me to ascend to the throne as your king, Finnegan by continuing the royal bloodline, is now His Royal Highness, the Crown Prince of Therantia. To be clear, this decision is not in response to the ongoing investigation into the suspicious death of Miss Bedelia Fielding."

"Thieving son of a bitch!"

Brendan roared and yanked back on Finn's arm, turning him into the fist he had flying toward his jaw. The taste of fresh blood on his tongue brought out his fangs as Finn snarled and snapped at his brother's attempt for a follow up hit, shredding the sleeve of his coat. Incensed, wild-eyed, Brendan turned to rail against the king, only to find Finn standing firmly between them prepared to defend their father to the death if necessary.

"Don't you dare talk about our mother like that," he warned, claws out and ready to rip into his flesh at the slightest provocation. "Time and place, Bren, and this is neither."

Eyes bulging, teeth out, shoulder seams ripping as his chest heaved. "Fuck your time and place! You and you whore conspired to take this from me, and this will not stand!" He snarled at Cora, who, surprisingly enough, did not react beyond shifting her eyes as the deposed prince was set upon by his aunt and several members of the Guard who dragged him away. "I will have my day!"

Cora pressed a handkerchief to his lip he hadn't even noticed was bleeding as a hush fell over the crowd, no one daring to speak until the SUV containing the irate wolf had left the premises.

"My son's outburst notwithstanding," King Niall picked back up like nothing had even happened, "this a joyous day for our family, and the shifter kingdom at large. Thank you all, again, for your support." The moment he stepped away from the mics, they were barraged by a rising tide of questions as the Day and Night Watch Guards surrounded them and herded them toward the waiting vehicles.

"That could have gone better," Finn murmured as Cora tilted his chin to attend to his bruised jaw.

She hummed in agreement, pressing a kiss to the uninjured

corner of his mouth. "Could have gone worse, though."

He sighed, leaning back in the seat and cuddling her against him in his lap, his cheek against her forehead. "You're right. You could've shot him."

"There is that."

CHAPTER TWENTY-TWO

AUNT GWEN

She wished she could say the screaming was unexpected as she came into the palace via her private entrance. Ahead of being the dowager duchess, she was the older sister of the king and as such afforded certain liberties that others would likely not be. One of which was a private entrance in a sequestered part of the palace that was otherwise unoccupied. It was an entire wing for her, as if giving her that instead of her rightfully deserved crown would appease her. Still, it kept her close to court, and the throne, and that was exactly as she'd planned.

The boys' mother dying had been exactly the boon she'd needed positioning her exactly as she wished to be. Also exactly as she'd planned. For Brendan, so desperately heartbroken at the loss, Gwen was a guide, a mentor, a mother figure, among other things who loved and supported him even when he made decisions others found selfish, or even downright reprehensible. She was his rock, and more importantly, she had his ear.

There was damn little in the future king's life that she didn't know about, and that was by design. Sometimes it was to foster connections he'd need later in his reign, and sometimes simply so she could have leverage over him when such things were required. Such was the case in that moment as she wandered down the hallway toward her darkened drawing room stepping over disembodied limbs and splatters of blood on damn near every available surface.

While the wolf in her was disciplined enough to overlook the terrified shrieks and pained wailing, the smell... ye gods, the smell was another matter entirely. Copper heavy and rich with proteins and adrenaline. Her fur and fangs were out by the time she hit the door.

Brendan's wolf was rangy, tall, unusually so at almost nine feet, black fur and bright green eyes. Well, normally black fur now matted in clumps of drying gore from his snout almost all the way to his tail. His was imposing figure even on all fours.

Currently he stood in the shadows by the cold fireplace at the far end of the room, up to his shins in bits and bobs and people's parts. He pulled his face from his latest kill with a snarl at the sound of her claws clicking against the hardwood. The blood dripping from his fangs only added to the horrific tableau.

"Put those away," she murmured as she surveyed the damage. Thank goodness all the curtains were drawn and the shutters long sealed. She left her Guards outside her wing of the palace, knowing they could only be paid to overlook so much. So far, she counted four torsos, nine legs, and three arms. "Is there any housekeeping staff left?"

He grumbled instead of speaking, biting into the flesh of a thigh defiantly, green eyes following her acutely as she did a circuit of the room. Brendan could be this way sometimes, petulant, entitled. It was a difficult set of traits to temper given that he was the crown prince and thus entitled to a great deal, however, he did not get to behave that way with her.

Gwen chuffed, a quick almost-howl that brought him snapping to attention. He watched as she clicked her claws at him and indicated, moving to heel at her side like a good boy. So long as she reminded him, he would always behave like a good boy.

"That was quite the show today," she murmured, not unkindly. When his eyes widened in terror, she shook her head and trailed her claws behind his ears until those same eyes closed in pleasure. "It's understandable, really. He stole from you. They stole the crown from you, my dear sweet boy, like your father did from me. And how do we treat thieves?"

For anyone else, that blood-soaked grin, with his head cocked to the side and tongue out playfully would have been heart-stopping. In Gwen it just aroused... pride, among other things.

"So, now we must decide, my sweet angel, how will we rid ourselves of this meddlesome Corvid?" At his grunt of confusion, she sighed fondly, lightly scratching his chin. "Because, the fastest way to solve your problem is to remove the baby from the equation. No half-breed mongrel, no crown."

She didn't mention that this was the correction of a mistake she'd made last time. Lacking the will to do what she must. There would be no such problems this time.

She walked slowly from her place by the hearth to one of her overstuffed armchairs on the other side of the room, away from the carnage, her nephew matching her step for step on all fours as she walked upright.

Perched on the fine damask, she changed forms again, human once more, but naked, with him on the floor by her side. It wasn't the first time Brendan had seen her like this. She needed to think. They needed a plan because the Corvid, unlike the Hircine girl, was smart, cagey. This would require cunning and careful crafting to get past the birdbrain's natural suspicious nature. It was difficult, but not impossible.

The stress of the day made it hard for her to think. She needed a bit of relaxation before she tackled that particular riddle. "Brendan?" He came up to a sitting position most obediently as she got comfy in the chair, ready to receive her next command. "Would you help your Auntie with something?"

He cocked his head to the side, lifting one paw then the other to show his readiness. Crooking a finger at him, she smiled as she spread her thighs. "That's a good boy. Now, heel."

CHAPTER TWENTY-THREE

FINN

The next few days were an absolute blur. Between meeting with advisors and the crash course on the coronation, he was now in the middle of planning a wedding. Two state functions within days of one another, they had to be completely insane.

Cora, thankfully, took charge of the majority of the wedding planning. He could see her Guard training coming through loud and clear in the level of precision and organization she expected from those participating in the wedding either as members of the family or part of the planning team. One of them jokingly referred to her as Generalissima and she told Vasi to put her in for a promotion.

Not to mention fielding media requests, putting out their official engagement pictures, and enduring endless discussions about the ring. Everyone wanted to know who she was wearing, how she felt about being the first mixed marriage in the history of the monarchy, and so many other things both great and small. It was a wonder they got either a moment's peace or a meal between them.

Cora's morning sickness had returned, unfortunately, stronger than before and the doctor had put her down for a couple days rest while her body recovered electrolytes via an IV port. Needless to say, pissed off did not even begin to her feelings about having to slow down to a more measured pace, but the one bonus was that more than once, Finn had returned from work to find his father and Cora spending time together, playing cards, chess, or backgammon, drinking tea, or even both in the library on separate couches reading magazines while wearing house slippers. That picture had gone directly onto the palace Instagram account.

Brendan, and Aunt Gwen, left the evening of the fight. Vasi informed him that their passports were checked in the Lisbon airport, and as much as it pained Finn to say it, he hoped they would never return. Life would be so much easier that way, though he was becoming accustomed to looking over his shoulder now, so there was that.

The overall feeling in the kingdom had lightened since the change of succession with the community at large feeling more hopeful than they had in a long time. Of course, there were some quarters who would have preferred his brother on the throne, but he suspected that had more to do with their perceived leverage over him than his actual ability to govern.

It had been going too well, really. The transition to crown prince, his public relationship with Cora, and even, surprisingly, his private one, too. After his flubbed proposal, he'd spent time making it up to her with flowers and her favorite tea that settled her stomach and her favorite late night snacks and cheesy movies when she couldn't sleep. The line between personal and professional was so blurred between them, it may as well have evaporated. There would be consequences, at the end of all this. Political, definitely. Emotional more than anything, though, but in the moment, it was very easy to let himself imagine a future together.

The morning her cell phone rang had been a good one, they'd awakened early and dined with the king, who was starting to feel remarkably better after so long in decline. Finn had been preparing to leave for work and Cora, feeling truly herself for the first time in a week at least and dressed to kill in her clingy azure sweater with a draped collar and black pencil skirt combo, had been preparing to lay siege to the wedding plans once more.

It had been a quick conversation, the look of confused suspicion on her face giving him pause. He waited until she was off the phone before he left for the day. "You okay?"

His concern only grew as she slipped a holster for her compact pistol seamlessly in the back waistband of her tight pencil skirt, and an extra knife he didn't even know she had with her into her purse. "Mookie just called. The alarm company for my safehouse just called my assistant and inform her there was a fire at my place. He's sitting off of it now."

"I thought it was still being renovated." He held the door to the hallway for her as they walked down the hallway to their waiting chauffeured rides.

"It is, hence my concern."

"You going over there?" He didn't like the idea of her going alone, but he also knew enough not to voice that concern. Instead, he held her coat as she slipped into it and threw on her scarf.

She shrugged. "I have a 10 A.M. with Shayla, the assistant wedding planner to discuss more fucking flower arrangements." He covered his mouth to hide his amusement at her irritation. "And then I'll head that way. I'll let you know what I find, okay?"

"Okay." He leaned down and kissed the corner of her mouth like he did every morning. "I'll see you tonight."

"Have fun storming the castle," she called after him as he headed down the steps to his waiting car. Driscoll waved at her as she got into the SUV they'd designated for her use and both pulled out of the palace grounds to start their days.

CORA

Finding a venue to hold this wedding had been a chore, between the needs for security, the fact that the Morrigan don't exactly have a church where one worships that does not involve extensive bloodshed, and the sheer presence of royalty, it would have been easier plotting to overthrow the government.

Barefoot in a field of spring violets was what she wanted, with a bouquet of white roses to honor the dead and red to honor the living. Lavender, mugwort, and rosemary were needed in all the arrangements, at least somewhere, even if they were hidden. Convincing a florist to honor those requests, however... A non-shifter florist was out of the question, though she wanted to make sure to use non-shifters for some portion of the event as a show of unity.

By the time she left her meeting, it was well past noon and she needed food before she became dangerous to everyone around her. She was so hungry these days, and for weird shit, too. Like fried chicken and sauerkraut. It wasn't natural and she was not a fan. Truly, she could not wait for the hormones the doctor injected her with to run their course.

Plus they made it hard to remember this was a job. She was doing a job, protecting the prince, and this wedding she was planning, this 'baby' she was supposed to be carrying, were all in service to that end. This wasn't a relationship, regardless of her feelings for him or the way he liked to snuggle with her on the couch after dinner or fuck her brainless and boneless in the mornings before they got out of bed.

Her mind immediately conjured his besotted expression as he watched her take apart and clean her pistol before putting it back in the bed under the pillow, not to mention the one she kept on her leg and the one in her bag. She was not part of his world, not really, and no amount of playing pretend would remedy that. No matter how real the feelings involved were.

She parked half a block from her safehouse. So far as her Guards were concerned, she was still with the wedding planner and her assistant had Samson drop off her ride for ease of escape. It was work to facilitate her escape, but it was necessary, if she wasn't going to bring any more people into the party than she had to.

Mookie had wanted to stick around for her, but her firm had other cases and he was needed elsewhere, so she'd dismissed him. There was a benefit to being armed to the teeth, and it wasn't like she was truly helpless at all, regardless of the height of her heels or the delicacy of her attire. She'd fight naked if she had to, just who she was.

The approach to the house was the same as it always was. A quiet street, rows of connected houses and interconnected lives. Cora had chosen this neighborhood for its nondescript charm. The only truly remarkable difference was the window boxes out front and the door colors. Hers, alas, was 'Molotov chic', or somewhat of a burnt toast aesthetic. Someone had come and tried to torch the house, and for some reason, there were no contractors to be found. Somewhere, somehow, there should have been guys there fixing and reinforcing the shot up walls and windows and now, repairing the door.

Keys out, she explored the ground floor and found windows open in the back, her french doors unlocked, toolboxes out and opened like their owners had just stepped out for a moment. It was... eerie. Upstairs, her bedroom was still in shambles, most of the holes in the lath and plaster were now patched with the Kevlar mesh over the steel frame replaced, but not sanded or painted.

"The fuck am I paying these people for?" she grumbled as she dialed her assistant's number.

Cora sensed the movement and twisted out of the way just in time to avoid the swing of a claw hammer, phone flying from her hands, stunned for a moment by the image of its head embedded in the sheetrock like it surely would have been her skull. Then she saw its owner, a wraith of a man with no hair in a threadbare NHRA shirt under a leather jacket and holey jeans, and grinned.

The Lacertine was tall, sickly thin but moderately muscular, with slit green eyes and a mouthful of sharp teeth that made for an unsettling grin in return, made even more so with the flick of his forked tongue.

"Missed," she purred as she turned to face him fully, pistol out and pointed at him. His thin frame filled the doorway and blocked off her access to the rest of the house. She didn't want to kill him if she didn't have to, but there would be no escape if she couldn't get past him.

He wrenched the hammer out of the wall and pulled a nasty-looking hunting knife from the back of his jeans, brandishing both like he might know what to do with them. "I won't this time, sweetheart."

"Come with it then."

When he rushed her from the door, it was all she could do to put one in his chest and one in his head. She left him twitching on the floor as she made for the stairs, stymied to see he'd brought several friends who had heard the gunshots and were running to his aid.

Unlike her neighbors. One of the features she'd had installed was soundproofing in all the exterior walls and those that joined up with her neighbors on either sides. There'd be no relying on them hearing a strange noise and calling it in unless, perhaps, they saw the clown car of motherfucking lizard men erupting on her front law.

The problem with lizards was that they were fast. Damn fast, and no respect for simple things like gravity or the fact that walls and ceilings were not fucking walkways!

"So rude!" Across the upstairs landing to the guest room with reptiles on her bearing down on her ass was not how she'd planned to spend the day. To be fair, it was better than picking out another fucking floral arrangement but still. Diving through the door, she slammed it shut behind her, locking it and shoving the empty wooden dresser in front to buy her some time. The door itself was also steel reinforced, but that wasn't going to keep them out forever. She needed a plan and quickly.

Her cell phone was out, dropped in the other room when she was attacked. Damn her training. She had enough bullets left to kill some, but not all of the intruders, so that wouldn't help her much. Any spare weaponry would have been removed by her team prior to the renovations commencing.

Her sense of urgency got a jump by the loud crash against the door that jostled the dresser incrementally. "A door breach? Are you fucking kidding me?" Three more solid hits were the answer that solidified her plan: fight wasn't an option so flee it must be.

The guest room had just one way out, the window overlooking the backyard and alley behind the house. It was locked, and alarmed, so hopefully when she opened it, someone would come. In the meantime, she tossed off her clothes in record time, firing a shot when the door opened slightly, and gratified to hear someone scream in pain in response.

"Look, lady, we're not here to kill you," a semi-reasonable sounding male voice with a Brooklyn accent called through the door.

"Your friend said otherwise."

Left standing by the open window, Cora was naked as the day she was born except for her engagement ring. When she shifted, she'd have to move fast to get it and take it with her. Damn everything else, that was non-negotiable. Perched precariously onto the ledge, she aimed her pistol at the door, taking out three more men as they crowded into the room.

She threw the gun once she ran out of bullets, shifting quick and snatching up here ring. "Like I told your friend," she called behind her as she dove out the window a six foot raven in full flight, "you missed!"

CHAPTER TWENTY–FOUR

BRENDAN

How in the absolute *fuck* did it take fifteen men to grab one woman, one fucking *debutante*? And then they *fail*? Brendan closed his eyes as he pulled a hand down his face, doing his very best to rein in his temper.

The first step of the plan and it couldn't even get off the ground. He'd sent a glamoured Lacertine to Portugal to accompany Aunt Gwen and let the heat die down, buying him time to think of a way to course correct. Losing his temper had lost him footing, socially, politically, but not the war. He'd spent the days in his aunt's section of the palace, skulking about and shaking off the absolute betrayal for the conviction of righteousness. This was his and he would take it back.

First, though, was setting a trap to nab a wily bird.

"I need you to walk me through this one more time." The Lacertine in front of him shifted from foot to foot, a story of fear from his flippy little tongue to his twitchy little tail. Brendan had half a mind to snatch it off, just to watch it regenerate. Of course, his aunt would not appreciate him decorating her office in blood like he did the dining room, so he refrained. For now.

"We watched the block and she pulled up in a black car by herself."

That was interesting. He kicked back in the chair with his ankle laying across his knee. "She was driving? Where were her Guards?"

One leather-clad shoulder shrugged. "Dunno. She was driving and parked way far away from the house. She was looking around when she walked up to the house like she was expecting us."

"Do tell."

"She didn't see us; we blend in real good. So we waited and followed her inside."

"All of you?"

The lizard rolled his eyes, which was kind of this weird creepy blink more than anything. "Except Larry."

"Was 'kill only if necessary' an unclear command?" he asked softly, again feeling the rage flow and his claws extend.

The grubby creature in front of him shook his head vehemently. "No! No, Highness. Not at all. It's just... Larry, he got excited. Got ahead of himself."

"And got killed for his troubles," Brendan finished for him. "And the rest?"

Head down, the younger man sighed. "It kind of all fell apart after that. She was a lot tougher than we'd been led to believe. She sure didn't fight like no society chick I ever seen."

That was an interesting tidbit. "Fine. Wait in the hall. Send in the vulture."

Driscoll entered, as attentive as ever. As minions went, he was at least prompt, courteous and occasionally worth a damn. "Highness?"

"I need you to tell me," he paused, sighing deeply as he organized his thoughts. "Why is it, a society princess like Cora Westgate knows how to fight like she's been in the special forces?"

"Well, she was a member of the Guard in Logistics."

He said that like those words were supposed to go together and make sense. His brother's girlfriend? A member of the Guard? "We talking about the same person?"

Driscoll nodded. "Yeah, about yea tall, incredible ass? Engaged to your brother?"

It was unclear to him which was more annoying: this new information or the person giving it. "I need you to find out why a glorified mailman turned socialite managed to kill no less than five of my men and then evade capture. Can you do that?"

Heels clicked together as he leapt to attention. "Of course, Your Highness."

"Good. Then kill the lizards on your way out, if you would."

"Of course, Highness."

FINN

He'd expected her to be back at the palace when he'd gotten off work, ready to rail against the unfair strictures placed upon her by having a massive royal wedding so close to a coronation. It was a daily thing for the two of them. She'd bitch about the wedding planning and he'd grumble about the coronation, and together, they'd unwind and decompress over whatever food they brought home with them.

Coming home to his empty suite was disconcerting. Not just disconcerting, jarring. Her scent was so faint, he knew she hadn't been home all day, so where was she? He dug his phone out of his pocket and dialed the Guard house.

"Xander, have you or Dev seen Cora?"

The silence that greeted his question made his stomach drop to the floor. "...We're on our way to you now."

Finn stared at the blackened screen of his phone for a moment in absolute bafflement. "Because that's not upsetting or ominous at all, really."

The decisive knock on the interior door made him jump and he opened it to a parade of three harried and haggard birds of prey in suits. "What happened."

His best friend passed a hand over his mouth and gestured to Xander as he threw himself into the armchair in the living room. "Cora went to her appointment today with the wedding planner, and she disappeared somewhere around noon." The blond man looked both pissed and apologetic.

"...that doesn't make sense. I thought she went to her brownstone after the appointment?" Raised eyebrows all around and Dev's frantic texting set off alarm bells. "Is that not what happened? Why were there no Guards with her?"

Vasi licked his lips. "We're not sure. For either question. Her driver went to pick her up at the designated time, but she wasn't there."

"You've been looking for her since *noon*?" He didn't realize he'd been yelling until everyone in the room flinched and cowered just a bit.

"Highness, I assure you, we've been doing everything we can think of to locate Cora," Xander avowed, looking like this whole situation was a personal affront he planned to rectify if it killed him.

"You'll pardon me if your assurances aren't doing a whole lot for me right now," Finn snapped, though the rest of his tirade was cut off by Dev's cell phone ringing.

Everyone in the room fell silent as the man stepped away to take the call, looking more and more serious as the quiet conversation continued.

"...thank you. Let me know what else you learn." He turned to the waiting trio and blew out a breath. "Why don't we all take a seat?"

Finn felt a blistering heat wash over him at the lack of direct answer. "I will stand, and you will speak." He did not like to pull rank like that, but goddammit, his fiancée was out there somewhere, and he needed to know she was alright.

Dev's dark eyes rounded as he swallowed loudly. "Of course, Highness. I sent men to her place to look it over." He blew out another deep breath before looking Fin directly in the eye. "They found signs of a struggle and a *significant* amount of blood."

He had no idea how he ended up on the couch, or where the drink in his shaking hand had come from, but the burn of scotch over ice was welcome as he came back to himself. "I... what are you doing to find her?"

Dev took a seat at the other end of the couch, her end, and looked like he'd just shot his own dog. "We're canvasing the neighborhood, checking traffic cameras in the area, but so far, we don't have anything yet. On the upside, it looks like there's way too much blood to be just one person, and none of it is Corvid, though it shows up messy and vaguely Avian."

"That just means she took some with her. If she was fine, she would have contacted me by now." Looking to Vasi, who was busy texting in the armchair, he asked, "Is there a way to track her?"

The owl looked up from his phone. "Like with her cell phone? If it was on, yes. It's not, we checked."

"Okay, but what about her handler?"

Confusion colored his dark features as his blue eyes narrowed. "What about her handler?"

"Would he have a way to track her?"

Xander came over and perched on the arm of the chair next to Vasi. "I mean, sure. It's possible. But we don't know who that is, so..."

"Nicodemos LeStrange. Do you know him? Her brother?" He hated selling her out like this, but desperation was now firmly in control of his decisions.

"Mos? You gotta be fucking kidding me."

CORA

Cora spent the rest of the afternoon in a heavily wooded area in the middle of the city not far from Fenway Park. It was the only place she could think of that was close enough to hide a six foot tall raven in broad daylight in February. Naked trees were definitely a consideration.

Shifting left her with two problems even as it solved the more immediate one of her kidnapping: she was naked if she changed back, and her animal form was damn noticeable. She didn't shift around humans because even though there were treaties and things in place, their world still had no idea what to do when what they thought was human most decidedly was not.

Once night unfurled across the sky and the streetlights came up in the city, she headed over to the safehouse she had Mookie and Samson stay in, over by St. Elizabeth's hospital in Aberdeen. It was a cute little two-bedroom townhouse in a nondescript court with seven other units that all looked like hers. Perfect for hiding in plain sight.

Mookie's car was parked out front and she knew Sam was still on the job, so she felt safe touching down in the backyard and shifting back. The key was kept under the pot that would eventually hold bright red geraniums in the spring in the hanging planter she'd made in college when she fancied herself crafty. It didn't count as a break in if you had the keys, right?

Mookie had a sweet face. Admittedly, until you got to know him, that was the only thing sweet about him. To strangers and the uninitiated, he had the disposition of a giant porcupine and the size to match. He was a hulk of a man with shaggy gray hair who, by virtue of standing anywhere, was the definition of looming. There was nothing about his size that would indicate he was a big old gray-striped tomcat, but he was a Felid through and through with ridiculous reflexes.

Reflexes Cora did not take into account when she broke into the house unannounced, which was how she ended up with a gun in her face.

"My bad," the deep voiced cringed as he took in her naked state before turning around, gun vanishing as quickly as it had appeared all in one smooth motion. "Sorry, boss."

In the darkened hallway, she could just make out his flannel shirt and old jeans he'd had on earlier. His lack of shoes said that she'd interrupted his relaxation time. "It was my own fault for not calling ahead, no harm no foul." She snickered at her bird pun, but Mookie only blinked at her. The nice thing about her people was weird was relative and no matter the time, they were there to help. "Thank you."

He looked over his shoulder sharply. "Thank me? For what, putting a gun in your face? You got some weird fetishes, boss."

Cora wheezed at his sideways attempt at humor. "Dude, today is not that day."

The smile never left his face as he nodded. "No worries. Let's get you some clothes."

She kept a couple changes of clothes in the guest room closet, as well as the more traditional safehouse features of ID cards, burner phones, money, and guns with extra magazines of ammo because that would not happen again. Having on a pair of jeans that fit and some old school Docs went a long way toward settling her nerves. Next order of business: a plan.

Mookie never turned on lights he didn't have to, and when he was home alone, everything stayed off. His jade green eyes were pretty in the daylight and let him see in pitch conditions. She drank a cold coke over ice as she powered up the burner phone at the kitchen table in the dark. The caffeine and sugar felt amazing, and damn but she was tired. And hungry. Seemed like anymore, she was always fucking hungry. "You got any leftovers?"

Mookie nodded and dug in the fridge until he pulled out a big glass bowl full of soup. "Pozole," he answered her silent question, batting away her grabby fingers as he went to heat it in the microwave. "You are not a heathen. Simmer down." She felt the urge to pout, but Samson's pozole was to die for, so cold or hot, she was down.

"You feelin' alright?" he asked as he slid the steaming bowl in front of her. "You look a little pale."

Coming from the giant Dominican dude who was sitting in the damn dark, that was quite the indictment. "I spent the better part of the day feathered or naked, in February, up a damn tree in The Fens. I've been better." She blew on her steaming spoonful of hominy-studded goodness and fell into culinary heaven.

Mookie spun a chair around and rested his chin on the back of it as he watched her eat. "You gotta go back out?"

She shrugged as she attempted to set a land speed record inhaling the bowl in front of her. "I have to. I... this job has gotten weird. Personal weird. And the guys who tried to take me are still out there. So I have to go protect the prince." She didn't say his name because she knew Mook would know instantly that something hinky was up in their relationship.

"Need to call your handler then."

She hissed in a sigh before blowing out a deep breath. That was quite the bind. "Not sure he can be trusted."

His green eyes glittered in the muted light coming in from the streetlight in the alley. "Why not?" he sounded personally offended at the suggestion.

Simple question. Messy answer. "I know who he is now."

"And?"

"I'm not sure I believe him." She pushed the empty bowl away and rattled the ice in her glass.

"He do something to you?"

"Yeah." Understatement of the century right there.

"Would you still call if you didn't know who he was?"

That was a question she hadn't thought of. "Probably."

Mooks sighed and pushed to his feet, turning the chair back around the correct way. "Then you need to set that shit aside for the greater good: the prince. The fact is, this guy, whoever he is, brought you in on this case to keep Prince Finnegan safe, which means right now you have the same goal." He nudged the burner phone toward her hand as he picked up the bowl to take it to the sink. "The rest of that shit you can fight about afterwards."

Damn him and his minimalist logic. "Fine!" She held up the phone and waved it at him as he left the room snickering. Then she dialed the number from memory, stunned when he answered after half a ring. "Who is this and how did you get this number?"

"Missed you too, Mos."

"Fucking hell, Coretta! Where the hell have you been? They are getting ready to put out an APB on you!"

"What? Why? And how did you know I was missing?"

"Vasi called me, and he's going to chew us both out when we're together next, so just keep that in mind." She didn't have to work to picture his snarling grin at that. "They said your brownstone had been firebombed and there were bodies inside?"

Not quite, but close enough. "I had some issues today."

He hummed in what she was sure passed for amusement with him. "Apparently. You leave your cell at the palace?"

"No? I had it on me earlier today. I had to ditch it when I shifted. Why?"

"We have a problem." She could hear typing on a keyboard in the background. "They're searching for you on the grounds of the palace because your cell phone pinged there ten minutes ago."

If her cell phone made it back to the palace without her... "Shit! They're trying to use that to lure out Finn! I'm on my way!"

She ran through the house, grabbing the keys Mookie held out to her from the chair in the living room, not even bothering to look her way. "Bring it back with gas!"

"Yeah, yeah."

CHAPTER TWENTY-FIVE

FINN

The upper floors of the palace weren't used very often unless
there was a summit of some sort, requiring them to house
multiple dignitaries. It was museum beautiful, but crypt quiet. He
didn't expect to find Cora up here, but once Vasi, Xander, and Dev
opted for an outhouse-henhouse-doghouse-style grid search, he
figured it wouldn't hurt. Her phone pinged on the grounds, so she
had to be there somewhere.

He'd started off with his security detail, searching the ground
floors and the terraces, but somehow, he'd managed to get separated
from them. No big deal, considering he was in his own house. He
only hoped she was alright and his father remained none the wiser.
The last thing the king needed was the added strain of worrying
about his future daughter-in-law and grandchild.

He'd just stepped out of the conservatory when Driscoll came tearing down the hallway at a breakneck pace. He came to a halt, puffing and out of breath. "Holy shit! There you are! Highness, you gotta come with me! It's Cora and it's bad! Please!"

"Lead the way."

They turned back the way the Guard had come, quickly coming to the end of the hall with nowhere to turn. The tall, skinny vulture turned and shrugged, both hands out.

"What's going on?"

"Sorry, Highness." And that was the last thing he saw.

VASI

"How do you lose *the future king*? Huh? How does that happen?"

He had long since given up the pretense of having chill and was just stripping bark off everything that stood still long enough. First Cora had gone missing, and now Finn? Xander was with the king, he was coordinating the search of the gardens and the woods, and Dev had gone to see to shoring up the perimeter. No one in or out until this shit is sorted.

"And has anyone seen Driscoll?" The bellowed question dimmed the murmur of the room as he looked at each of the faces manning the phone bank and consulting maps before going back out. The fact that the Guard he'd assigned to Cora had also gone missing worried the hell out of him. He hoped he was alright. He hoped they all were. "Anyone?" Instead of an answer, his attention was drawn to a melee by the front of the Guard house.

"You will let me in the goddamn door, or I will snatch the beak off your goddamn face!"

"I'd know that bitching anywhere. Let her in," he called over to the Guard who looked grateful that she was no longer his problem.

The future queen consort of King Finn of Therantia came

stomping through the door in a black pea coat over a black turtleneck, dark jeans, and a pair of well-loved shitkickers. Well, there was one problem solved. "The hell have you been, Commander? There are bodies and we have questions."

She shook her head, taking off her coat and throwing it across the desk artfully, revealing a black leather shoulder holster and a compact double stack pistol that all but screamed she was out of fucks at this point. "Those are gonna have to wait. We have bigger problems."

He knew ravens had a reputation as being magical, but what she psychic too? "You know about Finn?"

"Yeah, my cell phone pinging here was a trap meant to lure him out. Where is he? I need to see him."

Vasi had been in fear for his life twice before and standing within arm's reach of Cora Westgate in that moment was the third. "... I think you should sit down."

Gold eyes stared him down as the bullpen grew silent with anticipation. "I think you better start talking."

It didn't take long to catch her up, and she was surprisingly not nearly as ballistically pissed off as he'd feared. Ever the soldier, she immediately settled down to work the plan, combing over video of the grounds in search of anything out of place.

"Got him!" she called, standing up to grab her coat. "Top floor of the palace, last seen getting off the elevator. Let's hit it." He watched her pull her pistol out, chamber a round, thumb grazing the safety, knowing in his heart she was going to add to her body count very shortly if they didn't find Finn, and soon. "Anybody got a vest I can wear?"

CORA

Vasi held the door for her as she entered the palace. "Ma'am." He dipped his head in mocking deference and she lightly elbowed him in the ribs. "Ow! So mean!"

"Meh. You're delicate."

They headed straight to the elevator and headed to the top, eager to retrace his steps and hopefully find the errant prince. When the doors closed, he turned to her. "So... about today..."

"Short version is there was an ambush at my safe house. I shot a bunch of guys and had to make a quick exit."

He looked like he was making mental notes. "How'd they get your phone then?"

"I had to shift to make that quick exit out a second story window. It was pretty dicey, and they may or may not also have one of my weapons." That wasn't the proudest moment of her life, but she lived and was able to keep the engagement ring, so she'd take the win.

"Oh, that's nice." Like he was talking about the coming spring warmup and not the potential for taking fire as soon as the doors opened. "I'm gonna need the rest of that story later."

"No problem."

"What'd you do with the bodies?" he asked as the elevator dinged for their floor.

She quirked an eyebrow. "Nothing. They were there when I left."

"That's what I was afraid of."

The doors opened to silence, which only made her anxiety thrum that much harder. He shook his head, his acute night vision and hearing giving him no help at all. There was nothing at all to give them a clue as to which way to go.

"I go left, you go right?" she offered gamely.

He nodded, checked his weapon and moved to follow her command. "Holler if you need me."

The rooms were empty, as expected. Clean, to five-star hotel standards, no dust, no carpet fibers out of place, nada. Still, she checked each and every one just in case. In the closets, under the beds, not that she expected to find a man Finn's size in either of those places, but she also didn't want to find anyone else lurking that should not have been.

She would have missed it if she hadn't been looking, the tiny tail flick just above her. "Another fucking lizard," she snarled as she aimed her pistol at the shadow retreating across the hallway ceiling. She didn't want to shoot in the palace but hell.

The Lacertine was, again, too damn quick for her to feel comfortable opening fire, and she took off on foot after him. Ceilings, walls, windows, floor, didn't matter, he was moving and no matter how she chased him, he was ducking away. This would have been a helluva lot easier if she could shift, but she wasn't sure the hallway was wide enough to accommodate her wingspan, which would have defeated the whole purpose.

She was so busy chasing after him, she had no idea where she was in the palace when she lost him. It was a long hallway with tall windows on both sides, that let in the moonlight and the security lights outside, casting everything in between the stripes of light in stark relief. It wasn't a wing of the palace she was familiar with, but she figured if she kept going forward, she'd find her way eventually.

A flick of a shadow caught her eye from down the hall, and clawed hands that grabbed her arms and held her materialized out of nowhere. The bastard grunted when she drove her foot down her assailants shin, and another set of hands grabbed for her flailing feet. She felt the toe of her boot meet a chin, and heard a body hit the ground, but the hood they shoved over her head prevented her from seeing more.

FINN

The sharp pain in his face woke him, with the burning in his restrained hands and feet being the next things he noticed. Surprisingly enough, it wasn't the yelling.

"Christ! How hard did you hit him?"

"Highness, we barely tapped him, I swear."

Blinking, it took a second to orient himself to his new surroundings. Finn found himself in a large, mostly empty room, with windows down one side. From the collection of tapestries on the walls, it looked like the formal dining room in the palace, except he was pretty sure he remembered there being both furniture in there and a decided lack of decaying body parts. His brother, looking sharp in a deep forest green dress shirt with the sleeves rolled up, paced manically back and forth in front of him like he expected something.

"Bren..." he started, though he wasn't sure if he wanted to go the 'what the actual fuck' route or the 'why am I here' route, because clearly 'have you lost your damn mind' was off the table and in play. "Where are we? What the hell is this place?"

"Oh good, you're awake." He actually looked joyful as he stepped around semi-dry pools of blood in his Zegna loafers.

"The yelling made unconsciousness difficult. What the hell, man? Really. What the fuck?"

"Why couldn't you just die? Between you and father... Clearly that is asking far, far too much of the fates. Because all the methods we've used so far have come up short."

There was so much to unpack in that sentence, Finn would have flailed if he could move his hands. "Wait, what? What? You've been trying to kill Da? Who's 'we'? What?"

"Not important. What is important is that you're going to die here and then I will finally be able to take the throne without your interference."

"I don't understand."

"I'm unsurprised," he chuckled darkly. "Gods, I can't believe you think you can rule. I'd bet Cora is the brains in the relationship." Brendan licked his lips as he thought about it. "She's certainly the tits and ass of it. Brains is just an embarrassment of riches. We'll have to ask her."

"Wait, what? Is she here?" The hiss and sizzle of silver against his skin kept him mostly still, but if she was here....

"You're jumping ahead. In due time." His brother patted his shoulder like he actually gave a damn about him.

"Okay, really. What the fuck is going on? Why are we here?"

"I..." he sighed happily, "got tired of watching you slowly but surely take everything in my life. Absolutely everything. You've been doing it since we were kids."

"What is it you think I've stolen from you?"

"Besides the crown?" He blinked at him meaningfully. "What about our mother?"

The low blow knocked the breath out of him. It was no secret she'd died in a car accident, on her way to see him play hockey for the boarding school. At least once a day, every single day since, he'd wondered what life would have been like had he not begged her to come see him. Wondered if it was somehow his fault. No amount of therapy could fully repair the hole left by her untimely death. "That's not fair. You know damn well that wasn't my fault."

"Now you want to talk about fairness?" He cocked his head as he looked at him, searching his face for something before a sickly grin slithered across his lips. "Bring her in." He spoke to someone behind the chair that Finn couldn't see, no matter how he craned his neck.

"Where the hell are you taking me?"

Moments after he heard her voice, Cora's scent drifted in as she, in a hood, was forcibly escorted in the door by a thin-looking Lacertine with impressively sharp-looking claws, and... "Driscoll? Really?"

The vulture smiled broadly as he slammed the door and made Cora jump. She hissed as his hand drifted over her chest, groping her breasts before pulling out a pistol and aiming it at her head. "Impressed? You should be. I fooled everyone. Even the spy. I think once all this is over, I'll be putting Brețcu out of a job."

Finn snarled as the skinny man slapped her on the ass before advancing on him. "I will kill you for touching her."

The taste of fresh blood burst across his tongue as the Guard brought the butt of the gun against his cheek. "I'd love to see you try."

Brendan sighed theatrically. "I do wish you'd hold off. We haven't even gotten to the fun part yet."

"Apologies, Highness."

The black wolf yanked the hood from Cora's head, and she spit on him immediately. After wiping his face with a handkerchief, he backhanded her so hard her nose began to bleed.

"Now. If we've gotten all the unpleasantries out of the way..." He seemed to wait for her to respond, and upon her silence, he continued. "You, Miss Westgate, are not at all what you appear, are you? A spy? A soldier? The mousy little fledgling that used to follow me around while I was fucking your sisters? Did Finn know?"

Cora stood mute, chin raised and dark eyes defiant.

Unhappy with her lack of reply, Brendan wrapped his fingers in her hair and yanked her head until their lips were mere breaths apart. "I asked you a question."

"I knew," Finn volunteered rather than have her subjected to further torment. All eyes on him, he couldn't miss her blinking Morse code. Whatever was going to happen, he was going to bear the brunt of it. For her. "I knew, and I love her anyway."

"Unlike her family." He shook his fist, yanking her hair so hard he could see silent tears rolling down her cheek. "I wonder how Marius is going to feel knowing his disgraced little chick has come home to roost. And right under his nose, too."

He kept his hold on her but looked his way with a mocking grin. "Breaking all kinds of rules, aren't you? She's a Corvid, a divorcee... why not just run the crown over with a car?"

"I won't apologize for loving her."

"Or stealing my throne, apparently." He spread his hand over Cora's belly, claws clearly visible. "You've seen how we've dealt with the first threat to my reign. How do you think I'll deal with her?"

CHAPTER TWENTY-SIX

CORA

Brendan's hands on her made her skin crawl, but she had to focus on keeping it together. "The Fielding girl? What possible threat could a kitchen girl pose?"

His attention back on her, he yanked on her head again, her scalp screaming in protest as she focused on not attempting to twist out of his grasp. "Are you kidding? I told her to deal with the half-breed. I gave her money to get rid of it and she stole from me. She was still pregnant and was going to keep it. Could you imagine?" Then he snorted a laugh and stepped away from her, leaving her held up by the lizard behind her. "Who am I asking, of course you could."

Finn began to struggle against the bonds that held him to the chair, silver manacles digging into his flesh so deep she could smell the sear as they burnt into his flesh. "Your fight is with me, Brendan. Let her go."

"And leave a potential heir to the throne out there? Just out there, waiting to depose me? What *do* you take me for?" He turned to Finn with his hand out. "Not to mention how dangerous she is. Did you see what she did to Arthur's friends today?"

The lizard behind her tightened his grip painfully on the ropes around her wrists. "Your little bird caused a lot of problems today." He flicked his tongue out, dragging it up her neck until she cringed away.

"So the question in front of you, dear brother, is do I send her off for the lizards to take care of her or do I kill her here in front of you?" He tapped his index finger against his chin as he paced. "Or do I split the difference and have them kill her here? Decisions, decisions."

Blue eyes blazing, Finn met her gaze steadily. In her soul she knew he was going to do something stupid and shook her head minutely. Now was not the time for whatever harebrained scheme he had cooking.

Her reaction seemed to firm his resolve as he lifted his chin. "She's not really pregnant."

"The fuck, yo." Cora struggled against her bonds now, because she was going to march over there and kick his ass herself. "Why would you say something like that? What is wrong with you?"

He had the gall to look pissed at her. "Me? I'm trying to save your life!"

"And doing it badly! Please stop," She sighed, shaking her head. Slowly she felt her claws emerge, not fast enough to warm up her skin or startle the Lacertine behind her, but enough to delicately tease the hemp bonds they had around her arms. This was gonna cut it close since he decided to up the crazy-sauce in his brother.

Brendan paused and squinted at his brother for what seemed like a long time, shoulders jerking occasional with a tiny huff. Indignation or laughter, she couldn't be sure with his back to her, but given that she was teetering on that edge herself, she didn't blame him.

"She's... not pregnant."

Her incredibly-courageous-to-the-point-of-stupidity charge

shook his head. "It was my plan. I stole the throne from you and she only went along with me because I coerced her. Deal with me, not her. She's as much of a victim here as you are."

"And you expect me to believe this?" Brendan marched over to stand at her side, making a show of sniffing the air as he stared down his brother. "Even if I hadn't seen you two in person at my birthday party." He turned to her as an aside, "and I have never seen a more ravishing woman in my life," he puckered his lips in an air kiss before readdressing the issue at hand, "I am not. Fucking. Stupid."

In a flash, she yelped as he lashed out with his claws across her chest, slicing open her sweater and her skin from her collarbone diagonally to the top of her breast. All the predators in the room seemed to perk up as the scent of her blood flowing out of her spread. "I know what a halfling pregnancy smells like, the Hircine was not my first."

The wounds were superficial but stung and she hissed as he dragged his tongue across her lacerated flesh before flashing a blood-soaked grin over his shoulder at his brother. "Delicious." Brendan nodded at the lizard over her shoulder. "Have fun now."

A yell outside the door drew everyone's attention and was enough of a distraction for Cora to shred her bonds. Vasi came barreling in the door with Dev and a heavily armed contingent of Guards behind him as she reached back and broke the Lacertine's neck, leaving her the only thing between Brendan and justice.

A roar behind her, followed by a scream and a gunshot, distracted her but only for a moment and then she was on Brendan like he did her wrong. Just his luck.

Talons in his face and neck, she kept her attention on the soft tissues of his eyes, rage pouring off of her with every slice into his flesh. Every moment of fear for Finn, righteous fury for Bedelia Fielding, all of it pouring out of every punch, kick, and slash.

"Medic!"

Dev's voice sounded frantic, and Cora looked up to locate Finn, only to get knocked back, thrown almost all the way to the door by a force she didn't see until after she landed.

Finn in full wolf form, lit into his brother with an uncontained fury. Flesh ripping, snarls, and screams quickly filled the room as she knelt next to Vasily and pressed her hand to the gushing gunshot wound to his shoulder as Dev dragged both of them out of the room and shut the door so the medics could attend to the Commander.

The moment she handed off Vasi's care, Cora bolted back for the room. She could not leave Finn alone with Brendan, especially in that moment. Dev grabbed her arm as she turned the handle.

"You can't go in there."

"He won't hurt me," she promised, fighting the clawed grip he had around her bicep.

The falcon shook his head. "This has been a long time coming and has all the hallmarks of Lunacy. I can't let you go in there."

Cora shook him off and went to the door. "It's not a matter of 'let'. I'm not afraid of him."

"I'll have medics ready," he called after her. Probably for the best.

CHAPTER TWENTY-SEVEN

FINN

Blood, thick and heavy over his hands, so warm, flesh so soft and squishy, easy. The scent of death—old, new, coming—filled his lungs with each breath, igniting his soul. The boiling rage he felt in that moment, surrounded by the smell and taste of blood, drove him onward, heedless of anything else. There may come a time after this but that was not his to worry about.

Her fragrant essence shot through him like a bolt of electricity, bringing him to a halt as he breathed her. Her footsteps, cautious, heavy, slow. Facing her in his wolf form, he could see the bird she hid when she shed her skin. Breath coming thick and fast, she smelled like safety, home.

The raven hopped over to him, close and unafraid as he knelt over Brendan. Her bright yellow eyes held no judgement, no recriminations, her slight purrs and soft chirps, a kind of music to his ears. She was beautiful like this, feathers so dark they shone greenish purple in the light like an oil slick. Part of both the shadows and the sky, she was a part of him now too.

She stood next to him, nipped at his hand with her beak and gave him a cheeky grin before dancing away again. Just having her next to him brought him solace, a soul-deep peace that let him call back the rage that even still was darkening his vision and honing his violence to a lethal point.

The fingers he felt through his fur stunned him, Cora's shift so fast and subtle he didn't even sense it. Tall and proud, her perfect dark skin on full display as she stroked his muzzle and behind his ears then held a hand out to him.

"Leave him, Finnegan..." she cooed softly, hand out as she stood her ground. He ducked his head and her lips curled into a hopeful smile. "Come back to me."

Cocking his head to the side, he watched her. No tricks, no hidden agenda or manipulation. Just her with her hand out for him, as he was. Slowly he pushed to his feet, four feet, then two, his paw quickly transitioning to fingers that laced tightly in hers.

Both naked, and covered in blood, they presented quite a sight as they left the room and emerged into the waiting arms of the medics and a grateful Guard.

"You're are easily the bravest and craziest woman I know." Dev laughed as she was loaded onto an ambulance, clapping her on the shoulder.

"Hey!" the giant ursine medic barked sharply. He was the size of a compact car with a scowl so fearsome, she wondered if he had some grizzly in him. "That's your future queen. Hands off the merchandise."

Grimacing at their mutual breach of public protocol, Cora nodded at the medic. "Thank you, Commander." She winked. "I'll see you at the hospital."

Properly chastened, the brown-skinned man nodded, giving her a secret smile. "Of course. Ma'am."

FINN

The superficial wounds were already on the mend, thanks to his wolf nature. At least those not caused by the silver. Dr. Mo, the palace physician, wrapped his wrists in gauze. Burns that penetrated deep into the tissue, the pain was intense, constant, and the nurse promised to return with an IV full of pain medicine.

He'd prefer that someone return with news of Cora. They'd gotten separated after his recovery from Lunacy. He hadn't even known such a thing was possible, until her. Of course, a Lupine being able to break through silver bonds was a myth until tonight. Also until her.

Finn had no idea how he managed to break free, all he remembered was seeing her bleeding as the Lacertine started to drag her away and then nothing else until a raven walked beside him. His hands told of the rage, split knuckles healing slowly and blood under his nails. Whose, he had no clue and was pretty sure he did not care so long as Cora was alright. Xander had informed him about Vasi needing surgery for a gunshot wound.

It was so much to think about. More than just Brendan and Driscoll, but a whole network of people who wanted to kill him. And, he smiled as she was rolled in on a gurney, a group of people equally dedicated to preventing it.

"My Angel," he murmured as the medic parked her next to him, taking her hand as they promised to have someone in to see her in a moment. Once alone, he tugged her until she was curled into the bed with him. She'd fussed about his wrists and ankles but having her with him was the best balm he could think of and he would not relent. Her head pillowed on his chest, her hand in his over his heart, he felt all the residual tension seep out of him.

"Vasi's gonna be okay, if you hadn't been told. Shot nicked the top of a lung but otherwise not nearly as bad as it could've been."

"Good. He's a fighter. You two have that in common." He'd planned to see his best friend the moment the doctor turned him loose here. "And Brendan?"

She turned her face into his chest, sighing. "Still in surgery, last I heard."

Her soft hand petting his chest through the hospital gown broke his heart. She could have been killed tonight. "I still can't believe—"

"I know, baby."

"You saved me twice tonight," he whispered against her hairline.

"That's the job," she laughed, but there was clearly no joy in it.

"Just the job?"

Cora leaned up and kissed his bearded jaw. "What do you think?"

The warmth in his chest had everything to do with woman cuddled up in his arms. Her contented little sighs seemed to bathe him in a foundational peace. "I think you're amazing and I'm unworthy."

"Agree to disagree."

"Miss Westgate, I am so sorry for the delay—" a human woman in rose pink scrubs and a long white coat came bustling in and screeched to a halt when she looked from the empty bed to the one occupied by two. A short-haired Indian woman with a bright smile and a pretty face, her eyes were wide as she took in the two of them twined around each other. "Your Highness, I'm sorry to interrupt."

"Not at all, doctor. She has several lacerations on her chest that likely need your attention." He could feel Cora stiffen against him and kissed her forehead just to tweak her that much more.

"Thanks for that, sweetie," she said dryly. "Appreciate it."

The doctor smiled and looked down at her tablet. "The superficial wounds on Miss Westgate's chest are not my primary concern. I'm Dr. Nancy Sharma from Obstetrics? I was asked by Dr. Moallem to look in on you?"

"Oh."

XANDER

The silence of the royal wing was staggering in its depth. Each footstep echoed on the marble tile outside of the royal bedroom. He had a team of eight men spread out and stationed on the balcony, in the rooms on either side and across the hall, as well as at the ends of the wings, with orders to allow absolutely no one through, and as much as he wanted to be out there in the field helping Vasi and Dev, looking for Finn and Cora, his duty was first and foremost to the crown.

Once an hour, he entered the bedroom, just to make a circuit inside, check the doors and windows and then out again. It was two minutes, tops, but it was an added layer of protection for their monarch, because there was something seriously hinky going on and had been for a long while and His Majesty was way too weak to fight off any intruder who may attempt to take advantage of the chaos.

The royal chambers were dark, and while he would have normally sent one of the Strigians on his team in, Vasi had entrusted the king's safety to him and he damn well would look after him. He checked the lock on each window, each French door, adjusting the curtains to maintain the darkness.

A quick sweep of the closet left just under the bed to check and he was on his way back to peruse the halls. He'd be glad when he could get back out and get a status update from Dev, because the stress of not knowing was wearing on him.

Xander caught a strange reflection when he shined his light under the bed. It wasn't anything he remembered seeing and given that he'd already been in there several times, it appeared to be new. Rounding the bed cautiously, his ears caught a new sounds as he neared the sleeping king. A repetitive drip, not so fast that it appeared to be flowing but some sort of leak maybe.

One pass of his flashlight over his monarch's sleeping form had him flailing back, fingers clawing for the radio on his hip. Blood everywhere, out of his mouth, soaked his clothes and dripping from the corner of the sheet onto the floor in a dark but slowly growing puddle.

"Medic! I need a medic for the Crown! Stat! I need a medic to the Crown stat!"

CORA

Shit! Shit, shit, shit! The obstetrician was definitely not something she'd planned on confronting right then. "Sorry," she averred as she pushed to sit up in Finn's arm, hoping it would cover her shocked reaction. "It's been a long night."

She smiled kindly. "Of course. I'm going to go and get a fetal heart monitor to examine you and the baby, alright? I'll be back in a moment."

Cora was fairly certain the only hearts audible for miles were hers and Finn's as they looked at each other. "What are we gonna do?" he asked the moment the door closed.

Fuck! Fucking hell. Closing her eyes she pulled in on herself. "Alright, breathe. Think."

"I got nothin'."

She hushed him, folding and unfolding the problem in her mind like one of those paper finger games from elementary school. "We lost the baby," she said finally, staring into startled blue eyes.

"We what?" he sounded so breathless it could have easily been mistaken for real upset.

"We lost the baby," she repeated, following it through in her head. "Everything that went down tonight, I lost the baby protecting you and in service to the crown, we are heartbroken and ask for privacy during this trying time."

He blinked for several minutes. "You just came up with that?"

"Yeah?"

"Jesus you frighten me."

She rolled her eyes even as she smiled affectionately. "This is what I do. You got a better idea?" Hearing the doctor's voice in the hall, she tapped him on the chest. "Get ready to look bereaved."

Dr. Sharma, with her sweet face and kind smile, returned with an ultrasound machine and directions for Cora to lie on the empty bed. "Dad, you can be with her, but she really needs the room."

They moved around and she got into position with him standing by her head, exhaling a shuddering, nervous breath. Clutching Finn's hand in hers as the cool gel was applied to her abdomen, she muttered, "It's gonna be okay."

The doctor nodded reassuringly. "Oh yes, absolutely. This is just a routine check since you and the little bean had trauma recently. No reason to think anything untoward." She got situated at the machine and patted Cora's free hand. "Now, deep breath and relax, Mama."

For a long while there was silence as she ran the wand back and forth across her belly. It was hard to tell what anything was, but so far it looked like a field of absolutely nothing that moved occasional.

"I'm starting to get concerned," she said warily, mindful of the role she had to play.

"Nah," the doctor scoffed. "Nothing to worry abo--oh! There you go. There it is."

And in that moment the world came to a blinding, screeching halt. "There what is?" Finn demanded urgently.

Grinning broadly, the doctor stood up and pointed on the screen. "Right there. Now, in human births, this is way too soon to detect anything, but shifter anatomy is a bit... anyway. Would you like to hear your baby's heartbeat?"

At the same time, both Cora and Finn arrived at the exact same conclusion. "Holy. Shit."

All eyes in the room turned when the door banged open and Dev blundered through, out of breath, eyes rimmed in red. "Therantia weeps!"

"What?" Finn's hand tightened around hers even as he stepped away from her gurney toward the Guard.

"The king is dead," he huffed, leaning over and bracing his hands on his knees as he caught his breath. When he looked up again, he took a knee on the floor as he addressed Finn. "Long live the king."

About Alexis D. Craig

Alexis is a romance writer with a day job. When she's not out saving her little corner of the world, she's behind the computer typing away, taking care of her two heathen dogs, or enjoying the company of her family and friends. She's a craft addict with more hobbies than sense.

The author of the bestselling Behind the Blue Line series as well as numerous standalone pieces, she's been published since 2011.

You can keep up with her and my internet wanderings by heading over to Lexie's Lyceum on Facebook and @Dispatchvampire on Twitter.

WORKS BY ALEXIS D. CRAIG

Imminent Danger

Undercover Seduction

US Marshals Series:

Give Me Shelter
Bulletproof Princess

Behind the Blue Line Series:

The Ex File
Dead & Disorderly

Naughty Bedtime Stories-In Three Words (Anthology)

No Such Thing

Shifted Into Love Anthologies

Love Changes Everything
Lust In The Times Of Mardi Gras
Hotel California

Coming Soon

Mistletoe and Kisses (December 2019)

The Winged Guardian Series

Book 1: A Killing Moon

Coming Soon

Book 2: A Hunter's Moon